GEARS

BRACKEN RIDGE REBELS MC

MACKENZY FOX

Cover by: Mayhem cover creations
Exclusive photo by: Wander Aguiar Photography
Model: Chris Lynch
Formatting by: @peachykeenas -Savannah Richey
Editing and proofreading by: Mackenzie - nicegirlnaughtyedits.com
2nd proofread by: Kiki Edits
Alpha reader: Michelle (The Outgoing Bookworm)
Beta Reader: Alana S
ASIN E BOOK: B0BJL8J8JR

To my amazing team especially: Dakotah, Alana, Michelle &
Savannah I am truly the luckiest girl in the world x

AUTHOR'S NOTE

CONTENT WARNING: Gears is a steamy romance for readers 18+ it contains mature themes that may make some readers uncomfortable. It includes violence, mentions of domestic violence and rape (not graphic) coarse language...basically what the Bracken Ridge boys do best! And as always....LOTS of very spicy love scenes!

ABOUT GEARS – BRACKEN RIDGE REBELS MC BOOK 9

Blurb

Gears

I'm a Prospect.

Nothing special.

Nothing to anyone, except to her.

She's my V.P.'s sister, and she's older than me.

She's off limits.

And as much as I try to keep my distance, she keeps coming around.

Showing up places where she shouldn't be.

Like my bed.

It's no secret that she could undo me.

Take everything from me.

Like my soul isn't already tortured enough.

Now I have to betray my club.

But it may just be worth the fall. If it means I get to keep her safe and keep her in my arms.

Amelia

I shouldn't, but he's just too tempting.

Those hazel eyes.

His bad attitude.

The way he swaggers like he owns the world.

I don't know why I'm like a moth to a flame.

Why I have to have him.

Why I don't care about the consequences.

But when danger lurks and he has to make a choice,
will he be the last man standing?

Will we survive the aftermath?

That is, if the Rebel's enemies don't step in first.

Then all could be lost. Including my fractured heart.

And the man I love.

Forever.

PROLOGUE

THREE MONTHS AGO - GEARS

"Do you think you can fix it?" Amelia calls, when I lean back from the hood.

"Uh, I can but we need tools."

"Tools?"

I smirk. "Yep, the kind that are back at the clubhouse. Jump in, I'll give you a ride. If I leave you out here on the road at this time of night, Brock and Axton will string me up."

"I'd like to see that."

Something about the way she says it has me looking sideways at her.

Her eyes leave my body quickly, but I see it.

She was checking me out.

What the fuck?

I mean, Amelia is hot. She's every warm blooded man's fantasy.

But she's too pure. Sure, she might have a sassy mouth and she gives me plenty of lip, but she's sweet looking. Like butter wouldn't met in her mouth kinda sweet.

What I'd give to have that mouth on me...and she's

older than me, not quite a cougar because we're both in our twenties, but yeah, if I had the chance, I'd go there.

A hundred percent.

Sucks to be me when you're a prospect in the MC and can't touch any woman, especially a club sister, my VP's sister. They'd kill me.

I open her door and she climbs in.

I try not to notice the short skirt she's wearing and I wonder who she's wearing it for.

More to the point, why is she out here so late?

I start my truck, lucky for her I'm not on my motorcycle because I have vision of that skirt being rucked up around her hips.

Jesus. Get a grip already.

We make small talk in the car, which is mainly her peppering me with questions and me grunting a reply.

I don't really talk much to chicks, sure I bang plenty, but talking isn't really my thing.

Yet, with Amelia, I find myself listening to every word.

She works as a legal secretary in town and she's smart as fuck.

When I glance sideways at her, she's biting down on her lip.

The image goes straight to my cock.

I shouldn't be thinking like this, it isn't healthy for me, or my cock.

"Do you like being a part of the MC?" she asks, surprising me.

"Uh, yeah, of course," I reply, thinking it's a trick question. The last thing I need is her tell tailing on me and making my life harder than it already is.

"Even being bossed around by my brother?"

"Even then. It'll be worth it when I'm patched in." It's the truth. This club is all I got. They've been good to me.

2

"You'll get to do whatever you want," she goes on. "I bet the sweet butts will be happy."

I swallow hard. "Maybe I'm holding out for something a little classier?"

She laughs. "Uh huh, right. I thought pussy was pussy and it didn't matter where it was or where they came from."

Hearing her say those words, it makes me question that I've misjudged her all along. Here I was thinking she was as pure as the driven snow, and she's got a fuckin' potty mouth.

Well I'll be damned.

"That isn't exactly true," I say, trying to keep my voice even because now I'm picturing what I could do to her pussy. "Some of us have standards."

She laughs again, it's a nice sound. I don't hear Amelia laughing enough, I decide.

"Riiiiiight."

"Anyway, *sugar*, why do you care?"

She folds her arms over her chest. "I don't."

I want her to say pussy again.

"I don't know, it kinda sounds like you were makin' some kinda pass at me." Another favorite pastime of mine is giving Amelia shit.

"In your dreams!"

"Does it help if I tell you I have a big dick?"

She snorts with laughter. "God, I'm too fucking sober for this conversation."

My dicks hard.

"Yeah, me too. I could ask what you're doin' out here so late at night."

She sighs. "The girls and I had a movie night," she says, and I immediately think she's been doing anything but that. "I had to drive so I didn't drink."

3

"What did you watch?"

"Romantic chick flicks."

"Sounds riveting."

"I hate action films more than life."

I smirk. "That confirms it, we'll never be a thing. I hate romantic chick flicks and I like watching action films."

"That's a damn shame."

I glance at her again and she's hiding her smile.

Fuck she's cute. How have I never noticed this before?

Unfortunately, we pull up to the clubhouse in no time, the car park is all but deserted at this time of night.

I jump out of the truck and immediately jog around to her side, holding out my hand as she tries, and fails, to exit my vehicle graciously. Her skirts has ridden right up and I can see her black panties.

Holy Jesus, save me.

"How very chivalrous of you," she says, taking my hand as I help her down. With her other hand, she tries to tug her skirt down, but fails and I have to look away.

When our hands touch, a jolt runs through me. Her hand is soft, delicate.

She stares down at me as I try not to make it obvious I'm jonesing.

Instead I say, "I'm here to please, *sugar,* but it's probably not a good idea to wear short skirts like that and be climbing up into people's trucks."

She rolls her eyes, tugging her skirt down when she's safely on the ground. "I didn't know I was going to be stranded, did I?"

"For future reference, if a man can see your panties, it's too short."

"Are you complaining?" she fires at me.

"Hell no. If you ask me, there should be more short skirt wearing around these parts."

She shakes her head as if unsure what to do with me.

It's then I realize; our hands are still joined.

I pull away at the same time she does.

Fuck.

Her mouth opens and closes.

"Uh." I sound like a dick.

"Um, yeah."

"Tools," I tell myself. "I need to get tools."

Her lips twitch. "Tools."

I stalk off toward the clubhouse doors as Amelia follows behind.

Now all I can smell is the scent of her perfume, it invades my nostrils as I try to put one foot in front of the other and keep my hands to myself.

She's off limits.

If I get through tonight without dragging her up to my room so I can rip that skirt right off her, it'll be some kind of miracle.

GEARS

PROSPECT.

Another word for resident shit kicker.

I get all the jobs nobody else wants. The jobs so low, even the sweet butts don't get to do them, and that's saying something.

I can't complain. Hutch and the club gave me a chance, a fresh start, and it was one I've taken gladly. Anything to get out of the shit hole I was in.

When my old boss, Jack, started stealing from the Bracken Ridge Rebels last year, I knew it was time to jump ship. He stole the club's multiple shipments of junkyard parts, looking out for nobody but himself, but it eventually caught up with him.

Then again, Jack wasn't a nice man, not to anyone, including his kids and long-suffering wife.

If there's one thing I can't stand, on top of being a thief, it's a man beating on a woman. Maybe it's because I take pity on the weak because of my deep-rooted issues involving women, or it could be the fact I just don't like fuckheads. One thing I can agree on is that Jack had it coming.

The fucker deserved everything he got; beaten, broke, and run out of town.

When I decided to leave, I made sure I had all bases covered before I went to Hutch, the Rebels President, and told him what was going on.

Some may say being a snitch is the lowest of the low, but I know who's side I'd rather be on, especially when Steel, the club's enforcer and Sergeant at Arms, broke every single finger, including both thumbs, on Jack's hands when he got found out. That was just the beginning.

He's lucky they left him breathing, but he was forced to pay them back, with interest, and hand his car-wrecking business over to avoid involving the cops.

Some people are so fuckin' dense.

Needless to say, my loyalties to the club were rewarded, kinda. If you consider shit kicking to be a profession, then I am a master at it. I should know, I've had enough practice.

Starting from the ground up isn't so bad. At least if I make it to being patched in, I'll be able to do my own thing and have the loyalty of the club behind me.

I haven't had the pleasure of knowing what a real family is like, not until I joined this club.

Hutch is hard, but he's fair.

He doesn't take any shit, but why should he? He's earned the respect of the members and the people around him. I admire him, what he's built, how people look up to him and, above all else, the loyalty they show in return. He's proven to me there is another way, one that doesn't involve being a crook.

I might only be twenty, but I've lived what feels like a hundred years. I've seen a lot coming from a broken home, one where my own mother was taken from me in the worst of ways…right in front of my face. Maybe that's why I hate men like Jack so much. They only know cruelty and that makes my stomach roll.

For the most part, being a prospect is about keeping your head down and ears open. The menial tasks never end, and you only get a flogging if you do any crazy shit or don't know your place. I already got that down pat; I learned to be seen and not heard by age three.

I learned what it was like to be nothing, feel nothing, and have nothing. But I also had the love of my grandma, and even though she's in a retirement village now, without her, I'd be dead. She took me in when my mom was killed, and she raised me. Even when I rebelled and left to do my own thing, I never once took her for granted. I never will. She's the reason I still have a pulse. I owe her everything.

"Need you to get over to Kennedy's and help get the furniture off the truck and into the new place," Bones, the Road Captain, says to me as I walk in the door.

Kennedy is his ol' lady and the club's attorney, is moving her practice to a bigger office. All of which I've had the fun task of moving with the two new prospects, Buzz and Mac. Jax normally helps out, but since he recently got patched in, he has other obligations.

I only just finished hauling shit off a truck for Lily's salon, Steel's sister and Gunner, the clubs Treasurer's ol' lady. Gunner is a good guy, and he used to be the resident fuck boy, till he got a ball and chain and now he thinks he's a fuckin' expert on relationships.

I don't mind the salon, though. I stretched the hauling out for as long as possible because of all the cute chicks going in and out. I guess you could say the ladies seem to like me. I'm young, have a baby face, and they think I need to be fixed.

What they don't know is, I don't need or want to be fixed. This is who I am. I'm not gonna change. I stopped trying to live up to people's ideals and expectations a long time ago.

The only people I need to back me up is Hutch and my club, and the rest can go to hell.

"Gotcha, was gonna go get cleaned up…"

"No time for that. Brock's over there, and I'm already late."

Great. Just what I need.

Brock is the Vice President, and one of his favorite pastimes is keeping me in line.

Then there's Amelia. Brock's little sister. She's the real reason I'm eager to get washed up.

Not only is she easy on the eyes, she's also fuckin' smart and works for Kennedy.

I helped her with her broken-down car a month back, and when we made it back to the club, Brock and his brother, Axton, were all over me like a cheap suit. All I did was give the chick a ride. Albeit not exactly the ride I had in mind, but I can't go there.

If there is one woman on the planet who is off limits, it's her.

And she's absolutely fuckin' gorgeous.

Long legs. Curvy body. Tits that are a nice handful. And she's got the face of a fuckin' siren. Her mouth, however, she's a dirty little bitch. I'm sure she just antagonizes me to get a rise, but I've seen her checking me out when she thinks I'm not looking. What I would give to be able to shut that mouth up with my…

"You listenin'?"

I snap out of my reverie of Amelia on her knees before me, wearing her pencil skirt and smart blouse wide open as I wrap my hand in her hair while I fuck her mouth…*holy shit.*

"I'm good."

"So why are we still here talkin'?"

I shrug. "On my way."

Despite my fantasy about Amelia, running into her isn't always pleasant when her brothers are around. She gets to sass me, and I can't say shit back. When we're alone, however, I tell her how it is, and a part of me thinks she actually likes it. I bet she likes it rough. Chicks like her usually do. If only I could be the one to give it to her. It would be like all my dreams coming true, without the beating I'd get from her brothers. She may be a grown ass woman, but that doesn't mean shit.

Brock and Axton are very protective.

She's older than me. Twenty-six.

A cougar by my standards, and that gets me so fuckin' hard.

I get out of the club as fast as I can, jump on my sled, and take off for Kennedy's place.

Bracken Ridge is a small town south of Phoenix, Arizona, and while it has expanded in the last few years, it's still pretty small and traffic is non-existent.

I get there in under five minutes.

Brock's out front yelling at someone who was reversing the truck. When I walk over to him, he slaps me upside the head, his signature move.

"You're late."

"Don't blame me, blame those chicks at Lily's. They wouldn't let me leave. I can't help that they're all over me every time I go over there." Another thing I'm extremely good at is shit stirring.

"They shoulda tied you down and waxed your whole

11

body. That'd give you something to fuckin' complain about," he grumbles.

"Nah," I reply. "I like pain."

He gives me a disgusted look, and I waste no time getting the back door of the truck open.

"Girls know where they want shit," Brock says, just as Bones arrives, obviously having taken the scenic route. "Ask them before you go plonking furniture down. It'll save you a job movin' it twice.

I turn and see Kennedy and Amelia walking out of the office. It's a Saturday, so neither are in their work clothes.

Amelia is dressed in sweatpants with a matching sweatshirt, a fuckin' varsity emblem on the front of both, a ribbon in her hair, and three-hundred-dollar sneakers. I almost blow my load.

But I don't stare for too long; Brock has eyes like a hawk.

Most of the time, I ignore her and pretend she's not even there.

Bones swings an arm around Kennedy's neck when he sneaks up behind her, and she squeals. Grabbing her ass, he mutters something in her ear. She laughs and swats his arm playfully.

Amelia's eyes meet mine for a brief moment, and as I look away, she says, "Hello, Gears." It's the simplest greeting, but the way she says it, it's like a chick on a sex hotline.

I glance back at her and gave her a chin lift. "Amelia."

"Hi, Gears," Kennedy says as they approach. "Thanks for helping."

Bones rolls his eyes.

"Don't thank him, that's his job," Brock grunts, then barks more orders at the driver.

Of course, the women of the MC know exactly how

shit works around here, and Kennedy is one of the nicer ones. They don't have to acknowledge us at all if they don't want to, but for some reason, I think Kennedy likes me. Maybe because I get on with shit with no questions asked and women tend to like guys who get stuff fixed for them. Amelia, on the other hand, she's one I just can't read. She says one thing, then does another.

I tend to think she's a good girl who wants to be bad, though from what I've heard, she does like to party hard. Probably drinks champagne cocktails to wash down her caviar.

I snicker.

Everyone looks at me.

Sometimes I just need to learn when to keep my thoughts to myself. Especially when all I'm thinking is about Amelia's legs wrapped around my face.

I guess I really do have a death wish.

"Somethin' funny, prospect?" Brock arches a brow.

I shake my head, wiping the smile off my face. "Nope."

"Then stop gawkin' like a teenage girl and get the fuck up in here."

I don't miss the smile that touches Amelia's lips.

Lips I'll never have, nor will I taste.

It's the story of my life.

AMELIA

I KNOW HE'S TRYING TO IGNORE ME. I CAN TELL BY THE WAY he steels his jaw, like he's forcing himself to look away.

I don't know when this thing started between us, and I'm probably too old to have a crush, but something about him just tugs at my heartstrings, even when I know that's ridiculous. He's a wiseass, for one, with a huge chip on his shoulder, and thinks he's God's gift to women. And even though he's not allowed to touch the sweet butts or hang-arounds, they swarm him like bees to honey.

And, if the rumors are anything to go by, I know a little more about him than I probably should. Like the fact he's supposedly got a Jacob's Ladder piercing.

I try not to let my eyes drift south as I imagine it. I've never seen one before, and I cannot imagine what would possess a man to do something like that to his own penis.

Sexual pleasure, my mind reminds me. Ah yes, that.

It makes me curious; how much could a twenty-year-old actually know in the bedroom? I mean, it's highly unlikely he knows where the G-spot is...Just as I'm thinking it, he snorts out a laugh. I snap my eyes back to him, realizing he's not even looking at me. But my big brother, however, is.

As scary as Brock is to most people, I'm not afraid of him. I know exactly how he works. I know he's as annoying as any over-protective brother can be, but his heart is in the right place, even if sometimes I want to choke him.

When my other brother, Axton, was in jail for ten years, Brock took on the role of the overbearing brute of the family. In his eyes, I'm still his baby sister with pigtails in her hair who kicks the mean boys in the shins on the playground and isn't allowed out at night.

Sometimes it becomes such a drag.

"What?" I snap, glaring back at him.

He points a warning at me, and I roll my eyes.

"Seriously?"

"Seriously."

"What are we missing?" Kennedy interrupts as she glances from me to Brock to Gears.

"Absolutely nothing," I say, giving Brock a look.

If I want to check Gears out, while thinking about his Jacob's Ladder, then that's my business. One of these days, I'm going to explode, and I'll be sure to add my brother's face to the target practice dummy when I do.

The only reason I don't give him any lip is because it'll get Gears in trouble.

"Well, let's not all stand around here like a bunch of fuckin' wet mops. Need to get this shit inside so the girls can get back to work on Monday," Bones says, as the truck doors are opened wide, revealing all of our new office furniture, fittings, and shelving. There's a lot of it.

Kennedy does nothing by halves.

I've been her legal secretary for almost a year now, and I love it.

I had no plans to move to Bracken Ridge, but I guess I have always kinda liked it here, and when Kennedy offered me the job, I couldn't pass it up. I've never really been a city person, so being out in the country, away from the hustle and bustle, suits me.

I've got my own small condo, make good money, and have a nice group of friends. It's a pity the ratio of single men to women in this town is seriously lacking, but I guess there has to be a flaw somewhere.

Not that I have time to date, or even have a little fun. It feels like I haven't had any fun since college, and since I hang around the club most weekends and drink with some of the girls, there is zero chance of getting lucky there. Not when my brothers are hanging around with their hawk eyes. I'm considered a club member, or *club sister,* as the MC likes to call us girls who are the siblings or ol' ladies of the men. So, I'm off limits. And to a prospect, that's the equivalent to a deadly sin.

"Don't you have anywhere else to be?" I ask Brock, with my hands on my hips.

He turns to me, still barking at the driver and his passenger. "You wanna haul all this fuckin' shit yourself?"

Kennedy gives me a look which tells me to play nice.

"No, that's your job."

He gives me another disapproving look before telling Gears to move his ass.

Kennedy and I spend the next few hours bossing the men around, telling them where to put everything. Gears works quietly and efficiently. The one thing the prospects know how to do is to keep their head down and not speak unless spoken to. Though, I know from talking to him before that he has quite a bit to say.

He's not grumpy like Brock, or grouchy like Steel who scowls at everybody, or a comedian like Bones or Gunner.

17

I can safely say that, where Gears is concerned, he's his own crown of thorns.

"Didn't have to dress up for me, *sugar*," a voice behind me says.

When I turn, Gears is leaning against the door jamb. He crosses his arms over his chest, his tank stretching across his muscles as I fight at keeping my eyes on his. His hair is like its usual disheveled self, but today he has it half tied back. The honey shade of blonde and his hazel-colored eyes remind me that he is one mighty fine looking man, not that I needed the reminder. I'm all over it as is.

I assume my brother has either left, or he's busy, for him to risk talking to me.

Or, as I like to call it, flirt with me. And I don't mind one single bit.

"Luckily I didn't," I reply. "Though, haven't you heard? It's grey sweatpants season, not really fair that you didn't dress appropriately."

He smirks. His lips curling up slowly, as I find my heart rate accelerating.

"What is it with chicks and gray sweatpants?"

I snort a laugh. "Do I really have to explain?"

"Enlighten me."

I know he knows what I mean, he just wants me to say it.

"You mean, you really don't know?" *I wish he'd stop staring at me like that...*

"I'm pretty dumb." He points to the back of his cut. "Prospect, remember?"

I know he's not dumb, far from it, but I'll play along.

"That doesn't mean shit. One day, you'll get to be all grown up, just like the big boys at the club."

"Don't change the subject."

"Fine." My eyes meet his. "Women like gray sweatpants

because you can see the outline of a man's dick through the material, and it's hot, got it?"

He bites down on his bottom lip, and it's oh-so-sexy, as he tries not to laugh.

"So, by saying I didn't dress appropriately, do I take it that means you want to see mine?"

"Sweatpants or dick?"

"Both." He doesn't look away.

Holy shit. Did the temperature in here just go up by fifty thousand degrees?

"That's awfully presumptuous. Maybe I just meant you don't look all that comfortable in your"—my eyes drift down his body to his crotch—"jeans."

"I like the concept," he goes on. "But I'm not really a free-balling kinda guy, if you get my drift." He gives me a wink for good measure.

Oh, I do like this game... "I guess, depending on its size, it could get a little awkward..."

"Only if it's small. Which it isn't."

I cannot believe we're having a conversation about his penis. Somebody pinch me.

"So I've heard."

He pushes off the door jamb and comes toward my desk. The only thing separating us is plastic and bubble wrap.

"Those sweet butts been braggin' about me again?" He presses his hands down on my desk, leaning forward, pretending to check its weight as my mind wanders to why he would be doing that...

"I certainly hope not. I thought those sluts were off limits to you?"

"Now, now, no need for name callin'. Sweet butts have other friends who hang around, ones with loose lips, so it seems."

Oh yeah, I have no doubt he sleeps around…with a face and a body like that. Which is why this is strictly flirting. Nothing else.

I may as well go in for the kill…

"Actually, I heard you have piercings." My eyes flick to his again as I stand my ground, not moving even though we're literally a few feet away.

That smirk appears again as he straightens.

"Is that right?"

Well, now I need to know if it's true.

I nod. "Yup, and it always made me wonder why a man would have his most prized body part mutilated. Not to mention with a high chance of swelling or infection."

One eyebrow quirks. "Sounds like you're well versed in body mutilating. I never would've picked it."

"What is that supposed to mean?"

He reaches for me, but his hand doesn't reach my face. Instead, he pulls my ponytail, holding on to the ribbon with a small tug as he says, "You, in your varsity sweater, actin' like butter wouldn't melt in your mouth while askin' me about my Jacob's Ladder? Sugar, if you want a closer inspection, all you gotta do is ask."

My mouth goes dry as the heat rises in my face.

My panties dampen from him tugging on my hair.

And his words…holy shit…he has me drooling like a fucking dog.

Me in my varsity sweater?

I keep my cool on the surface…somehow. "If I wanted a closer inspection, I would've had one by now."

His lips twitch. He removes his hand, though it lingers as he cups my face. He smells like gasoline and a faded, musky cologne I can't place. Everything about this… *prospect*…sends my hormones into overdrive.

Okay, I know he's technically off limits and he's

young…six years younger than me…but with him still touching me, my body doesn't care at all. My panties are well and truly soaked…

"Baby girl, if I wanted you to see it, you wouldn't still be standing here."

I smile condescendingly. "Oh no? Where would I be standing, then?"

His eyes stare right into mine, and I feel a thrill of fear, mixed with lust, all rolled into one. "You'd be on your knees, takin' all of me with that smart mouth of yours."

My mouth opens and closes, words lost, as his thumb traces along my bottom lip. I want to suck it and tease him, just like he's teasing me, but I refrain. Just barely. "You'd like that, wouldn't you, Amelia?"

I swallow hard. "You have a dirty mouth, *prospect.*"

"Not as dirty as my mind right now."

I glance down his body. "You're hard, aren't you?"

I know I'm playing with fire, but the flirting has me too hot under the collar. I know I'm going to regret this because it won't go anywhere, and now, I'm frustrated and need friction, but I'm kinda lost in the moment.

"Nice sturdy desk," he comments, avoiding the question.

"Meaning?" I'm practically panting.

He brushes his thumb over my lips again, and this time I don't hold back. I bite the pad gently, his eyebrows furrowing as he watches me, devouring me with that look. Oh, he's into it all right, no matter what he claims.

I've never wanted anything so much; I don't even know what's come over me. *"Fuck,"* he mutters, his eyes never leaving my mouth as I move my lips over the tip and suck.

His stance is rigid, and I want to reach over and feel how hard and big he actually is, but there's still a desk between us, and secondly, my brother is likely in the very next room, and we could get caught any second.

His thumb goes deeper into my mouth as I take him, grazing my teeth along his skin. I don't know if I'm imagining it, but I'm pretty sure I hear him growl.

I suck on his thumb, my clit throbbing, as his other hand balls into a fist while he watches me.

"What's the matter?" I drawl, in between sucking. "Cat got your tongue?"

His eyes finally lift to mine. "No, but I'd love to have my tongue fuckin' your..."

"Amelia!" Kennedy hollers, her footsteps approaching.

Gears and I jump apart, like teenagers who just got caught making out.

He reaches down to his crotch and adjusts himself while I fight the urge to remain calm and in control, instead of unhinged and horny.

"In here!" I yell back as I busy myself with the filing cabinet drawers.

Gears doesn't even pretend to be doing something.

As soon as Kennedy walks in, she looks from me to Gears, then to me again.

"Cassidy brought us lunch," she says, trying, and failing to keep the smirk off her face.

Cassidy is Colt's ol' lady, another club brother.

"Don't mind if I do," Gears says, heading toward the door as I stare after him, then he stops and says loud enough for me to hear, "Feelin' a little peckish myself. Amelia's practically had me tied to the desk."

My eyes go wide as he disappears, and Kennedy stifles a laugh. "Sorry for interrupting."

"You weren't," I tell her, knowing that I'm probably beet red. "He was just helping."

She flicks her eyes back to the hallway again. "He has a

22

very nice butt, and a swagger that shouldn't be legal. Pity I'm taken and old enough to be his mom."

Remain calm.

I love Kennedy, but she's, my boss. And she's Bones' ol' lady, so I can't tell her shit.

No matter what the club sisters say, pillow talk eventually gets back to the club. And I don't want to risk Gears getting beaten because I wanted to have my way with him… *I need to get a grip.*

"He knows it," I add, throwing in an eye roll for good measure.

Then it hits me…he never did answer the question about his Jacob's Ladder, and now I can't help but wonder, even more so, if it's true.

It's insanity.

And I sucked his thumb…*what the hell is wrong with me?*

Kennedy smirks. "Just wipe that look off your face before Brock gets back," she says. "It'd be a shame to fuck up Gears's face. I quite like looking at it."

3

GEARS

I TRY TO TAKE MY MIND OFF IT, BUT ALL DAY, ALL I CAN think about is Amelia and her lips wrapped around my cock.

Well, in reality, it was only my thumb, but a man can dream.

I don't even know what the fuck happened.

It's her come-fuck-me-but-you-can't-have-me eyes, that's what it is.

Then she had to go on and talk about my dick.

I know we crossed a line, a very big line. But fuck me if she isn't the biggest tease I've ever met. There I was, trying to be all cool and shit, and she just went and knocked it out of the park by batting her goddamn eyelashes and sucking on my thumb.

I know I'm asking for trouble. As much as I want to, I can't fuck her. She's Brock's sister, a club sister, a woman, who, as a prospect, I can never have. And here I am panting after her like a fuckin' golden retriever.

I had lunch in all of two seconds, then split, went home, and fucked my palm in the shower.

Jesus Christ, the woman is going to be the death of me.

I barely made it to my afternoon shift, and when I did, Nitro eyeballed me like he knew exactly the reason I was running late. Nitro is my boss who runs the scrap and car yard now where I work. His ol' lady is Frankie, the local baby doctor and they have a kid together.

I have to admit, Nitro is pretty good to me, even though I know the yard better than he does. We've been working together for about six months. Jax and Gash, another member, help out when they can, and Amelia comes over to help with the books, which is just another thing that can't be happening any time soon. If I see her in the next twenty-four hours, I'm gonna bend her over the nearest desk.

She can't go around talking about my penis, and then expect me not to get fired up. Now all I can picture is her playing with my piercings when I ram my cock down her throat.

I'm not surprised one of the sweet butts was flapping her gums. The only thing with having piercings on my cock is that it often takes more lube, or foreplay, to get the chick ready.

The barbells aren't for everyone, though it feels so much better when she's into it. Most of the chicks I've been with are curious about it, and they end up liking it. And I like them touching it, exploring me like I'm some goddamn aberration. I'm not complaining.

I wonder idly how into it Amelia would be.

If I weren't a prospect, and Brock wasn't hanging around the building, I would've fucked her over the desk, just so she knows exactly what I'm about, and teasing me like a little bitch isn't gonna do anything except make me want her even more. I guess that was her whole objective; because she knows I can't do anything without getting into a whole world of hurt. The brothers in the club take that kind of thing seriously.

Which is why I'm pissed at myself. We went too far.

The more I try not to think about it, the more my mind drifts until it's all I can think about.

The only thing I can do is throw myself into work like a man possessed.

I've always worked hard; that's why Hutch hired me and let me be part of the club. He saw the potential in me, and he knows I never drag my heels. If there's something to be done, and in a hurry, the club always asks me first. Which means, I'm always fuckin' busy.

"You all right?" Nitro asks, when I've finished serving a customer.

"Never been better, why?"

"You look like you just won the lottery but had to share it with a hundred other people."

Am I really that transparent?

"Just been a long day, haulin' shit for Kennedy's new place," I reply. The man has a bullshit radar better than Axton's, so I gotta be careful. "Same shit, different day."

He snorts a laugh. At least he lets me bitch and complain, not like the others in the club.

"You hear about the new cook for the Burger Joint?"

I frown. "Nah, but don't tell me it's not opening now. I plan on eatin' there most nights."

Roxy, the chef at the Stone Crow, the bar the Rebels own and operate, has a prize-winning burger sauce that rival's competitors around the globe. It's even won awards. The recipe is so secret, it's locked away in Hutch's safe and only a handful of people know how to make it. Bracken Ridge Hot Sauce. It's making them a fortune.

"Fucker broke his hand in an accident and won't be starting since he can't work with one hand."

"Great, now I gotta find a new place to fuckin' eat. They banned me from the smorgasbord at the Crow." Fuckers. I'm a growing boy. I need grub like I need air and sex. It's a necessity.

"That's because you eat your body weight in food, for free."

I scoff. "Free? Gotta be kiddin' me, the amount of haulin' I do and shit shovelin'."

He smirks. "Been a long time since I was a prospect, but I'll take your word for it. Least you don't give me anything to kick your ass for, that's a plus." He squeezes me on the shoulder as he leaves.

What it is, is a fuckin' miracle.

I was always getting into some kinda mess as a troubled teen, and even when I became a man, trouble seemed to just follow me. I've cleaned my act up some. I needed to.

I got shit to do that's gonna take me away from the club. I might not even get patched in, but that's the risk I vowed to take a while back. I always knew that at some point in time, what I had to do would creep up, and it's why I can't get too close to anyone. Though that's proving hard because from what I can tell, the club seems to like me.

Fuck knows why. I guess I just have a knack at keeping my head just above water and shielding the people around me from what's really going on.

It's what I know.

It's how I roll.

It's how I'll probably be for the rest of my life.

Nothing can get in the way of what I have to do. Loyalty.

It comes above all else, the Rebels know that. I'd never do anything to put the club in jeopardy. It's why I'll have to leave, at some stage.

Trouble is, I don't know when, and I can't tell anyone why. I just hope Hutch, of all people, won't be too disappointed in me. I don't know why I care that much.

Maybe because I never had a real father, or a father figure, and Hutch is a man to look up to. A man who I admire even, not like Jack, or the other dead-beat dudes I've had in my life over the years. A part of me longs for the family I never had, but the other part needs revenge.

It runs through my blood thick and cold, reminding me every second that, as much as I like this new life I've created for myself, it's all temporary. All of it.

It's also why I can't let things go anywhere with Amelia. Aside from the fact I'd be buried out in the desert before I even got to lay a hand on her, I should've known better than to do what I did.

I could lay the blame that she's older than me, that she was the one corrupting me, but that would be a lie. We both know I started it, and we both know we have sexual chemistry. For what it's worth, I think we'd be good together. In fact, I know it.

I get back to work so Nitro can clock out, all the while my mind is on Amelia.

But like most things in my life, it's a fantasy, nothing more.

∾

I stare at Hutch. "Say what?"

He looks up from bottom of the glass he's nursing. "You got a problem with that, son?"

I try not to grimace, but the thought of being the new dish pig at the Burger Joint doesn't exactly fill me with joy. Especially since it's opening night and they're already down the head cook. Now Roxy is going to have to work her magic and be in two places at once. Which is fine, what do I care? But now it impacts me, it ain't that fun. However, I can't let Hutch know that.

"Nope."

"Glad to hear it." He indicates for Axton, who's serving behind the bar, to refill his drink. "Gonna be a fuckin' shit-show. We're down servers, but luckily the girls offered to help."

"The girls?"

He flicks his eyes to mine. "Deanna, Sienna, and Amelia."

Oh, fuck.

I've been avoiding Amelia like the plague for the last few days. She hangs out at the club a lot, and since I live upstairs, avoiding her hasn't been easy. And I feel like a fuckin' wuss. All she did was suck on my thumb.

"Nice of them to offer to help," I say, knowing it sounds lame, but he's still watching me.

Deanna is his daughter. She's a few years younger than Amelia, and much, much wilder, or so I've heard, since she doesn't party at the club for obvious reasons. Sienna is Steel's ol' lady and works for him at his garage and workshop.

He was the first of the brothers, aside from Rubble, who's married to Lucy his ol' lady, to get snagged and tied down. Steel dislikes most people, aside from Sienna, and he's nuts about his rescue dogs, Lola and Rocky.

"Just remember you're there to work," he grunts.

I frown. "Know it." Frankly, it's insulting. I know my place, and it's well below his daughter and the other club girls.

He wags a finger at me. "Better know it. Deanna, unfor-tunately, takes after me when it comes to behaving, more so than her mother."

I snort a laugh. Everyone knows Hutch's ol' lady, Kirsty, is a fox. Hell, I'd still go there. Not that I want him to know that.

"I'll make sure they're okay, boss."

He gives me a side-eye, then shakes his head, amused. "Clearly, you don't know my daughter. She'd corrupt the devil himself if she had her way."

"What I meant was, they'll be safe…with me."

He focuses on me for a second, realizing I'm serious, then gives me a chin lift. "Appreciate it."

I've always, from a young age, felt the urge to protect women in my care. My mom, before she died right in front of me, and my grandma. Above all else, I despise any man who lays a hand on a woman. Not happening on my watch.

I'm not the tallest of the brothers, but I'm solid. I can take a hit, and I can hit back fuckin' hard.

The brothers know I'm one of those fuckers who just won't stay down. If it means I hurt in the morning, so be it. To look out for girls, it would be a privilege. Even if I can't stop thinking about Amelia day and night, regardless.

She's got me under her spell, and she did it on purpose. It's cruel, really, because if she did spend the night with me, I'd make her forget all about playing games.

I imagine her gagging on my cock. Yeah, that'd shut her up.

She usually has quite a lot to say for herself, but even I can admit that she was at a loss for words that day in her office.

It also makes me a little mad because I don't like the thought of her talking dirty like that with anyone else. Sure, she's not mine and never will be, but in my fantasy, Amelia only talks dirty to me and nobody else. In fact, in my fantasies, Amelia does a lot of things that she'd never do in real life.

It makes me wonder if she'd actually be up for any of it, if given half a chance, or is she all talk and no action?

Something tells me that she's a little in between.

Friday comes around too fast, and though I've no idea why one of the other new prospects can't fill in, I don't argue. I do what I'm told, no questions asked, even if it means being the resident dish pig. And here I was thinking my days of shoveling shit were numbered. I guess not.

I haven't even been on the receiving end of one of these famous fuckin' burgers during the testing phase, but if they're anything like the grub that gets served up at the Crow, then it's gonna be the busiest burger joint in Bracken Ridge.

When I get there, the kitchens in a mad panic.

Kirsty's at the helm, Deanna is rolling out meat patties, Sienna is buttering burger buns, Cassidy is putting fry boxes together, and Amelia is cutting up tomato, lettuce, and onion on a chopping board.

I stroll in and take in the situation. Nobody looks up.

"I've never seen so many beautiful women in one room," I say loudly, grabbing an apron off the hook.

Everyone looks at me simultaneously, and for the first time in as long as I can remember, it's like someone's happy to see me.

"Gears, thank God," Kirsty says on a relieved sigh, looking like she might faint.

I tie the apron strings behind my back and give her a chin lift. "Is everythin' okay, Mrs. H?"

For the first time since I've known her, she looks flustered.

"No, it's not. The Chef's sick. There's a lot of prep to get ready before tonight's opening. People are already waiting outside, the cooler isn't cold enough, it's a disaster."

I frown. "What happened to Roxy?"

"Came down with the stomach flu," Deanna pipes up. "So her Sous Chef had to stay at the Crow and keep the restaurant open. Which means, opening night is down to us."

"What about Buzz and Mac? Surely they can come help."

Deanna gives me a side-eye. "They're already setting up the tables and chairs and running across town to get more supplies. Bones and Brock had a last minute haul in Phoenix. Gunner had to help Lily at the salon, Colt's fixing the cash drawer because the server isn't reading properly, and fuck knows where Steel is…"

"He's working late at the garage," Sienna pipes up.

"So, who's cookin'?"

"Us," Kirsty replies.

My gaze flicks to Amelia. She looks away the moment our eyes meet.

So we're back to this.

"Not to sound offensive, but can any of you cook?"

"Not for two hundred people," Sienna cries, looking more and more frustrated by the second. "I mean, I can flip a burger, but there's more to it than that."

"I can't cook for shit," Deanna admits.

"I'm okay with a deep fryer," says Cassidy.

"Do these hands look like they cook?" Kirsty waves her leopard print nails at me.

I look back at Amelia and give her a chin lift. "What about you, Amelia?"

Amelia looks up from her chopping board. "My specialty is Ramen noodles, the kind you add hot water to."

"Doesn't sound very convincin'," I muse, folding my arms over my chest.

"What about you, Gears?" she fires back. "Is this the first time you've even been in a kitchen?"

Wiseass.

"It may surprise you to know that I'm a pretty good cook."

They each look at me skeptically.

"Do you have other hidden talents we're not aware of?" Deanna snickers.

I shoot her a look, and her mom chooses to ignore her.

"What do you mean by, *other?*" Cassidy rolls her lips.

"Yeah, Deanna, please elaborate." I raise one eyebrow.

"I would, but Mom probably doesn't want to hear all about your sordid sexcapades."

Kirsty rolls her eyes at me. "Kids forget we were young once," she says to me. "And that her father is a very virile man."

The girls, all but Deanna, splutter with laughter.

"Ew, Mom, that's disgusting," she groans, pulling a face. "Can we have one conversation where you don't mention anything about you and Dad doing it?"

She shrugs. "Just telling it like it is."

I bite my lip, trying not to laugh my ass off. I mean, go Hutch, seriously.

"So?" Sienna questions, looking at me. "Can you cook, Gears?"

I don't really want to give all my trade secrets away, but I can do a little more than flip burgers.

"That's for me to know," I reply, "and for you to find out."

Kirsty turns and gives me a stare down that would rival the Devil's Mistress. "Gears."

I glance at her. "It's burgers and fries, how hard could it be?"

"It takes coordination," Deanna helpfully chimes. "You know what the locals are like around here. If someone has an awful burger on opening night, it could be the end of the Burger Joint before it's even begun. They'll go running back to Burgers R Us before the weekend is out."

Women are so fuckin' dramatic.

"I'm sure y'all can come up with somethin'. I mean, you don't want me cookin' shit for openin' night."

"He's right," Amelia says, as I glance at her. "I think we can manage, between all of us, to get this show on the road."

"I think we have a cook-off," Kirsty announces.

I shake my head. "A what?"

"A cook-off, to determine who can cook the best burger."

"For all we know, you could have another hidden talent," Deanna says, giving me a wink.

So they've been talking about me. My cock is legendary around here, it seems, all because I have piercings.

"I'm not agreein' to this." I chuckle.

"Yes, you are," Kirsty tells me.

Of course, ol' ladies can't tell club members what to do, and up until this moment, I wasn't aware they could tell prospects what to do either. But here we are.

And Kirsty is kinda scary. I'd bet she knows how to use violence, or worse, she could threaten to tell Hutch I wouldn't participate.

I run a hand through my hair. "I came here to wash dishes."

Kirsty throws a dish towel at me. "And now you're gonna cook a burger like you never have before."

"Wait." I hold up a hand. "Who the fuck am I competin' against?"

Sienna raises her hand. "Trust me when I say, I really don't want to do it."

"I'll burn a burger patty too," Cassidy puts in. "Just so it evens up the playing field."

"How the fuck am I bein' roped into this shit?" I complain, wondering if I made a run for it, how many of these women would tackle me to the ground.

Each and every one of them seems stressed. More to the point, why are they all being left to deal with it. Then again, I wouldn't want to eat anything being cooked by Steel or Rubble or any of the brothers, for that matter.

"Out of the goodness of your heart?" Sienna says sweetly.

I snort. "Right. You know you can't make me do this. I've been told to do dishes, and that's it. Ain't nowhere it says that I gotta be cookin' shit just because the cook didn't show up and Roxy's got the stomach flu."

"But what if you actually got through service," Amelia says, "and Hutch finds out we didn't have to close after all."

"Or I take the fall when it all turns to shit," I reply, knowing this has to be a factor.

Kirsty shakes her head. "We're family here, Gears. We don't do shit like that."

A cook-off does sound kinda fun. "Fine. But I get to drink beer, and I don't have to do dishes if my burger is the best."

I've no idea what the fuck I've gotten myself into, but I guess I'm about to find out.

4

AMELIA

WE ALL AGREE. GEARS'S BURGER IS THE BEST, AND JUDGING by the smile on his face, I think he's quite enjoying the attention.

In all honesty, I've never seen someone work as fast as he does.

There might not be much creative genius that goes into making a burger, but somehow, he makes it look easy, and he puts it together like it could be in a food magazine.

I'm surprised and also a little taken aback. After the whole thumb sucking incident, I've been questioning what the hell happened, even when I know why he's been avoiding me ever since.

I've always known he's a little aloof, and has a big chip on his shoulder, even when he masks it well. But I also know that when it comes to the crunch, Gears is loyal and reliable.

Two qualities that seem lacking in so many others these days.

Yet, some of that allure to him is because I know he's

forbidden. And he's younger than me. That in itself is enough to halt me in my tracks.

Am I usually attracted to a man who isn't even of legal age to drink? The answer to that is no.

But Gears is much older than his years. There's something about him that tells you he's lived a very long life in a short time, that he's also possibly seen too much. Maybe that's why I'm attracted to him, because my friends always tell me I like to try to *fix* guys.

Something tells me that I'm unsure if Gears needs to be fixed, but then again, knowing my track history with men, I should stay the hell away and not poke the bear.

It never gets me anywhere.

But do I ever learn? Hell no.

I'm a sucker for a pretty face, a smooth line, and a man I can't have.

Two hours into service, I feel like Gears is at a freakshow.

All the boys from the club stand there watching him.

He's got burgers lined up on the grill, and as fast as I'm laying out the buns and putting all the other ingredients inside, they're being wrapped up, put in a basket or a takeout box, and disappearing before our very eyes. And Gears isn't even breaking a sweat.

"Is he even human?" I hear Colt mutter.

"Beats me," Steel grunts.

"He looks like Gears," Gunner says, rubbing his chin. "But he's not actin' like him. For the first time in his life, he's bossin' women around without gettin' his ear chewed off."

"Shut the fuck up and let him work," says Hutch, who's like a hawk looking down from his perch.

Gears ignores them, calls out the next order number, then I pass the bag to Sienna and she staples it to the front and puts it through the serving window. We have a production line.

"I think someone needs to get him a drink," Rubble observes.

"Nah, alcohol will only slow him down," Gunner replies. "He's on a roll. Don't need to be distractin' him."

"I meant water, dickface."

"If you're so concerned about Gears looking fatigued, you could just get cold water for everyone," I retort, annoyed. "There're pitchers out front."

"Great idea," Hutch agrees, then nods to Gunner.

"What am I, the fuckin' errand boy?" he grumbles.

"Just shut the fuck up and go get the crew water," Hutch replies, as Gunner reluctantly makes for the door. Kirsty flounces through it a second later, but the moment she sees all the boys standing around, she frowns.

"What the hell are all of you doing just standing there?" she demands, hands on hips.

I roll my lips.

Another reason I love this club; women have more of a say than they do in other clubs.

Hutch isn't a soft man by any means. In fact, he's a little intimidating, but I've known him a while, and I know he respects women. He doesn't let anything bad happen to the women of the club, including the sweet butts. In most MC clubs, the sweet butts are the least respected of all, but most women in general are second-class citizens and nothing more than walking pussies who are only needed for one thing. At least at this club, you know you're safe.

Kirsty may not be allowed in church, but she certainly has an influence in and around the club.

"We're observin' honey," Hutch replies.

She shakes her head. "If you're not going to help out,

then I suggest you all get the hell out of the kitchen. We're trying to serve here, and you're in the way."

Hutch's eyebrows raise.

"She looks like Kirsty," Gunner says, behind her with a pitcher of water in one hand and a stack of glasses in the other. "But she's not actin' like her." He plants a kiss on the side of her cheek as she smacks him upside the head. "I like a woman with a bit of spirit, Mrs. H."

Gunner is the club flirt and just being in his presence is good for your confidence, though he's taken now with Steel's sister, Lily, he still likes to break hearts wherever he goes.

"And I'd like you to all get the hell out," she reaffirms. "Or you'll be seeing more than my spirit. More like my foot up your ass."

He pouts, then laughs, setting the water on the counter.

"You heard the lady," Hutch says, his voice booming across the small space.

Steel grumbles, giving Sienna a kiss on top of her head as he passes.

Hutch swings an arm around Kirsty's shoulders. "That didn't really mean me, did it?"

She turns to him, kissing him chastely on the lips. "You bet your ass it did."

He looks at her adoringly. "Fuckin' smart mouth." She rolls her eyes, shoos him out, and then pours everyone a glass of water. We're too busy to even do that menial task ourselves.

I turn to Gears. "So, you're a hustler?"

He's stayed quiet this whole time, concentrating on the orders, but he finds time to amuse me.

"What makes you say that?"

I roll my eyes. "You didn't need a cook-off. You won hands-down."

He gives me a sideways glance. "I didn't really want the job."

I snort. "Looks like you've got it, whether you want it or not."

He wipes his brow. "My grandma taught me how to cook."

I'm caught off guard. I know so little about him or his family life, but just the way he says *my grandma,* tells me he thinks of her fondly.

"What did she teach you to make first?"

"Pasta," he says, smiling at the memory. "Carbonara. She liked all the bad shit; butter, cheese, cream, you name it, if it was on the naughty list, then grandma was all over it."

"What about your mom? Was she a good cook?"

He freezes, his back suddenly rigid as he flips the burgers on the grill. I immediately know I've said something wrong.

"Uh, I don't remember," he says, recovering quickly. "She died when I was six."

I bite my lip and wince. *Shit.* I've put my foot in it again.

"Shit, Gears, I'm sorry."

He shrugs. "I barely remember her."

"What about your…" I stop. I'm intruding. Then again, I've always had a big mouth.

"Dad?" he scoffs. "I don't know. He left the minute he heard my mom was pregnant. My grandma raised me after my mom was killed. If it weren't for her, I'd probably be dead by now, too."

After my mom was killed? My eyes go wide. I don't know if he realizes he just said that. He keeps flipping burgers as Sienna meets my eye from across the workbench.

I'm in shock. I know he's from the other side of the

tracks and he'd had a rough childhood, but not as bad as that.

"I'm so sorry, I never meant to pry."

"It's all right."

He doesn't meet my eye, and for the rest of the night, we pump out another two hundred and fifty burgers, and he never says one more word about it.

The tension in the air has changed since he brought up the details about his mom. I feel a sense of remorse come over me, wondering what that would be like, losing your mom at such a young age. I may have had ups and downs with my own parents, but I've only ever known a loving household, where I was protected. Granted, my dad being ex-military sheltered me a lot from the outside world, and he was tough on my brothers, and distant with me. I relied on my mom for all the love and attention my father just didn't know how to give.

We've come a long way over the last few years, especially with Axton getting out of jail. It finally feels like we're a real family again. Dad and Brock are also in a good place, after years of displacement.

By the time the last order goes out, we're sold out of patties and everyone is exhausted.

The overall vibe from the customers is that the Burger Joint is a hit. Every single burger and fry that went out tonight was enjoyed and the feedback positive. All because Gears kept the kitchen running.

In a weird kinda way, I'm proud of him. Like he really excelled tonight and showed he can do more than just shit kick at the scrap yard.

After Hutch is done patting him on the back, beaming from ear to ear as he talks about how everyone is loving the place, I go to the cooler and come back with a beer and hand it to him.

"Think you've earned one of these," I say with a soft smile.

He looks up and gives me a chin lift. "Thanks, sugar. I think if I never see a burger again, it'll be too soon."

"Hey, he's not old enough to drink." Gunner laughs, passing us by, giving Gears a huge slap on the back that makes him splutter his beer everywhere.

"Fuck," he mutters, wiping his shirt and his chin. "Thanks, fuckin' pretty boy."

"Hey, listen, about the other day…at the office." His eyes meet mine, then he gives me a look that says *don't go there.*

Funny, I've never been very good at listening.

"Amelia…"

"Things have been weird between us," I say in a whisper. Not that the others can hear, since they're all out in the cafe, celebrating. "We used to be able to joke and share a few laughs.

"Yeah, because you've been avoiding me."

I snort. "More like *you've* been avoiding *me.*"

"Don't you think that's probably the best course of action?" he goes on in a hushed tone. "Considering who you are and who I am."

Do I let him know that I'm into him? That would be weird if he wasn't into me, but then I remember what he said to me. *"You in your varsity sweater, actin' like butter wouldn't melt in your mouth while askin' me about my Jacob's Ladder? Sugar, if you want a closer inspection, all you gotta do is ask.*

And then the whole growl when I sucked on his thumb, wishing it were his cock. Just like that, I'm hot for him all over again.

"I think some rules were meant to be broken."

He snorts a laugh. "Not these rules, babe."

You'd be on your knees, takin' all of me with that smart

mouth of yours. A shiver goes down my spine at remembering his words.

"You were into it, Gears. Admit it."

"I was momentarily blinded by your beauty. I lost myself for a second. It won't be happenin' again."

I stare at him, unable to fathom how he comes out with these things. It's like he literally has no filter.

"You were?" All I heard in that sentence is that he thinks I'm beautiful.

He shakes his head. "Babe, we can't."

"So why say all of that, then?"

"To tease you."

I give him my mean girl stare. "That isn't fair."

"Who said life's fair?" He shrugs, nonchalantly. Oh, I get it, the walls have gone back up.

I saw him be vulnerable earlier, and now he's making up for it by being a douche.

I poke him in the chest. "Funny, I thought you weren't afraid of anything."

He snorts a laugh. "Who told you that?"

"I can see it in your eyes. You do what you want, with no consequences."

"That just goes to show how much you really don't know. As a prospect, the club owns me. I can never do what I want."

"Including me?"

"Including you."

"You won't be a prospect forever." I don't know what's come over me, or why I even say it. But let's face it, it's the truth. That makes me think that he's right; he was just teasing me to get a rise out of me.

"No, but Axton and Brock will always be your brothers."

I shake my head. "Wow. You had so much more grit

44

when we were talking about your Jacob's Ladder. Now it's all about what my brothers think and what they'll do."

He stares at me. "You can't stop thinkin' about me, can you?"

I immediately look down at my shoes. *What the hell? Why am I like this with him? Why does he have the ability to turn my insides to mush each and every time?*

"You're such a smug asshole, do you know that?"

He moves closer to me, shooting a look toward the doors that separate us from the rest of the club members.

"You have, haven't you?"

I swallow hard. "Have I what?"

He glances down my body, his eyes assessing every inch of me. "Touched yourself."

I feel my cheeks burning with a flush.

Indeed, I have, but I'm not about to admit that to him. It's his fault anyway; he's the one who instigated the flirting.

I open my mouth, then close it again.

He smirks. "Thought so."

"Well, take a good look, *prospect*," I fire back. "Because it's as close as you're ever going to get to finding out."

He steps closer, caging me in against the kitchen bench and the sink, so we're momentarily out of eyesight from the door.

"I'm not denyin' that I want a taste, Amelia. Truth be told, I touched myself too, thinkin' about you."

My heart beats so loudly in my chest, I think it's going to burst out of my body and explode.

He did what?

"But, we gotta be smart. You're a woman with a real career, an expensive car, a nice place. You're upper class, in another league, and I'm a nobody. I kick shit for a livin' and that's probably what I'll always do. All I'm gonna be

45

good for is a quick fuck. If that's what you want, I can do that. All I gotta do is bring my shovel, though, so when I'm done, your brothers can bury my body out at Shotgun Canyon."

I stare at him. "Why do you always say shit like that?"

"They would bury me, it's the truth."

"Not that," I admonish, aware our bodies are almost touching and my clit is on fire. I want him to press his body into mine so I can feel his cock, see if he's hard for me like he was the last time. "The part about me bein' a stuck-up bitch and you apparently being a nobody."

"Never said you were a stuck-up bitch, but you are a woman so far out of my orbit, you could be the fuckin' moon."

I shake my head. "Look at what you did tonight, Gears."

"I don't need a pity party. I also don't need a mercy fuck."

Tears sting my eyes. "Is that what you think this is?"

"You looked at me differently after I told you about my mom."

"I'm sorry," I stammer. "I was in shock...you said...you said she'd been killed."

"She was murdered," he replies, his eyes boring into mine. In their depths, I see something I've never noticed before; pain, a lot of it. "Does that mean I get a blow job and a fuck?"

"That's not funny."

"Wasn't meanin' it to be, but I'm nobody's fool. I know you probably think I need fixin', right? Because I'm so endearing or some shit. Trust me, *sugar*, I've been hearing that my whole life. It's just a face. I can make you think anything I like. What does that make me?"

"Human?" I counter. "It makes you human, Gears."

He snorts. "You don't wanna hear that shit."

I stare at him. "I'm sorry about your mom, that's horrible."

"I don't need sympathy. I should never have even said anythin'."

"Then why did you?"

"Because I knew it'd be the fastest way for you to high-tail it away from me."

I frown, my hands balling into fists. "Why would you do that?"

"Because I can't have you, Amelia!" he whisper-shouts in face, his eyebrows furrowed.

"I can't fuckin' have you, and if I do, then I'm a dead man. Don't you get it?"

"I get it, trust me. I've been controlled by the men in my life for as long as I can remember. I've been shielded and protected like I've been wrapped in cotton wool, and that's all great in theory, until you go out into the real world, and you have to hide things from your family because you're too scared they'll take things away. Not being able to live your own life in fear of what your brothers will do or how they'll react to every decision you make is like walking on eggshells your entire life."

"So why did you come to Bracken Ridge?"

I shrug. "I thought it'd be different now I'm out of school and have a good job, my own place...I'm not ungrateful." I whisper the last part. "I love my brothers, and my parents, but I'm like a ticking time bomb, Gears. I need to live my own life."

"Then maybe you need to leave."

The silence hangs between us.

Tears sting my eyes. "Leave?"

He steps back, running a hand through his hair as he does. I grab onto his arm. He doesn't flinch or pull away, instead, he cups my face with one hand, one knee going between my legs as I gasp. "I'm sorry about all of that, but you're a young, beautiful, and amazing woman, Amelia. You could have any guy you want. And like I said, I won't be *that* guy. If I weren't in the MC, I'd be happy to be your fuck boy mornin', noon, and night. But that's how it is. That's how it's goin' to stay, until I'm patched in."

I push him backward. I don't want him to see how much rage and shame I feel.

Rejection. Once again.

I always do this to myself. I always pick the guy I can never have. But with Gears, it feels like nothing else ever has. The way he looks at me...the way he says *sugar...*

"Fine. Stay away from me, and I'll do the same."

"Amelia."

"Don't, Gears. I've got the message loud and clear."

I push past him and stride out of the kitchen and through the throng of bodies. I need to get some fresh air.

How humiliating.

But what was I expecting? Him to throw the club in for a roll in the hay?

I've no idea what the hell is happening to me or why I'm acting this way.

But one thing I do know for sure is he's not going to drive me from the life I've built here.

No fucking way.

From here on in, I make my own decisions. Nobody else gets a say.

If they don't like it, they can go jump off Shotgun Canyon.

5

GEARS

TWO WEEKS LATER

"I DON'T KNOW," I SAY TO HUTCH. KIRSTY SITS ON HIS KNEE as they both talk to me in his office, away from the prying eyes of the club.

"What do you mean, you don't know?" Hutch quirks an eyebrow.

"I mean, I don't know what I can fit in. I still work six days a week with Nitro." They want me to be the full-time cook at the Burger Joint. I don't want to sound ungrateful, but I've got so much on my plate, I don't know how I'd fit that in as well as my other duties.

"You'd give up the yard," Hutch replies, his eyes meeting mine. "The prospects can help Nitro for the time bein', and that leaves your days and nights free."

I palm the back of my neck. "It's an amazing opportunity."

"It's more money, too," Kirsty says. "And you'd get to move out of the clubhouse into better digs. Right, sweetie?" She turns to Hutch.

He gives me an eye roll. "He's still a prospect," he reminds her. "What do you plan on doin' with him?"

"He could take Axton's old room above the Crow. He and Stevie are moving onto Brock's property, and Roxy is moving into Stevie's apartment. It means Gears would be closer to work, can fill in at the Crow when needed, and look after the place now that Axton isn't there as security at night."

Stevie is Axton's ol' lady and she manages the local pub, the Stone Crow where Axton runs the bar.

"The whole idea behind a prospect, honey, is that he lives at the clubhouse until he's patched in and has earned his dues. That won't be for a while yet."

"Why the hell not?" she counters.

He gives her a stern look, but before he gets to answer, she plows on. "Don't look at me like that, and don't you dare say it's *"club business,"* Gears did an amazing job on opening night, and he's been pitching in on the weekends when he could've been resting. The kid never sleeps."

"Next you're gonna say let's patch him in right now."

She purses her lips. "Take it to the table, but we know what has to happen. He's much better value at the Burger Joint and we both know it."

"Glad I've got my ol' lady on your side," he mutters. "Or I might think I need a new advisor. I don't know how Brock would feel about you becomin' the new VP."

She slaps him on the arm. "Don't take that tone with me."

"I should put you over my knee." He looks over to me. "But that's for later."

I clear my throat. "With all due respect, I'm happy to keep helpin' on weekends…"

Kirsty shakes her head. "We've been lucky with Roxy back from the dead, but she's spreading herself too thin, and she's needed back at the Crow. It makes sense for Gears to have his own place, Hutch, and Axton's apartment

50

is empty. That makes it nice and easy. Part of his prospect duties can be to secure the Crow at night, now that Axton isn't on site. It's win-win."

Fuck. Go Kirsty.

Having my own place, as a prospect, would be a dream come true. It's not something I ever expected would happen, not like this.

"You're lucky my ol' lady has a soft spot for you," Hutch mutters. "Trust me, if she didn't, we'd be havin' a different kind of conversation."

This is Hutch. He doesn't get mad at his woman for talking club business in front of me, or making it clear what she thinks, especially when we both know that she's making sense.

Sometimes it really does take a woman's touch.

In so many ways, she reminds me of my own mom, from what I can remember of her.

The trouble was, my mom got caught up in some heavy shit that she couldn't get out of and ultimately it claimed her life.

I saw her beaten to death right in front of my eyes.

I swallow hard.

Don't think about that here. Now isn't the time to lose it.

After my conversation with Amelia, I've been feeling pretty shitty these last few weeks.

I don't know what the fuck went down with us, but I know I did the right thing.

She wants a walk on the wild side. She wants a fuck boy. She doesn't get it.

I don't know when it was that I fell for her. Maybe it was the first time I laid eyes on her. Or the time I fixed her car. Or the time when she paid me any attention. Who knows.

But, the fact remains, for some unknown reason, Amelia is my downfall. She will break me.

She'll break my walls down.

She's the reason I can't fuckin' concentrate on anything. Putting one foot in front of the other seems like a hard enough task without having to relive her words to me the night she stormed out.

Even though she'll never admit it, she knows it's for the best. She knows I'm not good for her, that, in her eyes, I'd just be using her for sex. I'm good at sex. I know how to use my body to make a woman feel pleasure. That's the easy part. The part that I suck at is when I switch my brain off from just sex to actually giving a fuck about the person. With her, it's different. It isn't just about sex, even though we've not done that yet. And I don't know how to do anything else. I don't know how to surrender this part of myself that so badly wants to be held and loved. It's talk. I've never had anything more than casual fucks, and I know with Amelia feelings come into the equation. Love isn't something I can give her.

It's not a strong way to think and no way for a biker to act. It's fucked.

But I can't deny something about being around Amelia makes me want to tear my walls down and have at it. To let her see the parts of me that I let no one else see. Even when I know deep down, she'd never cope with it. She doesn't want to see that side. Nobody does.

She wants to see the wild, kinky man-whore who knows where to touch to make her scream. All. Night. Long. That I can do. But the rest? The rest is just plain scary.

"I like him because he's honest," Kirsty interjects, pulling me out of my reverie. "He's a hard worker; he's proved his loyalty. The boys like him, the women—"

"Let's not talk about the women." He points at me. "Which isn't a free pass to start thinkin' your ass is above the rules, son."

I try not to smirk. "I would never think that."

He watches me for any obvious signs of smart-ass before he looks back to Kirsty. "Anythin' else my queen requires?"

"Yes, but there are children present," she whispers, loud enough for me to hear.

I chuckle. "On that note, I'd better be off," I say, going to stand.

He kisses Kirsty chastely, then looks back to me. "We'll discuss it at the table. So, to be clear, you'd be workin' full time for the Burger Joint, and helpin' at the Crow when they need it." Kirsty slaps him on the arm again. "Oh, and movin' into Axton's place. On probation, though, no fuckin' parties or wild chicks and shit. It's a onetime only offer…don't fuck it up."

I can't help the smile that spreads across my face. "Love everything you just said."

Kirsty beams at me as I give her a chin lift. "Thanks, Mama Bear."

"You're welcome, sweetie. Congratulations."

"Mamma Bear?" Hutch balks.

I quickly leave as I hear him say, "The fuck? I thought you were my Mama Bear?"

"Shut the fuck up and let me play Nurse instead. Seems like you've got some wounds that need to be licked."

Then I hear him groan.

I shudder. It's bad enough imagining old people doing it, but those two? Fuck me, they're like a couple of teenagers.

As I pass by the bar, Summer, Gunner's sister, waves. "Hey, Gears," she says.

She's cute. Tall and lanky with short blonde hair and blue eyes. She's the quietest of the group and hasn't been around the club that much with going back to school.

"Hey, Summer, how's it goin'?"

"Don't suppose you can help me change the kegs over?" She's also the only one who ever speaks to me with any respect around here.

"Sure thing."

"Thanks. I usually get Ginger to do it, but she's off sick."

"When did you get back into town?"

"Spring break." She shrugs. "And I'm moving back permanently. I've secured a placement at the hospital."

"Cool," I say. "Though, don't college kids usually go off and have fun on spring break?"

She smiles wistfully. "Not those with no college fund. Luckily, I have a brother who looks after me and helps out more than he should. Besides, I like it here."

I wonder what that must be like. Being an only child, I never had the opportunity to know about having siblings, only shitty cousins who used to try to beat me up when Grandma wasn't around.

"Well, good for you. Guess it beats the city any day of the week."

"I heard you were a big hit at opening night," she goes on. "You saved the club from having to postpone and lose a lot of business."

"You could say that, though the window washer would've got the job over me, if they'd had the option."

She laughs. "You're being modest."

"They just liked the hot sauce; the club got a deal to ship it to England and stock it in some fancy store."

"For real?"

I nod. "So I'll know I've really made it when I get the

sauce recipe. For now, it's still a trade secret, locked in Hutch's safe."

"Something to live for."

I grin. "Definitely."

I switch the kegs over quickly. I'm already late to finish up my shift with Nitro. I don't know if he'll be glad to see the back end of me, but cooking at the Burger Joint isn't so bad, and it has air conditioning.

The part about me moving into Axton's, though, that has to be the best fuckin' news I've heard in a while. The clubhouse isn't that bad; it's better than my last place, but unless the sweet butts come and clean up, the place can get like a pig sty if it's left up to the prospects. Especially after parties. And they don't come and clean prospects rooms, unfortunately.

Luckily, I'm actually pretty neat and tidy. I don't like things out of place, and I always make my bed. I guess some habits die hard, or maybe Grandma just instilled it into me that you can't start the day off right with an unmade bed.

On the way over to work, I can't help but think about Amelia and our last conversation again.

How she stormed out on me and her parting words… *Fine. Stay away from me, and I'll do the same.*

She acted as if I'd burned her, and while I never meant to hurt her, I know I was leading her on and I should've quit. I should never have told her I touched myself; in hindsight, that was a little TMI. Maybe a part of me wanted her to fuck the consequences and take the lead. Not that I'd normally let a chick do that, but Amelia is unlike any woman I've ever met. With Amelia, I want her to do bad things to me. I want her to lead me astray.

I'd let her guide me into hell if it meant I'd get to touch her, even just once. Tasting her, fuck, I'd die. Her soft, sweet skin, and those legs wrapped around me while I take my time fuckin' her slow. She makes me so goddamn crazy.

And that's what it's like being around her; it's like my skin is on fire whenever she's close. It's like a goddamn inferno.

I run a hand through my hair the second I'm off my motorcycle, kicking the stand down. I've let my hair grow out, much to the club brothers' amusement, and since then, I've been the butt of everyone's jokes. As long as the chicks around the club like it, that's all that matters.

I wonder what Amelia thinks...not that she'd care now, since she hates me.

For all I know, she could be telling her besties shit that could get me into trouble with the club, but she doesn't seem that vindictive. At least, I don't think so.

Whenever I've thought about her in these last few weeks, I get this pain in my chest. I don't know what the fuck that's all about. I also don't expect to see her at Deanna's poker night, not that I got an invite, but another one of my shitty jobs being a prospect after work is to do menial shit that's beneath me; like drop takeout to the club girls while they play cards, get drunk, and try to fondle me.

Tonight, it's pizza because the Burger Joint is closed on Tuesdays. Meaning, my one night off is never sacred, no matter which way you look at it.

"Gears!" Deanna squeals, hugging me in a tight embrace as I almost drop the pizzas while she squeezes me around the middle. "How the hell is it hanging?"

"Uh, it's hanging just fine," I reply. "Where do you want these?"

Please just take them out of my hands so I can go.

She's clearly had a few rounds before I arrived, so when

she finally let's go, then apologizes for hugging me, she drags me by the elbow into her sitting room.

"Girls, the entertainment has arrived!" she announces as I glance around the room.

Kirsty. Sienna. Cassidy. Lily. Lucy. Katie from the beauty salon. Angel; Brock's ol' lady. Amelia. And Kennedy and Stevie can be heard in the kitchen laughing as they get the snacks organized.

"Wow. I've died and gone to heaven," I say, giving Kirsty a wink.

"Leave him alone Deanna," Kirsty mocks. "We don't need you scaring the poor boy away before he can commit to taking on the Burger Joint."

Oh yeah, it was voted at the table. So I'm officially the new cook at the hottest gig in town.

I start Saturday night, so I'll celebrate my birthday cooking burgers on a grill and sweating over a hot stove. It's not like anybody actually cares about a prospect's fuckin' birthday anyway.

I can spend Sunday moving from the clubhouse to Axton's apartment, since he's officially moved all his shit out.

"Are you sure he's not the entertainment?" Katie smiles, sizing me up. She's cute. She hangs around the club sometimes with Lily, but she's not really my type. She's not tall, with honey colored hair, and curves in all the right places.

I gyrate my hips, still holding the pizzas while all the girls fall about laughing, cat-calling like a bunch of deprived hens.

All I really want is Amelia's eyes on me. I want them all over me.

"You know, I was thinkin' about takin' a job in adult entertainment," I say when I finally get to place the pizzas down on the kitchen bench. "But I chose to stay here so I could be fawned over by the most beautiful women in Bracken Ridge instead."

Sienna snorts a laugh. Lily claps her hands. And Angel just rolls her eyes like she's heard it all before.

"Smoothness will get you everywhere," Sienna says when she's finished laughing at me. "But I'm surprised nobody tackled you for the pizzas. We've worked up an appetite."

I notice they're all congregated around the coffee table in the lounge, the dining table set up to play poker, but they haven't started yet.

"What are y'all doin'?" I squint at the screen as Amelia quickly slams the lid shut.

"We're setting Amelia up on a dating app," Deanna chimes happily.

Suddenly, I hear the blood pounding in my ears.

What the fuck?

Keep calm.

Do not react.

Breathe in. Breathe out.

"Do those things really work?" I find myself asking, feeling myself breaking out into a sweat.

"Ask Katie, she's the blowjob...I mean, dating app queen." Lily laughs as Katie swats her on the arm.

"I am not!" she retorts, her cheeks coloring.

I snicker, but my eyes flick to Amelia. She looks away the minute our eyes meet.

What in the actual fuck does she think she's doing?

I feel a sensation rising within me from the pit of my stomach...what the hell is that?

Jealousy?

I don't know. I've never had the feeling before, and I'd remember if I did.

"You don't wanna go on those apps," I say nonchalantly.

"All you'll find on there are guys who wanna get into your pants."

"Maybe some of us just want a hook-up?" Amelia fires back at me, unable to keep quiet any longer. *There's my girl.* "A fuckboy who's in it for no other reason."

Snorts and snickers ring around the room, even Kirsty has a little chuckle to herself. So much for mother hen.

Using my words back at me? She's sunk to a new low.

"Amelia! I've known you since you were a teenager," Kirsty admonishes, taking a big guzzle of her wine. "I don't want to hear about random hook-ups or anything else close to it."

"Oh please, Mom," Deanna counters. "We all have to hear about you and Dad's sexcapades until our ears are bleeding. This isn't shocking news."

"I think you're better than that," I say to Amelia. Her annoyed face doesn't deter me, nothing can. "And it sounds dangerous to me. What if the guy's a fuckin' murderer, or rapist, or one of those guys who likes to hang out in the park and flash people?"

"That is extremely unlikely." She shakes her head and folds her arms over her chest. "Anyway, I don't remember asking you for permission to pry into my private life, *prospect.*"

"He's got a point." Cassidy shrugs. "You can't be too careful these days."

"You said a mouthful there," Lucy agrees.

"Don't forget what happened to me," Lily pipes up. "I was drugged on a blind date and the guy almost got away with date-raping me." She looks over to Sienna. "You saved my life, sister."

Sienna smiles warmly. "Gears is right, you can't be too careful, not these days. If we learned anything from Lily's experience, then we should be making sure we're safe."

I can't help but notice Amelia looking very uncomfortable.

"Hold on," Cassidy says. "That doesn't mean we can't have a little fun in the process."

"Exactly what does your kind of *fun* entail? Not that I think I want to know," I mutter. Trying to smooth over the fact that Amelia will be on a dating app over my dead body.

"Right, you're a virgin, isn't that right, Gears? They don't let you get the goods out, not even for the sweet butts." Angel laughs.

"Am I that transparent?" I mock.

"Well, she could always do one better, and find two dates," Lucy, who clearly has no filter, singsongs. "Or three. In fact, she could start her own harem, then pick and choose who she wants to play hide the sausage with."

Everyone laughs, except Amelia, who throws a handful of popcorn at Lucy as I stare at her, willing her to challenge me with her gaze.

Not gonna happen.

My mouth feels dry as I make my way to the door. If I don't leave now, I'll haul her over my shoulder, and carry her out of here caveman style.

I can't have her, but that doesn't mean another man gets to enjoy her.

Nope. I'll fuckin' rip his throat right out of his neck.

I crack my neck from side to side. "Well, ladies, I hope you have a nice night." My eyes flick to Amelia's. "Enjoy the poker game."

She scowls at me as I turn to leave.

"Thanks for the pizza, Gears," I hear Sienna, the only one with any manners, call out.

"God, he's so cute," someone else says, Katie maybe. "Is it true younger guys can go all night, without, you know…"

"Ejaculating?" I'm sure Kennedy finishes, laughing. "Take it from a woman who has a younger man, it's true."

"He's a looker," Kirsty agrees. "But you know he's a prospect, ladies, and you know what that means…"

I shut the door, feeling like I should somehow feel violated, yet my anger and annoyance are all that flood my very being.

I pace the hall, unable to leave. I pass Frankie on the stairs and give her a chin lift. She's carrying a bowl of something that smells like chili.

"Hey, Gears," she says.

"Hey," I reply, barely giving her a look.

Taking the last few steps two at a time, I jump on my sled and race over to the scrap yard. I don't like disturbing Nitro late at night, so I'm relieved to see his car isn't in the lot. Perfect.

I open the gate, unlock the office, and go to the diary on the desk where Nitro writes important numbers. Amelia has come over to help with the paperwork a couple of times…maybe he has her number written down…*Bingo.*

I punch the number into my phone and before I even leave the office, I'm typing out a message:

Don't even fuckin' think about goin' on that website, sugar. If you wanna test my patience, then be prepared for the consequences.

Before I can even think twice, I hit send.

6

AMELIA

I STARE AT THE MESSAGE IN COMPLETE SHOCK.

What the hell?

I glance around, but nobody is paying me any attention because everyone's finally settled into playing poker after devouring pizza and most of Frankie's chili.

Who the heck does Gears think he is?

I know now for sure that he's just playing games with me, and I don't like it.

I should ignore him.

I shouldn't give him the time of day.

But I can't help it when my fingers take on a mind of their own and I start a reply.

Me: Since when in the hell do you get to tell me what to do?

Instantly, it says he's read the message. The gray bubble begins to form, telling me he's replying.

Gears: Like I said. Don't push me.

I'm actually so mad right now, I could go kick his pretty face in.

Me: How did you get this number?

He doesn't reply.

I stuff a mouthful of chips into my mouth as I form another reply.

Me: If you think I answer to you, *prospect*, then you've got another thing coming. Hear me, let it register: leave me the hell alone.

Gears: A few weeks ago, you wanted to fuck me. Now you're all mad because I tried to do the right thing.

I snort. Deanna looks up at me, and I smile sweetly. I don't need anyone knowing I'm texting him.

Me: You're only saying that because of what Deanna said about going on a dating app.

Gears: Is it true?

Me: That's none of your business.

Gears: As a member of this club, it's my job to protect you.

I shake my head. He is clearly delusional.

Me: You told me to leave.

Gears: So that's what this is all about?

Me: Note to self: the world doesn't revolve around you. I'm sure that will come as a shock to you. It'll rival that huge chip you have on your shoulder.

Gears: If I see you on a date...

My heart accelerates at his words. I feel that tingle through my body, the possessiveness hitting me deep in my core, and it makes my pussy throb. *Jesus, he undoes me with the click of his fingers. Well, I will not succumb to his idiotic demands, nor will I stoop to his level.*

I can't help it though when I write: **What are you going to do about it?** I know, yet again, I'm playing with fire.

The gray bubble appears again, then disappears, then appears. This happens several times before the next message comes through.

Gears: I'll kill him. And you'll be punished.

I clench my thighs, knowing full well he's getting me wet. *Punished?* Oh God, yes.

I mean, no. NO! This is bad, very bad.

Me: Don't make promises you can't keep.

Gears: I've got a compromise. If you're up for it.

I lick my lips, sitting up a little straighter in my chair as Lucy starts to deal the cards.

Me: Go bore someone else with your petty taunts.

Then, the bubble doesn't appear. *Shit.*

I check my phone five minutes later. Nothing. Twenty-minutes. Nada.

He's got me so pent-up with rage and want that I can't fucking see straight. I'm not concentrating on the cards, barely going through the motions.

I want to know what he was going to say, but now I can't ask him.

Two hours.

Three.

He's literally driving me to the brink of madness.

It's not until I'm getting ready for bed, hours later, three shots of tequila down and nothing better to do, when I crawl into bed, switch the light out and toss and turn for the next hour.

I sigh, annoyed with myself, then roll over and grab my phone.

I text him before I can think any more about it.

Me: Fine. I've had enough tequila to make me drunk enough to ask what you meant.

Instantly, the gray bubble appears.

Fucking asshat.

It's like he knows he's winning this stupid game I wasn't even aware I'd signed up for.

Gears: We can't date.

Me: Duh.

Gears: I can't touch you.

Me: Get to the point, I'm aging here.

Gears: I want to see you. *All* of you.

I frown. What in the ever-loving fuck is he talking about?

Me: Speak English, for fuck's sake.

Gears: I want to watch you. On camera.

My eyes go wide as I sit up in bed. *Watch me?* Like...a cam girl?

I stare at the screen and read his words over and over again.

I've never done anything like that before, obviously.

The thought initially makes me cringe and want to slap him silly. Then, when I think about it and feel my pulse quicken, I realize that my inner kinky self is nodding her fucking head eagerly.

Me: Are you insane? I have to make it sound like he's lost his marbles. He has this nasty habit of flirting with me until I'm practically begging for it. Then he pours cold water on my head and puts all the flames out.

Gears: It's the perfect scenario. We aren't breaking any rules. We don't even meet in person.

Me: I'm pretty sure we're breaking all of them.

Gears: Amelia. I want to see you, and you know what?

I take the bait...

Me: What?

Gears: I know you want to see me too.

My mind races as I think about seeing him naked. Thinking about him touching himself, like he already told me he did, sends shock waves right through me. And knowing I did that to him, well, that makes it that much sweeter.

Me: Do you have a Jacob's Ladder? I blame the tequila for asking again.

Gears: Do you want to find out?

I take a few deep breaths. I know I do. In the darkest depths of my fantasies, I watch someone live, not like porn, but like a cam guy kinda thing. Friends of mine have done it in college, and while the idea always sort of repulsed me back then, this somehow speaks to my libido like nothing else. It's like a spark just ignited inside me.

Imagining him fisting his cock…

Say yes. Say yes.

I press the button on my phone to lock it and don't reply.

I can't do this.

I cannot even believe the damn conversation went on for this long. He's so far out of line…

My body, however, is on fire. My nipples are taut and my pussy's slick with arousal.

I want to see him so damn much. I can't deny it.

It's so erotic.

We can't see one another.

We can't speak.

We can't touch.

But we can do this.

We can watch each other.

Maybe if I let him go first…

I don't look at my phone again for the rest of the night.

If I sleep this off, then maybe it'll be like it never happened.

Good plan.

Wishful thinking is always in hindsight for a reason.

The next morning, as I'm getting ready for work, there's a message from Gears.

Gears: Did you think about it?

No good morning, or how are you doing, or did you sleep well, or anything like that.

This man is infuriating.

I take a sip of my coffee and contemplate my reply.

I mean, am I completely forgetting this man texted me to say that I'm not allowed to go on a date with another man, and if I do, he'll kill them?

In the light of day, sober, things seem a little…less erotic and more sketchy. I mean, people don't do this kind of thing, only in romance novels and, well…porn, right?

I can't let humiliation win over this time. If Gears thinks he can make me look like an idiot, yet again, then he's got another thing coming.

Me: I fell asleep. What does that tell you?

A few moments go by before he replies.

Gears: You're saying that because you think I'm playin'

Fine. I take the bait.

Me: Aren't you?

Gears: I can assure you; the complexities of the female body are not something I joke about

I splutter my coffee all over myself. Jesus Christ.

Gears has me seriously unhinged. Of course I'm thinking about it. I couldn't get to sleep last night because all I could replay in my head was a scene of watching Gears jerk himself off while I touched myself, enjoying the show.

Gears: Or maybe you like the idea of watchin' me? That can be arranged.

My mouth goes dry. Well, that sounds a little more appealing than me taking my clothes off in fear he'll screenshot me and ruin my life. Not that I think he'd do that. If he wanted to live a normal life and not be chased down by my family or the MC, then I doubt he'd be that stupid. But the worry still remains in the back of my head.

Maybe I don't have to show my face?

I internally slap myself. I should end this. I should tell him to go get fucked and not message me again. I could threaten him with telling Hutch. Or Brock. But I know immediately that's all hot air. I'm not going to do any such thing.

The dirty ho inside me loves everything he's saying. She's intrigued. She wants to see him naked. She wants to have this nasty, dirty little secret nobody else knows about.

Me: You mean, watch you jerk off? Well, that's telling it like it is. Let's just cut right to the chase.

Gears: Unless you want to watch me make burgers instead?

Me: This is wrong.

Gears: Only because your mind's telling you it is. Pretend we're strangers. Who met in an adult chat room, and we really don't know one another.

Me: I can see you've got this all planned out.

Gears: I've been thinking about it all night.

I pause. Should I? Oh, what the hell... **Me: Did you touch yourself?**

Gears: Yes.

Holy shit.

I squirm, pressing my thighs together tightly as I imagine it.

Gears: You get me so hot, Amelia. You always have.

My eyes go wide.

Me: Always?

Gears: Since you first came back into town.

Me: That was a year ago.

Gears: Before that.

Me: When?

Gears: Christmas before last. You were wearing a snowman sweater with tight leggings and your hair was up in a messy bun.

I stare at his words.

That was two years ago.

He was only eighteen then…my mind knows this is so wrong…but he's of legal age…that's not so bad…right?

Me: That is slightly stalkery

Gears: I've always had it bad for you, sugar. Never thought you'd give me the time of day.

Me: I wish you weren't in the MC

I hit send before I even realize what I typed. *Shit.*

Of course, his reply comes back immediately.

Gears: Why's that? Would you do bad things to me without the guilt?

Me: I'm not answering that.

Gears: Because we both know it's a yes.

We both know it is definitely a yes.

Gears: You should know. I'm up for anything. I have very few boundaries. I'm only into adult females, just to be clear.

I sit at the island bench and stare at the screen, mesmerized and unable to stop.

Me: So, you like kink?

Gears: If she's into it. Do you?

Me: I've never been with anyone that kinky before.

No, but my pussy is begging me to let him have at it.

Gears: What a shame. You have a beautiful body.

I've never really seen myself as someone who is that beautiful. I mean, I think I'm okay. But I'm taller than most, which means I usually stand out when I really don't want to. I have curves but small breasts, and I have kind of small features that I'm not really sure go with the rest of my face. I wish my lips were bigger, but I'm too chicken shit to get fillers. But, I do have clear skin and it can be pretty if I moisturize properly...

Me: I'm glad you noticed...in my snowman sweater

Gears: *laughing emoji* Nothing gets me more worked up than chicks in sweats, especially snowman sweaters

Me: Now you're just being nice.

Gears: Oh, trust me, sugar, if I had you for a night, I'd be anything but nice.

I take a long breath, puffing out my cheeks as I exhale. I am not going to go to the bedroom and use my clitarator on myself before work. No, I'm not. I'm stronger than that.

If I give in and orgasm to Gears's dirty talk, then what won't I do?

Gears: G2G. Need an answer soon.

Me: You're a persistent little shit.

Gears: Babe, you've no idea.

I click my phone to lock it and sit back in my chair.

Am I actually contemplating this?

Watching Gears touch himself?

I mean, I wouldn't have to get naked, and I don't plan to. But if he wants to...who am I to stop him? I can't help the flush that comes over me when I imagine him lying back on his bed, naked, jerking himself off as I watch.

And I can only guess that that was just the tip of the iceberg where his dirty mouth is concerned.

I liked every damn second of it.

Even if I won't admit it to myself.

7

GEARS

Playing it cool has always been something I've been moderately good at. I can fake it. I can be surprisingly patient, but not when it comes to Amelia's answer.

I'm not a patient man where she's concerned.

Maybe I did threaten to kill anyone who even thinks about dating her, and then I'd punish her, that part I will definitely do. She might not understand the depths of my depravity yet, but she will if she agrees to my request. She'll see the good, the bad, and the ugly.

I'd never hurt her.

I'll do whatever she wants.

I have no limits. Well, I do have one; Amelia with another man. That would send me over the edge, because now that she's infused in my every waking moment, I can't get her the fuck out of my head.

This plan is fuckin' genius. Fool proof, as long as she sticks to the rules.

If she doesn't want to show her face, I get it, but I don't give a fuck. In fact, the more I think about it, the more I know this is a rite of passage. For both of us.

Not touching her will be a nightmare. Not seeing her would be even worse. But I'll take whatever I can get. If she wants to see me getting my thrills and coming all over myself because of how she makes me feel, then so be it. I've nothing to hide. I want her.

But if I get to see her naked too…fuck. I'd die a happy man.

I wait an agonizing day before she replies back to me. It's like she knows she has me right on the edge of reason and I'm beyond salvation.

Amelia: I've thought about what you said.

I rub my chin. If she wasn't going to agree, she wouldn't be replying, would she?

Me: And?

Amelia: This is just between us, right?

A grin spreads across my face. My pulse quickens. My cock twitches. *Oh, fuck yeah.*

Me: Of course.

Amelia: What about those other prospects?

Me: I don't associate with them outside the club, and even if I did, this is between you and me. You're mine, Amelia. I don't want another man thinking about you, much less looking at you.

I wait for her to challenge me, to tell me I'm a fuckturd for being so possessive, but when she doesn't, I have to wonder if she actually likes the idea.

Amelia: How do we do it?

My dick strains against my pants. Thank fuck I'm in my bedroom and not around any of the brothers. When we talk like this, I'm instantly hard. And, being a fairly big guy, I can't exactly hide it.

Me: FaceTime is easiest.

Amelia: I'm not getting naked.

Fuck.

74

I run a hand through my hair.

Me: Okay.

Amelia: So, I can watch you?

I smile. I can only hope when she likes what she sees, it'll encourage her to be a little more adventurous.

Me: Yes.

She doesn't reply.

Me: What do you want me to do?

The gray bubble appears and I'm glad she hasn't taken off.

Amelia: I want to watch you pleasure yourself.

It pleases me she wants to see my cock.

I couldn't ask for anything more.

Me: Done. When?

Please say tonight.

Amelia: I can't tonight. I've got drinks with the girls...it'll be late.

Me: I'll be up. I'll be up all fuckin' night waiting for you, babe.

Amelia: You're eager.

Gears: You have no idea.

Amelia: It's a date.

I let out a slow breath and try to control my breathing. The idea of her watching me, even if I don't get to see any of her, makes me want to get down to business right here, right now. Fuck tonight.

Instead, I say, **Text me when you're alone tonight.**

Amelia: Okay.

And that's it.

I bite down on my lip as I lock my phone. She fuckin' agreed?

I feel like the luckiest man on the planet.

Just as I head downstairs, I run into Brock, of all people, and a jolt of panic goes right through me for a moment.

He stops and looks at me. "What's up with you?"

Is he a goddamn mind reader?

"Uhm, nothin', just cleanin' up. Gettin' ready to go do some prep at the Burger Joint."

"Roxy wanted you to swing by and pick up some sauce and she's got a tray of lettuce for you."

How fuckin' thrilling. "I'll head on over there now. I'll need to borrow the cage."

The MC has a van we sometimes use for smaller deliveries, and now that I'm cooking five nights a week at the Burger Joint, I've been using it a lot lately.

"Take the van."

"Thanks."

I get past him. I need to be out of here before he realizes I'm planning on palming my cock over his little sister tonight via webcam. Of all the people I did not want to run into, it's him.

"You sure you're okay? You look a little pale."

"I've got allergies," I call over my shoulder, needing fresh air like I've never needed it before. If I don't get out now, his bullshit radar will go off.

I wish I felt guilty, but I don't.

I'm a grown man. She's a grown woman.

If I weren't a prospect in an MC, I wouldn't give a shit what her brothers thought, but that's not how it is. It's not how it'll ever be. I don't want to make life difficult for her, but the temptation is just too much. And she wants this as much as I do, as much as she won't admit it to herself.

To get involved means sacrifice. I would go against my club.

I don't have a heart, so in some ways it'll be easier. I'll play the game. We'll have fun. And when my time comes and I have to leave, she'll know it's for the best. They all will.

She fuckin' blows me off.

I stare at my phone and try not to let my temper get the best of me. She hasn't even texted me.

I'm past the point of being annoyed. Now I'm just curious to know what got her attention all night that she stood me up. Did her nerves get the better of her? Did she find someone else to hook up with? Anger boils deep within me.

Drinks with friends?

She's at Zee Bar.

It'd be a little bit stalkery of me to go and find her, but I am a little extreme. Something else she doesn't know about me.

Maybe it has something to do with the fact that I was an orphan at six and saw my mom bludgeoned to death. I hid in the closet and covered my eyes. After that, I shut my feelings off so nobody could reach me, except for my grandma. Which is why she's the one I hold up high on a pedestal. I'd never want to disappoint her, but sometimes revenge just eats away at my very being until it consumes me.

All of this is just to pass the time. Until I fix things. Until I can breathe again.

Even if being with Amelia is a far-off dream, she can do better anyway. I don't plan on using her, or hurting her, not intentionally, but I do want her.

None of that is a problem anyway because she doesn't feel the same. Sure, she may want my dick. She may want to see me naked and panting for her, but she'd never want to see the real me. The fucked-up mess I really am. Nobody wants to see that shit.

I don't think.

I take off on my sled to go down to Zee Bar to see if she's still there, because I really am just that pathetic.

When I get there, even though I know I'm dressed in my usual attire; my prospect cut, Henley and jeans, I walk right on in, like I own the place, and sit at the bar.

There're no rules about not wearing club colors, but it's definitely frowned upon.

It's not like Bracken Ridge has any rival clubs that'll come in and start a turf war.

I can sit in a goddamn bar and drink a beer, underage, if I want to.

The chick at the bar eyes me, and I'm waiting for her to ask me for I.D., but luckily for her, she doesn't.

I turn my head, trying to look around discreetly for Amelia without getting caught.

The bar is pretty empty. Double fuck. It means I'll be easier spotted, not that I give a shit what Amelia thinks about me looking like an obsessed stalker, but the other girls of the club may become suspicious as to why I'm drinking at a swanky, tapas wine bar right at closing.

I don't have to wait too long.

She's still here. In the restaurant.

And I can see Deanna and a few others, and some guys I don't know.

I crack my neck.

So she really did play me after all that?

What a fuckin' idiot I am for believing it.

I neck down my beer, my hands shaking as I will myself not to go over there and break someone's face.

The rage in me boils. The monster lurks.

I stand, and just as I do, my phone buzzes. Pulling it out of my pocket, I glance down.

I swallow hard as I read the text.

Amelia: Are you still up?

78

I glance back to the restaurant. She has her back to me; she hasn't seen me. I keep walking toward the bathrooms, where I can get a better look at her without being seen.

Me: I'm always up when it comes to you.

Amelia: I'm still at Zee Bar.

I know.

Me: Better not hear you were talkin' to other men.

She does that thing where she shakes her head, and I know she just gave me an eye roll.

Amelia: What is it with you being weird about me talking to other men? I am single, remember?

Me: Not if we do this thing.

She frowns. I like that she's ignoring all the people at her table. The only thing stopping me from going over there right now and dragging her out of here, is the fact that I'll never be allowed back in the MC again. It's not like I can say I was protecting her. Half the club girls are here.

Amelia: You like your rules, don't you, prospect?

Gears: I want you to get home.

Amelia: Bossy.

Me: You know you like it.

She brushes one hand up and down her arm. *She's touching herself.*

Me: You've been thinking about this all day, haven't you?

She doesn't respond right away, because someone starts talking to her, momentarily distracting her.

Amelia: Cocky much?

I grin at my phone.

Me: Always. And you didn't answer the question. Well, I can answer it from my end. I've not stopped thinking about it all day. About her. About what we could be doing, in secret.

It's calling to every sense in my body, luring me in, making me fuckin' crazy.

Amelia: What if I said I have.

Me: I'd believe you.

Amelia: Have you?

Me: Why don't you get home and I'll show you.

Then, she pushes her chair out, says something to Deanna, who nods, then turns and heads directly toward me. She's making her way to the bathroom.

I move farther down the hall, out of sight, as she walks into the ladies.

What I want to do is stalk in there, demand to know where the fuck she's been all night. Take her by the throat and press my aching cock against her plump, firm ass. I fuckin' should. She deserves it. Teasing me like this, making me wait. But I don't do any of those things.

Instead, I wait. Wishing I could do so much more. Willing myself to be patient. Telling myself not to go in there and blow my cover. I'm sure she won't appreciate me accosting her in the bathroom stall.

I wait for her to say something else.

A few moments later, she reappears. I watch her ass and her long legs disappear back down the hallway, back to her table. Then, my phone buzzes again.

Amelia: Twenty minutes.

I smirk.

Me: I'll be waiting.

I feel a carnal need run through me at what we're about to embark on. And it feels so goddamn right.

If I can't touch her, can't be with her physically, then this is the next best thing.

Even if deep down I know it'll never be enough.

8

AMELIA

My palms are sweating as I take the cab ride home.

The way he reels me in with his demands, it appeals to me on another level, one I wasn't aware I even had in me.

Better not hear you were talkin' to other men.

I should be more bothered by that statement. All the men in my life are over-protective as hell and it annoys the shit out of me, even when I know they mean well. But when Gears does it, my body literally hums for him.

I can't explain it. I feel a rush of heat, the telling sign of wetness between my legs every time he takes charge.

We shouldn't work, we *can't* work. And yet, I find myself racing home so I won't be late.

For him.

Because I want to see him like this. I want to see him lose control.

It's so dirty.

So forbidden.

So damn hot.

As much as I try to make it seem that I'm unaffected by

him, he knows the truth. He knows he does something to me, or we wouldn't be in this predicament.

It's a game to him, I get it. But I like the game, and I want to play.

The deepest desires in me have come to life, and by the time I make it home, pay the cab driver, and let myself into my apartment, I'm feeling very horny.

I kick my shoes off, don't bother to turn on the lights, and go straight to my bedroom.

My heart racing, my skin flushed and heated, I sit on the end of my bed and contemplate this one more time.

I'm a little buzzed from the alcohol, but I know what I'm doing. I know I want this.

I look down at my phone just as a text comes through.

Gears: You home yet?

My heart is racing so loud that I feel the blood pound in my years. I reply with shaky hands.

Me: I just got home.

The bubble appears as I stare down anxiously.

Gears: What are you wearing?

Me: Seriously?

Gears: I thought you might want some conversation first...

I'm about to reply when my FaceTime buzzes. *Shit.*

I switch the camera off and answer.

"Hey," I say, trying to make my tone sound normal.

"You hidin' from me, sugar?" his sexy voice drawls. The screen is dark. I can't see him, but it's not on mute.

How have I never noticed how seductive his voice is?

"No, I...Well, I'd be lying if I said I wasn't a little nervous. It's not like I've done this before." Suddenly, I wonder if he has...

As if reading my mind, he says, "Neither have I."

"So you've never rang one of those hotlines?"

He laughs. "Nope."

"What about a cam girl?"

"Thought about it."

Wow. Honesty.

"Not gonna lie," he goes on. "I've subscribed to pornhub. I'm a man, after all."

I feel my pussy tingle and my mind starts to wander again. I don't know what to even say to that. I mean, I've watched porn before, but I don't subscribe to it. Clearly, I'm behind the times.

"You still there?" he asks after a few moments.

"Yes," I reply, still trying my hardest to sound natural.

"Want to know what I'm wearing?"

I stifle a laugh. "Sure."

The camera changes and his face appears.

Jesus Christ. He looks so damn good on camera.

He props up his phone and leans back onto his pillows...so he's in his bedroom...and he's shirtless. I stare at his broad, muscled chest. He has a large eagle tattoo spread across it and his abs are ripped. *Fuck me, he's gorgeous.*

"You gonna be shy, Amelia?" I press my legs together at his tone as he smirks. "You want to see me, don't you?"

I bite down on my lip as he sits up a little. He still has his jeans on, but he's kicked his boots off.

I swallow hard. I've got to give him something, or he might decide to can this whole idea.

"That's why I'm here, isn't it?"

He smirks at my sassy tone. "Not gonna let me see you? Not even your face?"

"Let me see more of you first."

He licks his bottom lip ever-so slightly, then comes

closer to the camera. "You want to see me? You gotta tell me what you want me to do."

Shit. This wasn't part of the deal!

So, he wants me to talk dirty to him?

I slide back onto the bed, kick my shoes off, and slide under the covers, still dressed.

Propping my pillows up, I get comfy.

"I want you to…"

He gives me a fuck-me look that just about melts my panties off as he waits for my instruction. *God, this is so hot already…*

"I want you to take your jeans off."

He purses his lips. "Your wish is my command."

He very slowly and deliberately reaches for his button and zipper, then agonizingly slow, he unzips his jeans. The whole time, he stares at the camera. Every brutalizing second that goes by, I feel the throb between my legs grow stronger.

He palms his cock through the material, then smiles softly, lifting his hips off the bed as he shrugs his jeans down…just his jeans…his white boxer briefs stay on. Then he kicks his jeans all the way off.

"This what you want, sugar?"

I stare at his cock through his underpants. It's such a mighty sight that a mewl escapes me.

This is like nothing I've ever experienced before.

His bulge does carnal things to me.

"Touch yourself," I rasp.

He complies. Moving one arm behind his head as he leans his head back, his other hand slides down to his cock. He palms himself, all the while staring right at me, even though he still can't see me.

"You want more? You gotta be more specific," he whispers. "Tell me what you want to see."

I do want more. I want to see if he has that Jacob's Ladder we've had so many discussions about. The thought thrills me.

This is so wrong, but oh so right.

"Put your hand under the elastic," I say, my voice shaky. I move my hand to one breast and begin to knead, but it's not enough. I slip my dress off so I'm only in my underwear.

Taking my bra off, my nipples are erect and needy. Needy for him.

He does as I say, his hand disappearing into his briefs.

My mouth is so dry as I watch him fondle himself.

"Fuck," he moans, rubbing himself slowly, his eyes closing for a second.

"Talk dirty to me," I command. I blame the last shot of tequila.

"Need your hot little pussy on my dick, sugar," he groans, his eyes opening again. "Need that sweet pussy on my face, ridin' me till you're squirting your juices on my tongue."

Holy fuck.

I pinch my nipple and a groan leaves my throat.

His eyes focus a little more. "Are you touchin' yourself, Amelia?"

I squeeze my thighs together…I can't masturbate like this…*can I?*

I drag the spare pillow next to me and prop my phone up, my other hand now free.

"I like watching you," I whisper as I peel my panties down. "You're so hot, Gears."

I think he likes the praise; he gives me a chin lift. "Wish I could see you, babe. Bet you're so fuckin' beautiful under those clothes."

No. I…I can't.

Ignoring him, I say, "Pull your pants down, all the way."

He bites on his lip and then complies, tugging his briefs down to his thighs. His cock springs free, and I suck in a breath.

He is fucking big.

His cock bobs as he palms himself, pulling on the end as I stare.

And…he has a Jacob's Ladder. The bolts are visible as he strokes himself slowly.

Settling back against the pillows, his fists his cock, his abs flexing every time he strokes himself.

"Fuck, Gears."

"You like my cock, sugar? Look how hard you've got me. Gonna fuckin' explode."

I slide my hand down to my pussy. I'm so wet it's ridiculous. I begin to circle my clit, staring at his monster cock, barely able to believe it or that we're doing this.

"So, the rumors were true," I muse.

"About my piercings or my cock being huge?"

"Both."

He gives me a shit-eating grin, his strokes long and slow as I stare at him in wonder.

He's so goddamn hot my phone might melt into a puddle, and I won't be far behind it.

I know I'm close, but I can't let him hear me come.

"You gonna be my dirty little slut, Amelia?"

My eyes snap open as I let his words sink in. All it does is fuel my orgasm, my need for him. It burns through my veins like lava.

"Oh," I groan, my wetness out of control as I watch him. Craving his touch, not this phone screen.

"You want my cock inside you, sendin' you to heaven and back, don't you?"

I insert a finger into my pussy. "Yes," I moan.

He likes it. He starts to speed up. "Imagine this cock inside you, Amelia, givin' you what you want. Pumpin' your pussy, your ass, fuckin' that smart mouth of yours. I'd bury my head between your legs until you're beggin' me to take you."

Jesus. I close my eyes, pinching my nipple harder as I start to climax. "Yes," I whisper. "Oh, yes…"

His hand jerks up and down, skating over his Jacob's ladder over and over, and all I can think about is that cock inside me and how it would feel with metal massaging my insides, sending me over the edge.

"Tell me," he chokes out. "Tell me how much you want it."

"Fuck me," I groan, inserting another finger as my thumb presses against my clit. "Gears…oh God…oh…" I lose it, my orgasm hitting so hard I'm seeing stars, and I'm panting as I try to be quiet and not let him hear, my fingers slamming in and out of me frantically.

"That's it, baby, milk my cum, milk me, Amelia, fuck…"

He pumps faster, harder, his face a sight of pure ecstasy as he chases his release. I watch as his cum spurts out all over his stomach as he starts to slow. It's the sexiest, most erotic, surprisingly beautiful thing I've ever seen. And I did that to him.

"Holy shit," I mutter.

He closes his eyes, his hand working to a stop, his release spattered all over his chiseled abs.

"That was so hot," he groans. "But next time, I need to see you."

"Gears…"

"I need to see your face when you come, if nothin' else."

"I can't…"

"You can, and you will," he says. "Or we can't do this again."

I bite my lip, marveling at the fact he's in no hurry to go clean himself up.

"I'll think about it."

"No. You'll do it. Tomorrow night. A bit earlier since I have to get up at six."

"Getting a little demanding." I chuckle. Though, really, I'm just trying to deflect.

He gives me a look. "Sweet dreams, Amelia."

"Goodnight, Gears."

He leans toward the camera. "You sound so fuckin' hot when you come."

The screen goes black.

I stare at it and then down at myself, naked and panting.

This is ridiculous.

Flopping back onto the pillows, I groan.

This is so unfair.

No man has ever gotten me this hot.

And the dirty talk...*his dirty little slut?*

Why was that so damn arousing? All I could imagine was him behind me, slamming into me while we do it doggie style, one hand at my hip, the other around my throat.

I throw the pillow over my face.

My hand wasn't nearly enough. I need more.

I need him. But I can't have him.

A few moments later, I reach for my top drawer. I need to finish the job, and even then, that won't be enough.

I pull out my favorite pink dildo, and I get off in record time as I think about what just happened and how hot he looked, how his dick is perfect, just like the rest of him, and he liked it when I told him what I wanted.

And I do want it, so very badly.

Gears is a complete and utter conundrum.

And all I can think is, I can't wait for the same channel tomorrow.

9

GEARS

I JERK OFF AGAIN IN THE SHOWER. I CAN'T HELP IT.

Her voice.

Her fuckin' voice, calling my name, while she fucked herself.

How I wish it were me so fuckin' bad.

I want to go to her. Lay on top and give it to her hard and fast, just how she wants it. And I know she wants it. I know she wouldn't have been able to take her eyes off me as I touched myself. To be honest, it was damn hot, even though I couldn't see any of her.

I can barely get anything done the next day. All I want to do is see her, even if it's just a glimpse. But I don't.

I have a shift at the grill but get home around eleven.

I grab a beer from the fridge, take a quick shower, and while I'm still in my towel, I text her.

Me: I'm ready to see you.

If she thinks she's backing out of it after she saw all of me last night, she's got another thing coming.

It surprises me when she replies almost immediately.

Amelia: That was pretty hot last night.

I smirk.

I want to play.

Me: Pretty hot?

Amelia: Okay, very hot.

Me: You got off pretty quick. I like that. Already, my dick is hard and ready for her. I want her between my legs so badly…

Amelia: I enjoyed the show.

Me: Glad to hear it.

I set my phone up on the side table, tilted to face my bed, and I call her on FaceTime.

She picks up with the damn camera off again.

"Hello, Gears."

"Hello, Amelia."

"How was your day?"

I snort a laugh. "Long and tedious, thanks for asking. How was yours?"

"About the same. I couldn't concentrate for some reason."

My dick twitches.

"Yeah?"

"Uh huh."

"You like bein' my dirty little slut?"

Her voice is quiet and breathy when she says, "Yes, I like it."

Fuck. I almost shoot my load.

I reach under my towel and cup my balls, then my dick. "Got me hard already, babe."

"Show me."

It's like music to my ears, but I've got news for her: she's not running the show.

"Nope. Not until I can see you."

"Gears…"

"What? You get to see me, but I don't think this counts as prospect duties."

I hear her laugh and I can't help but shake my head, smiling. I've been fuckin' smiling like a pussy whipped mad man all day.

"I've never…I've never done this before."

"And you think I have? Come on, show me." I stop touching myself. Instead, I spread my legs, not letting her see under the towel, and lean back on my hands.

I know what my body does to women. I work out. I keep myself trim. They like the six-pack. And they like my cock. It's begging to be let out. Even if it's not inside her sweet pussy, a man can dream.

A few seconds later, her face appears.

I can't help the grin that spreads across my face. "There you are."

"This is wrong…" she starts.

I shake my head, pulling my towel aside. Her eyes drop to my dick, and she gasps.

Her reaction makes my cock swell even more.

I pull the end of my tip with one hand, lifting my cock slightly as my other hand cups my balls so she can see.

"So fuckin' full for you, sugar."

Her eyes stare down at my hand in disbelief. "Your body…it's insane," she whispers.

"Sit back, let me see you," I say.

I fondle myself, but I don't rub. If I do that, it'll be over too quick.

As I run a hand through my hair, her eyes lift to mine, but she mainly concentrates on my hand, and my cock.

"Don't be shy," I go on. "It's just us, Amelia. I want to see that pretty face, those beautiful tits, and that sweet pussy."

She sits back, revealing that she's wearing a soft pink,

mesh camisole. I can see her darkened nipples through the material.

"Fuck," I groan, gripping my cock. "Need you so bad, babe. Touch yourself. Let me see those tits, Amelia."

I sheath myself, hoping she'll show me more, my mind begging to see everything.

She takes a deep breath and moves the camera again, revealing more skin. One hand moves to cup her breast, the top part of her face out of the frame. I won't push it, but my need to see her face while she climaxes trumps every other desire.

Her fingers play with her nipple, pinching and squeezing as her other hand comes to the other side, squeezing and cupping her tits. I need to see her flesh…

As if reading my mind, she drops the straps on her camisole, and the material floats down her arms, her breasts coming into view, but her nipples are still covered.

"Show me," I demand. "Fuckin' show me your titties, baby. Show me how you get yourself off."

She groans, pushing the camisole away so her perfect, round tits come into view. Her nipples hardened peaks as she pinches them again and throws her head back.

I strangle my cock watching her, trying to keep my movements slow so I don't come.

My balls are so tight. She's so damn hot.

"So fuckin' beautiful," I mutter.

"Gears…" she groans, pulling at her nipples as I watch, precum leaking out of my tip.

"Tell me what a dirty little slut you are, Amelia."

"Gears…"

"Say it."

To my surprise she does. "I'm a dirty little slut."

"You're *my* dirty little slut, say it." She hesitates, one

hand disappearing down her body. I know she's touching between her legs. "Say it!"

"I'm *your* dirty little slut."

"Open your eyes," I demand. She does, and those stunning blue irises meet mine. "Look at what you've done to me." Her eyes flick down to my cock, so hard it's painful. "That hot little mouth suckin' me off, swirling your tongue over my tip. You gonna take all my cum, Amelia?"

"Y...yes," she cries.

"Show me your cunt," I grit out, fisting myself harder.

"No, Gears…"

"Fuck." I squeeze my cock, moving my hand faster. I need release. "Need to see that pretty pink pussy. Gonna drive my cock into you so fuckin' hard, in and out, bendin' you over from behind till you're screamin'."

"God, Gears…oh God…"

She throws her head back and climaxes. I get to see her face and it's beautiful, lost in the moment of pure ecstasy.

Her getting off gets me off. I'm spurting my hot cum all over myself as I watch her tits jiggle while she continues to pump herself with her fingers.

I groan, milking myself of every drop, imagining I'm ramming my cock inside her while she cries out, telling me how big I am and how much she wants it.

"How was that?" I gasp, letting go, my legs still spread wide as her eyes open.

I'm sprawled out, my towel beneath me, and I'm a fuckin' mess.

"So good," she breathes.

It's never gonna be enough. I need her body so damn bad.

"I need to see all of you," I tell her darkly. "I need to see those fingers inside you, then your vibrator, tomorrow."

"I can't tomorrow," she cries. "I've got dinner with my parents, and I'm staying over for a few nights."

My cock is almost hard again from the thought of her doing this under her parents' roof.

"So, they go to bed at some point, don't they?"

"Gears..."

"Don't you like it?"

"Of course I like it."

"So, what's the problem? Don't tell me how wrong you think it is, because I know from what I just saw that you loved every minute of it."

She bites down on her lip, her face flushing as she covers her tits back up.

"I'll try, but I can't promise anything. My Dad has ears like a hawk."

"So?" I shrug. "You'll have to learn to come quietly, won't you, sugar?"

She purses her lips and I try not to torture myself, imagining them around my cock. "There you go, getting all demanding."

"Tomorrow." It's not a question.

"I'll text you when I'm free."

I grin, leaning forward to end the call. "Good girl."

The screen goes black.

Running a hand through my hair, I take a moment to appreciate this small but wondrous victory. She's so goddamn beautiful. Those tits, round, soft, and perfect. I want to spurt my cum all over them, mark her, make her mine.

I've got to be patient, but my need to fuck her for real is growing. It's dangerous how much I want her, making me want to fuck the consequences. Even when I know that's not possible.

Focus, I tell myself. *Don't fuckin' blow this.*

That's something I can't afford to do.

Time isn't my friend, even though when I'm with her, the demons go away.

They don't claw at me. They don't beg me to give in to the dark side. Around her, I can keep them at bay. Around her, I feel more like myself than I ever have, but getting too close is a mistake.

No matter what happens, I have to leave my feelings at the door.

I fell for her the first time I saw her, all those years ago. I never dreamed I'd get a chance, but even if it is like this, I'll take it. Unashamed, I will take anything she offers me, even the crumbs.

10

AMELIA

Seeing him in person, after what we did, makes me feel self-conscious.

His lips twitch as I glance between him and Brock.

"Amelia? Have you not had enough coffee this morning?" Brock questions with a huff.

I'm thrown off kilter. Obviously, I knew there was a high chance I'd see him at some point, but I thought if I stayed away from the club that I'd be able to avoid him for a bit longer.

Seeing his smug face after knowing what we did, and the fact I got off and he got a full view of my tits, makes my mouth dry and my feet feel bolted to the floor.

Then I remember his dick...

"I'm fine, thanks for asking," I sass back, trying to act normal.

"Well?" he prompts. "Where the fuck do you want this fuckin' thing?"

I wasn't expecting my brother and Gears to be here in my office, moving my new desk and bookcase around. The new prospects were supposed to be doing it, but now they're helping Steel at the garage.

"Just over by the window," I say, feeling Gears's eyes on me.

I try not to stare as they move the bookcase over to the wall, my eyes glued to Gears's ass. I also try not to notice every single thing about him, but it's impossible. He's absolutely everywhere; in my senses, in my thoughts, and as if that isn't bad enough, he's now standing a few feet away.

My mind idly wonders what might happen if Brock wasn't here…

Gears is also wearing that look I know so well and it spells trouble.

I can't look away, but I also shouldn't stare, not with Brock in the room. I know that Gears will be enjoying this a little bit too much.

Last night was so hot. I feel this genuine thrill run through me when I think about him sprawled on his bed, legs spread, fisting himself while watching me. I don't think I've ever seen or felt anything so sexy in my life. In fact, I know I haven't.

He's everything I know I shouldn't want. Even though I know the risk of getting caught will be disastrous, I deliberate how long we can keep this up without touching each other for real.

Gears loves the club. I know he wants me, but he respects my brothers, Hutch, and the MC, and I know he won't risk it for me.

I'm sure, to him, I'm just a toy. Somebody he can't have and that's what makes it all the more appealing. It's just sex. It's not like he has any real feelings for me. Wouldn't that be naive.

Brock looks at me again quizzically. *Shit.* I realize he's asked me another question.

"Sorry," I say. "Late night." The words slip out before I even realize what I've said. Of course, Brock, being the nosy, bossy big brother he is, will want to know exactly what I was doing last night. So before he even has a chance to ask, I say I had drinks with Deanna like that explains everything.

He rolls his eyes and turns to Gears. "Are you just gonna fucking stand there, bro? Or are we gonna get this done?"

He walks silently to the edge of my desk and picks up one end of it while Brock lifts the other. Of course, my eyes trail along his strong arms, his muscles flexing with the weight of the thing. With both their backs turned, I can have a good look.

It's not like on the cam, where we can let our deepest desires run wild. Here, we have to pretend. This is real life, and in the light of day, he's so much more than I ever perceived.

My eyes flick down to his ass once more, just as he turns his head to look at me. I whip my gaze away quickly.

"This where you want it?" he asks as my eyes dart back to him.

It's an innocent enough question, but I know the meaning behind it. My clit throbs, wanting his touch, no, *needing* it. I have to keep up the pretense when I'm now picturing him bending me over my desk and fucking me like an animal.

All the while, he stares at me with an innocent expression. One that doesn't show any signs that I saw him naked last night and he came all over his chiseled abs, milking his cock while he grunted in such an erotic way, I will have the memory etched into my mind forever.

I clear my throat. "Perfect," I say, my smile tight.

"Anythin' else you need?"

I turn away. "I think I'm good, thanks."

"Well, speak up now, or forever hold your peace," Brock chimes. "While you've got him pinned down, may as well use him."

My eyes go wide, and I see Gears smirk ever-so slightly. Bad choice of words, big brother.

"Could you move the filing cabinets next to the bookcase?" I say. "And I've got a couple of heavy boxes containing books in the reception area that need brought in."

Brock nods as they cross the room.

I wish my fucking body could catch up to my brain, which is telling me to *give it a rest already!* The pulsing I feel between my legs cannot be denied. And here I was thinking my workplace was a safe enough place where I could just work and not be distracted by all things Gears.

"Knock, knock," Deanna says, walking through the door.

"Hi," I reply. "What's going on? I thought you were in Phoenix until after the weekend."

She gives Brock and Gears a wave. "I was, but there was a change of plans."

Deanna is one of my best friends and has been for years. I'm a couple of years older than her, but both growing up in the club, we've bonded.

I feel guilty she knows nothing about Gears, and even though I trust her implicitly, it's too risky. I know she won't purposely tell anyone, but she could get drunk and accidentally blab to somebody. She's not called loose lips for no reason.

Oh, I know she'd be into it, and she'd probably applaud me and want all the details, but with Hutch being her dad, it's too close to home.

"Thought you might like to have lunch?" she asks. "Looks like you've worked up quite the appetite."

I snort a laugh, since the boys have literally done all the lifting. "Sure, sounds like a good idea."

"Oh, before I forget," she says, her tone lowered as she steals a glance at Brock. "Lars was asking about you."

Lars is one of the guys from the bar the other night. He's kinda cute, not that I really talked to him very much. Deanna and I were too busy having shots.

My eyebrows raise. "He was?"

She nods. "Uh huh."

Out of my periphery, I feel Gears looking over to me. Even though we're talking quietly, and Brock is not paying us any attention, I know Gears is listening.

"What did he say?" I press.

"He asked me if you had a boyfriend."

I swallow hard.

I know I have every right to speak to whoever I want, when I want, but I also know Gears won't be happy hearing that, not after the warnings he's already given me. And it makes me want to play with him just a little bit.

A delicious chill goes through me at his jealousy, even if he hasn't earned the right to tell me what to do and who with. Far from it. But this is a game we're playing after all, and a deep, dark part of me likes it.

"Of course I told him that you're single and you wanna mingle." She laughs wickedly, earning her an eyebrow raise from Brock.

I roll my eyes, lowering my tone again. "He's the dark-haired one, right?"

She tuts. "Honestly, Amelia, it's no wonder you don't have a boyfriend if you can't even remember what he looks like."

"We had a lot of tequila that night," I remind her. *The night I first saw Gears naked.*

I know right here, right now, Lars doesn't interest me. Not at all.

Gears, on the other hand…count me in any day of the week.

"Don't blame alcohol. You haven't been interested in anyone since Eric."

Shit.

I do not want to talk about my ex here, not with Gears listening in and my brother in the room.

I know, without even sparing Gears a glance, his nostrils will be flaring. I also don't want to run the risk of his threat to stop this if I even so much look at another man. *Asshole.*

"You can talk. How's Cash going?" I throw back at her, smiling devilishly.

Her eyes go wide as she mouths, *"Seriously?"*

Cash is the New Orleans Rebels' President. Yes, he's a badass, and a silver fox, oh, and he's one of her dad's best friends. Just a little taboo, but hot all the same.

"Very funny," she mutters.

"Don't talk about me, when you are clearly not going to make a move yourself."

"You're deranged, you know that?"

"Does this mean you're not buying lunch?"

"I will, but no more coffee for you."

"Don't change the subject."

"Brock," she mouths.

I shrug. "So what? He's busy."

"I'd rather talk about a double date with Lars and his friend Chad."

"It could work." I try not to smile to myself.

Play along. Just see what Gears's reaction is. It's not like he owns me, for God's sake...

"Wait, so we will do a double date?"

"Maybe."

"You could act a little more enthusiastic, Amelia."

"I said I'll think about it. He is pretty cute, and he did have a nice ass."

"There you go. He also has pretty eyes and drives a Mercedes."

A moment later, I feel my phone buzzing in my pocket. Casually, I pull it out and read the message. It's from Gears.

Don't even fucking think about it.

I stare at the message, unable to tear my eyes away, because if I do, I know I look straight at him. I don't reply. I don't give him the satisfaction.

"Maybe next weekend?" I say.

"That's the spirit."

"And he's younger than me, right? So, that means he's got stamina."

Deanna chuckles, and we both giggle like schoolgirls.

Another message practically burns a hole in my hand...

Gears: Very funny. How about I go find Lars and break his damn neck?

He continues to fuck around with the filing cabinets like nothing is even happening. I'm impressed. Brock is none the wiser.

"There's a new club in Phoenix. We could go clubbing," Deanna suggests.

It sounds like the worst idea I've ever heard, but unfortunately, Deanna is still at that age where she likes to party. Unfortunately, after Eric, my partying days are well and truly over.

Adulting sucks, and so does nursing a broken heart.

My phone buzzes again...

Gears: I will follow you to the city. There is nowhere you can hide from me, and then I'll fuck that smart mouth of yours, rammin' my cock down that pretty throat until you say you're sorry.

Once again, he has the power to render me speechless.

I steal a glance. He's not looking at me, he's talking to Brock. That's strange. I never knew men could multitask. I'm impressed. Usually, they can only do one thing at once.

I also realize I'm wet, and it's all because of him and his dirty mouth and possessiveness.

This time, I decide to reply back.

Me: Aw, don't be jealous, *prospect*. I only have eyes for your Jacob's Ladder, remember?

I click my phone off and glance up at Deanna, trying hard to fight the smile on my face.

At least I think I'm funny.

"Amelia," Brock hollers to me. "Gears will grab the rest of the boxes and do anything else you need him to, but don't be too long about it. He's got shit to do back at the yard."

"Thanks, bro," I reply as he leaves, Gears following behind him without looking at me.

His stance is rigid, his shoulders slightly hunched.

Deanna's phone rings, and she glances at it. "Sorry, babes, I gotta take this. It's a client who's needy as fuck."

Deanna runs her own interior design business and is doing very well for herself, but she's always busy.

I give her a smile and take the opportunity to quickly grab my purse and make my getaway. I do not want to be stuck in here with Gears, especially with the comments I just made.

Just as I get through the door, he's barreling through it, almost knocking me over.

I don't wait to find out where he's putting the boxes, I keep walking, but I don't get far.

I feel a hand wrap around my waist, and the other around my throat.

Holy fuck balls.

"You like to tease me, sugar?" he growls low in my ear.

I gasp.

His proximity. His scent. The way he's holding me flush against him, his hands gripping me tight. Again, that thrill goes through me.

"Gears," I whisper. "Not here."

He ignores me. "Don't even fuckin' think about meetin' another man, you got me? Or I'll bend you over that desk and fuck you into next week, and I don't care who's watchin'."

"Right," I snort. "I'm sure the MC would completely understand why you did it."

"Think I fuckin' care?" he rasps, really riled up.

Oops. I poked the bear a little too much.

"You know I told you once, bein' buried out in the desert might even be worth it to taste that sweet pussy of yours," he goes on, his hand at my hip gripping tighter.

He's hard. I can feel his dick pressed up against my ass.

I bite my lip as a moan almost escapes me.

"Not here," I whisper again, my body betraying me as I press back against him. A low, guttural sound rumbles in his chest.

"Why not here? You wanna play games, let's play."

"I'm not playing games, Gears, but the fact is, I am single, and guys are gonna want to date me."

"Not while I'm still breathing."

Fuck, that's so hot.

"You have no claim over me," I remind him. "You're a prospect."

He pushes into me, and this time, a mewl does leave my throat.

We both hear Brock's motorcycle start up and I almost sag in relief. As thrilling as this is, I wouldn't want either of us to get caught. He pulls me back into the room.

The hand at my hip moves down my body.

"Gears?" I breathe. "What are you doing? Deanna is right outside."

"Don't give a fuck," he mutters, reaching down as his hand squeezes my ass.

Then, I realize what he's doing.

"We can't!" I cry.

"Shh," he tells me. "You'll take whatever I have to give you, Amelia. Say it."

I close my eyes, my body melting into his. *I want him; there's no denying it.*

"I want it," I whisper.

He grunts, satisfied, pressing me against the wall. One hand reaches up my thigh and around to the front of my panties…which are soaked.

"Fuck, you're so wet."

"Hurry up!" I spit. "Deanna will be back any second."

He reaches his other hand from my neck down to grasp my breast.

"I told you before, Amelia, you're my dirty little slut," he says, his hand reaching into my panties as I spread my legs wider. When he circles my clit, I almost buckle under his slightest touch. "Say it."

I close my eyes. Every single nerve in my body is about to explode.

"Say it!" he growls.

"I'm your dirty little slut," I whisper on a moan.

He runs his nose up my neck, then bites down gently, his fingers, like magic, swirling over my nub. I'm a hot mess, grinding back against his dick as he inserts two fingers and starts to fuck me with them. I explode in about two seconds, coming as quietly as possible, the blood pounding in my ears as I hold in my screams.

"You like it hot and dirty," he whispers. "Remember tonight, or so help me, I'll come to your parents' house and climb through your window, and this time, I'll fuck you with my tongue."

I've never been so turned on by a man's words before in my life, but he has the ability to render me a quivering mess. And I need more.

He spins me around to face him. I watch as he brings his two fingers to his mouth and sucks on them.

My mouth parts…

"So fuckin' sweet," he whispers as I watch him with my heart racing in my chest…then I hear Deanna.

Gears smirks, then takes off, pushing past me out the door.

I shove myself off the wall and adjust my skirt.

"You coming?" Deanna calls through the open doorway.

I roll my eyes to the sky. "Oh yeah," I mutter, grabbing my purse from the doorway. "I'm coming all right."

This man will be the death of me, I swear it.

11

GEARS

I wish I felt bad. Remorseful even. But touching Amelia has the opposite effect. It makes me want things I can't have.

It made the blood boil in my veins that much hotter.

I know I'm reckless. Brock was still in the fuckin' building, and instead of walking away like any smart, or even sane, person would do, I made her come with my fingers instead. Added to that, her bestie was right outside the door, able to walk in at any second.

I smirk at the thought.

The way she responded to me was like heaven. Her body is so tempting, it's on a whole other level.

She makes me want to do things I should definitely not be doing in public, not in her office, and certainly not in the presence of her brother, who may actually kill me if he finds out.

What's worse; I now have to work the night shift tonight at the Crow, which means I can also use the time to officially move upstairs, so my plans to see her have changed.

To say I'm pissed is an understatement.

As soon as I get patched...*maybe things can change...*

Am I kidding myself?

If Brock wasn't there, and Deanna, would I have actually fucked her against the wall? For anyone to see or hear...I can't answer that honestly, because I know the truth.

I know when I'm in the moment, it's hard to regain control. It's hard to not just take what I want and fuck the consequences. And it doesn't help matters that she was into it. Rubbing her sweet ass into my dick like she doesn't know what that does to me.

I swear to God if I see her with another man, I may actually go to fuckin' prison myself. Nobody else is laying one finger on her. *She's mine.*

If I can't have her, then fuck me, nobody else is going to either. That's a promise.

I'm fucked the next day because, as I've had little to no sleep, I have a shift tonight at the Burger Joint.

I have to admit, it's better grilling burgers than being at the cafe, and now that Kirsty has more staff helping and I've got a short-order cook coming, it's lightening the load.

The short-order cook, Larry, is opening Friday and Saturday, which means I'll finally get some time off. My prospect duties won't end until I'm patched in, obviously, but I know this is a test from Hutch and the club to see if I'll pass or fail. Of course, I've never failed at anything in my life. I'm not a quitter.

It's late when I finally kick my boots off the next night and jump into the shower.

I've been so busy today running around like usual that I didn't even get time to message Amelia, and she didn't message me. Maybe she's gone cold after the incident in her office.

I know I pushed the boundaries, but it wasn't like she didn't enjoy it. It'll be something I keep etched into my brain until the end of time. It was perfect, just like her.

Me: You free?

Amelia: Hello to you too.

Me: Had a long day.

Amelia: We should probably talk.

Here we go. I was kinda waiting for this.

I decide to act dumb instead...

Me: About what?

Amelia: What happened in my office.

I suck down a couple of mouthfuls of beer and lean back in the recliner.

Me: What about it?

Amelia: Gears, it was risky.

I feel my heart racing at the idea that she doesn't want to do this anymore, that I will really never have her. Even if that is a given, I still don't like the thought.

Me: That's what you get for trying to make me jealous.

She starts to reply, then the grey bubble disappears. A few moments later...

Amelia: You act like you own me.

I do. You just don't know it yet.

I know how she feels about that, about how all the men in her life try to tell her what to do and how to do it, but this isn't like that. I would never do anything she didn't want to. But, if she thinks I'm gonna stand there and listen to her talking about some other dude and do absolutely nothing, then she's messing with the wrong guy.

I may not be able to do anything about it when my VP's standing there, but I can certainly do something when we're alone.

Me: After what I did to you, can you blame me?

Amelia: That was so hot.

A grin spreads across my face.

Me: I need to see you.

Amelia: I'll say goodnight to my parents. Give me a few minutes.

I drink the rest of my beer and crack open another, bringing it over to the bed as I take my shirt off, leaving my jeans on as I lay down and turn on the TV. I immediately mute it.

About ten minutes later, she calls me on FaceTime.

When her lovely face comes into view, all the stresses from the day melt away.

As usual, she looks beautiful. Her hair hanging loose around her shoulders.

"You like being the bad boy prospect as well as shocking me, don't you?" she throws at me as I rest my free arm behind my head. Her eyes follow the movement; she's checking out my body. I grow about ten feet tall under her attention, and my dick hardens in response.

"Yes, but in my defense, you were actin' a little too interested in this douchebag who isn't goin' anywhere near you."

"Ooh, you're so cute when you're jealous."

"It's cute you think I'm kiddin'."

We stare at one another. She bites down on her lip, and I feel my dick twitch at the sight. Yet, I'm not gunning it to get my clothes off because something's off with her. *Something's bothering her.*

"What's up?" I press when she doesn't respond.

"Nothing."

She's lying.

"Everythin' okay with your folks?"

"Are we going to chat now, like we're besties?"

Okay, I haven't had much to deal with bitchy Amelia, but there's a first for everything.

"No, just makin' conversation."

"And here I was thinking you only want me for one thing."

"For the record, I never said that, sugar. We don't have to get naked if you don't want to."

Then I see it…she's been crying…and she's been drinking.

I lean toward the camera as she looks down then back up at me.

"What?"

"Your face is red and puffy."

"You're such a charmer, Gears. Way to make a girl feel good."

I ignore her. "You've been cryin'. Who made you cry?"

"Why does it always have to be someone?"

"Because that's how these things work, don't they?" Though, what the fuck would I know, I haven't cried since I was six.

"Don't you want to see me?" I know she's trying to change the subject.

I frown. "I want to know what's up first."

"I don't want to tell you," she snaps. "I need to see you do your thing."

Woah. Okay.

"My thing?"

"Get your cock out, Gears."

My pulse races, even though I am actually concerned about her.

"Not like this…"

She drops the camera lower, and I get a clear vision of her pale pink, see-through bra. Her tits barely contained in the cups, her deep crimson nipples puckered.

I swallow hard. Her body is an instant aphrodisiac.

My dick strains against my zipper.

"Fuck," I hiss.

I can only see the bottom half of her face as she bites down on her lip again and pulls one cup down, then the other. Her tits on full display for me.

"Jesus, sugar…"

My hand moves down the front of my jeans to adjust my dick.

"Touch yourself, Gears. Let me see."

I tilt the camera down. My jeans are already unbuttoned and open, but my hand remains on the outside, rubbing my cock.

She settles her phone down, then with both hands, she cups her tits together and plucks at her nipples. I just about lose it. I've never wanted anything so bad.

"Do you want to fuck these?" she purrs.

"Fuck yeah," I answer without hesitation. I shrug my jeans down, my dick poking out the top of my underpants as I cup my balls and continue to massage myself.

"I want your hot cum, Gears," she whispers.

Holy fuckin' shit.

"Amelia," I groan.

She moves the camera again, so I can see between her legs. The pale pink lace hides nothing.

Her pretty pussy is visible as I lean back and get my fill of her.

"Finger yourself," I tell her. "Wanna see that pussy, baby."

One hand slides between her legs as she feels herself, the other hand still cupping her tit as I stare from one to the other.

I pull my underpants down past my thighs, my cock

116

swollen and ready to fuck. I wish it wasn't fucking my own hand, that's for damn sure.

She gasps when she sees me, not that I can see any of her face now, but I can see her beautiful body.

"Don't hide from me," I tell her. "Wanna see your face when I make you come."

I fist my cock, closing my eyes momentarily. When I open them again, she's swiped the thin scrap of lace aside and cum leaks out of my tip when I finally see her bare pussy.

"God, Gears…" she groans, her fingers swirling through her slick folds, circling her clit as I stare at her. "That feels so good, talk dirty to me, please make me come, make me forget…"

Forget?

I slow my strokes. I don't want to blow it right now, and I will if I keep this pace up.

"Wanna push my cock inside you, sugar, fill that tight little pussy, fuck you from behind while I spank that naughty little ass."

She hisses, her fingers moving faster. *"Yes…"* she whispers. "Yes, Gears…you're so big, filling me up, I can't take it…"

"Put your fingers inside, tell me how good it feels, tell me how good my piercings feel inside your hole."

She inserts a finger, then two. I watch as her pussy takes her fingers, and I feel like leaping off the bed and driving to Phoenix, just to fuck her.

"So good," she murmurs as she fucks herself.

A few moments later, she pushes her tits out and spreads her legs wider as she climaxes, almost silently, her fingers moving in and out and her thumb circling her clit until she's panting, legs trembling.

"Open your legs," I growl.

She does, her fingers still inside.

"Take them out," I tell her.

She does so.

"Suck them." She hesitates. "Suck them, Amelia."

She puts her two fingers into her mouth and sucks. I groan, and my hand squeezes my cock tighter.

"That was so good," she whispers. "I want your cock in my mouth, Gears."

"Oh fuck."

She swirls her fingers around her clit as I watch. "Taking all of you, taking your big, fat cock down my throat."

"Amelia."

"I won't stop, not until I suck out every last drop. I want it, I want it so bad…"

Fuck me, she is a bad girl.

My hand is working overtime, my balls ready to blow as I start to spurt. "Fuck, yeah, baby…*fuck…*" My orgasm hits me with intensity as my cum shoots out all over my torso.

My cock literally aches for more of her the moment I finish. This will never be enough.

"You're so hot when you come," she says, her voice all breathy and sexy.

"I need to see your face next time," I pant. "I need to see all of you."

"You did see all of me."

"Not all at once."

"Fussy much?"

I sit up, dick still in hand. "For you, I'm not fussy at all."

"Famous last words."

I stare at her; her vulnerability being masked. I recognize it well; I just don't know what the problem is.

"Next time, I want to see you use your dildo," I mutter, even though I want it to be me inside her, not some piece of machinery.

"I have to go," she mumbles, yawning.

"Goodnight, sugar."

She yawns again. "Goodnight, prospect."

She hangs up as I lie there for a few moments, wondering what the hell just happened.

Not the sex part, that part was fuckin' glorious. It was her. Something upset her greatly.

And I won't stop until I find out what the hell it is and fix it.

It might not be my job, but it's certainly my duty. She's part of the club after all.

Not that that's any excuse, but I'll run with it.

She can't hide. I won't let her.

The club throws a surprise party for my birthday on Saturday. Since I didn't tell anyone, including Amelia, to say I was shocked was an understatement.

The whole club turns up, along with sweet butts and hang-arounds.

Gash and Bones accost me at the pool table as I try to take my shot.

"Thought you'd be gettin' your dick wet by now," Bones says, earning a snicker from Gash, one of the newly patched in members.

"Just because it's my birthday, doesn't mean they'll let me bone sweet butts," I remind him.

He holds a finger in the air. "Ah, that's right, you're still a fuckin' numb nut at...what are you now...seventeen?"

I roll my eyes. "Twenty-one, not that I'd expect you to remember that age, *old man.*"

"Boys are givin' you a free pass," Gash goes on. "One night only, ain't that right, Bones?"

He tips his drink to me. "Any sweet butt in this room, tonight only."

I take my shot, sinking the ball as big tits Bambi comes up behind me, rubbing my ass with one hand. "Nice shot, Gears," she purrs, pressing her tits into my back as I stand upright.

It's like every prospect's dream. Allowance to fuck any woman in this room under sweet butt status, and all I want to do is run and find Amelia and give it to her instead. Except, she's not here. And thank fuck for that, since I'm already pretty drunk.

"Be nice to him, Bambi," Bones tells her with a grin. "It's his first time."

I punch him in the arm as he pushes me back, all the while, Bambi runs her hands along both my biceps, squeezing them as my dick awakens.

I want Amelia.

"Better show him how to roll on a rubber," Gash adds, like he's hilarious. "Then draw a map to your pussy."

"Funny fucker," I mutter, pushing him as well.

I turn as Bambi wraps her arms around me. "Want to go fuck?" she purrs in my ear.

I swallow hard.

My body screams *yes.* Take her. Fuck her. Use her. It's what she wants and it's what I need.

But I know this won't quench the thirst I have for the only woman who can hold my attention.

And she's not here.

She presses her tits into my chest. They're big and

beautiful, and normally, I'd waste no time in dragging her out the back to bend her over the nearest available surface and fuck her like a caveman. These women have been teasing me for long enough. To my astonishment, another sweet butt, Candy, comes over and whispers in my other ear, "Want a threesome, prospect?"

Holy Mother of God.

I know I probably look like a deer caught in headlights as they both wrap themselves around me. And I know that, between these two, I look like the pussy because I should fuckin' want this just as much as they do. "Let's play some more pool for a while," I suggest. "If we go now, I'll miss half the party. Plenty of time to get naked."

I've no intention of screwing either one of them, even if my dick screams *fuckin' idiot!* at me over and over. They go off to get some shots and I see Axton from across the pool table.

He gives me a chin lift.

My heart literally leaps in my chest when I see Amelia crossing the room. That was a close fuckin' call. I'm glad she didn't see or hear what the sweet butts offered me, she'll never know that I turned them down because even now, I can't deny it; all I want is her.

She walks right up to the pool table and places the chalk at the end, indicating she wants the next game.

I can't help the grin that splits my face in two, not that I need her brother watching on while I eye fuck her and wish it was her coming up to my old quarters with me.

She's wearing a short and tight nude colored dress with high heels. Her legs look fuckin' gorgeous.

"You look pretty," I tell her, knowing that could earn me a punch in the face. When I glance sideways toward Axton, he's busy kissing his woman, Stevie.

"So do you." She gives me a grin.

"You're not a pool shark, are you?" I quirk a brow.

She shakes her head. "I wouldn't tell you if I was."

Touché, Amelia.

I sink the next ball, my opponent, Dalton, from Steel's garage, loses again. He shakes my hand as I turn back to my girl. Well, my cam girl, anyway.

She throws the triangle in the middle of the table. "Rack 'em up, *prospect.*"

I crawl to bed. Alone.

Amelia and I never happened, not that it *could* happen, her fuckin' brothers were hanging all around her all night, and all I got to do was watch her as she acted all goodie-two-shoes.

I should never have started this.

That night when her car broke down and I brought her back to the club to get parts to fix it, I knew she was trouble. We shared some kind of fuckin' moment and it's had me confused ever since. Of course, yet again, her brothers ruined it because they were having a poker night and I almost got my face caved in because she came in with me. I swear fuckin' chivalry is dead.

But tonight…shit got real.

The sweet butts ended up elsewhere, thank Christ, although it was slightly satisfying seeing Amelia's pissed off face when Candy draped herself around me throughout the night.

I don't want Candy, as easy as it would be to bang the living daylights out of her, and Bambi, I know it will never fully satisfy me, not like having the girl I really want.

Rolling down on my bed, I groan when my head hits the pillow.

I shove an arm over my face, and I know I'm gonna be feeling this tomorrow.

It was unexpected I'd get a party thrown in my honor, which is another reason I love this club. Even when you're the resident shit-kicker, Hutch never wants you to feel like you're on your own. And fuck knows I've been on my own for such a long time, I almost forgot what it was like to have family around me. Speaking of, I gotta go see my grams tomorrow, she insisted. Not that I'm gonna be in any fit state to have any kind of conversation after the amount of tequila I consumed tonight.

I hear my door creek open. I don't even open my eyes.

"Go away," I mutter, knowing that even if it is Candy or Bambi, or both, I don't really want it...unless...*Amelia?* I shrug it off. That's never gonna happen. Torturing myself, however, is something I've kind of perfected.

I feel the bed dip.

"Who is it?"

"Your birthday girl," she whispers. Whoever *she* is.

"Unless your initials start with A and end with A, fuck off."

A hand goes to my waistband, my belt buckle pings open, my zipper lowers, and I suck in a harsh breath.

Maybe a blow job won't be so bad, if that's what my mystery woman is after. If I open my eyes now, and see Candy or Bambi, I may just throw them out on their ass, and it'd ruin the fantasy going on in my head that it's Amelia.

She crept up here, into my room, to suck me off.

My dick hardens.

"I want you, *sugar*," I mumble. "I only want my sugar."

My jeans get yanked down and my cock springs free.

She moves her hot little hand to my cock and starts to pull me off. I groan, *fuck yeah.*

It's not like Amelia is coming here to relieve my frustration, so why shouldn't I enjoy it?

I know somewhere deep down it's wrong to think about another woman while another tends to your needs, but if I just don't think about it...so, that's what I do...

12

AMELIA

I FIST HIS COCK AS I WATCH HIS BREATHING GROW LABORED. His chest rising faster as I play with him, marveling at how good he feels in my hand. His thickness, his size, it's glorious. That Jacob's Ladder…finally, I get to see and feel it and it turns me on like nothing I've ever experienced.

Yes, I snook up here. The party is still going on downstairs, but Brock and Axton have both left. Instead of hitching a ride home with Deanna, I chose to pretend to keep partying, and make my own private escape…upstairs, to Gears's room.

He might think he's in charge with this arrangement, but he can think again. No way is he the only one who gets to color outside the lines; lines that were drawn in the sand because we can't cross them.

I can't go another day without feeling his warmth, his touch, and yes, I may have had a few cocktails myself, but I know what I'm doing… and I need this…so damn much.

I can't wait to get him in my mouth. I'm like a giddy college kid all over again. Leaning down, I start to suck his tip, laving him with my tongue, and smiling as he groans.

His arm stays slung over his eyes, and he still wears his cut, with no shirt on underneath, in typical Gears style. He doesn't give a fuck, and he's so goddamn beautiful, too pretty to be a biker.

When I saw those two sweet butts all over him, I'll admit, it made my blood boil. Acting like I'm okay with every horrible thing he's doing is like torture, yet somehow, I've become really good at covering it up. On my face, you'd never know it affects me, that I want to rip those other girls' throats out with my bare hands, that I want to wrap my arms around his neck and kiss him, have him pull my body to him as we flirt and carry on, without anyone questioning what we're doing.

That goal seems far off. I push it aside...*it's just us now.*

"Fuck, baby," he groans again as I take him farther into my mouth, my tongue swirling around the underside of his cock, where his piercings are.

He's so much bigger in real life. His dick is like a work of art, but better.

I wrap my hand into a fist as I go deeper, sucking him up and down, bobbing my head as I straddle over his legs and rub myself against his knee.

"Just like that, *sugar...*"

It's erotic to think he's imagining me, despite the fact that he really doesn't have a clue who it is. I push that thought aside. My other hand cups his balls as he makes noises I've never heard a man make. I make a meal out of him, bobbing faster, jerking him as I get myself off at the same time. My orgasm is building quick because I've been hot for him all night. That, along with the jealousy, is feeding my lust for him like a nuclear explosion.

He's mine.

I'll knock those chicks out if they come near him again...okay, I won't, but the thought of doing so is sobering. Just the fact he came up here alone instead of with them has my heart soaring…not that my heart has any part in this thing we have going on. *Strictly sex,* I have to keep reminding myself of that…daily. More like hourly.

I lick all the way down his erect cock, loving how he tastes, loving how he groans and starts to pump his hips. One hand reaches down to my head, and I don't even mind when he balls up a fist and starts moving my head up and down along his length.

"Yeah, baby. Oh, that feels so good, sugar. You're takin' it like my good girl."

My pussy throbs. I start to really move my hips, my clit brushing against his knee in a mixture of pleasure and pain. *Who am I kidding?* Everything with him is pleasure and pain. I can't have him, that's pain enough.

We're both playing with fire, but if we want to get technical, he started it.

I take all of him all the way to the base, until my gag reflex kicks in, and I pull back. Repeating the process, I slow things down so he feels all the sensations, but Gears has other ideas.

"Fuck, baby, keep doin' that. Oh, *sugar,* take all of it, my greedy little slut."

I quiver, shaking as I feel my orgasm building at his dirty words, then, he pushes in farther, fucking my mouth as I unravel and start to come, sucking harder as I garble a moan, my entire body on fire as I shake.

"Gonna come in your mouth," he groans. "Stop suckin' me if you don't want—" He starts to spurt in my mouth and I lap him up, licking every last drop. His cum dribbles down my chin as he groans, and the sound goes all the way to my core.

I pull out, letting him go with a pop, wiping my mouth with the back of my hand as I stand.

"Mmm, that was delicious, *prospect...*"

Biting my lip, I pull my skirt down and head for the door, but just as I do, he sits up frantically. His eyes meet mine across the room.

"Amelia?"

I blow him a kiss as his eyes go wide. "Happy Birthday, Gears."

I giggle, then high-tail it out of there as he tries to move off the bed. His jeans are halfway down his thighs, and I hear a thud, assuming he fell off the bed. Then he curses as I take the stairs two at a time and run out to the parking lot before anyone can see me.

Luckily, I spot Bones and Kennedy leaving and hitch a ride with them before Gears can even come looking for me. With smug satisfaction, I sit back and wait for his reaction.

Point to Amelia.

I don't even make it home before Gears is texting me.

Gears: Sugar. You did a very bad thing.

I sit in the back of Bones' truck, my senses on high alert and tingling at what I just did.

Me: Didn't look too bad from where I was sitting.

Gears: Shoulda told me.

Me: And why's that? You're no fun.

Gears: Because I would've pushed you off me, turned you over, and fucked all that dirty talk outta your mouth.

My body lights up as I read the message, feeling elated and pleased with myself.

Me: Like you didn't enjoy it.

Gears: Need your pussy, *sugar*.

Me: Technically, anyone would do, you were drunk.

Gears: Anyone *won't* do. I didn't fuck those chicks. I want you. I want your pussy.

Me: You can't have mine.

Gears: Only on camera?

Me: That's how this game works. Those are the rules, we agreed.

Gears: You just broke the rules.

Me: So did you.

Gears: I warned you, and you didn't listen, so I punished you. You talk like a dirty slut, then I'll treat you like one.

I swallow hard, glancing up to the front. Bones and Kennedy hold hands and she adjusts the radio to another channel.

This whole secret rendezvous is exactly what gets me going. And I want more of it. Teasing him is like a full-time job and I don't know how I'm going to be able to stop.

Me: You like it. That way, you get to punish me.

Gears: Don't go getting any ideas, Amelia. I stick to my promises.

Ooh, he used my first name. He must mean business.

Me: Like going on that double date?

Gears: Just test me and see what happens.

A shiver runs through my body. The fact he only wants me turns me on even more. I know if I'd have stayed, we would've crossed that line with no way back.

Me: Challenge accepted.

I can just imagine him growling.

Gears: You don't want to see me when I'm mad.

Me: You won't hurt me.

Gears: I'd never hurt you, but I will tie you up and spank your ass if you so much as look at another man.

The vision of me tethered to his bed, panting and

begging him as he makes me wait, it has me wet and ready all over again.

I've never felt so sexual in all my life, and it's because of him.

I like the praise.

I like the fact he loves my body, that he wants to please me. It's like my pleasure comes before his own, which is rare for a man.

Me: What if I touch another man?

A long pause ensues as I wait, breathlessly, for his answer.

Gears: I'll cut his fuckin' hands off.

Me: Relax. I'll be good...*for now.*

Gears: What is that supposed to mean?

Me: Nothing.

I smirk, thinking I've got the upper hand, when the reality is, we both know he has me where he wants me. I don't need my throbbing core, or my racing heart, to tell me that. I already know.

If he wants to take things to the next level...I'd let him...which is why I gave him a blow job and ran. It was risky, but the act itself, well, it's something I'll keep in my memory because it was perfect. Just like him.

It's just sex. Yeah, yeah, shut the fuck up.

On Sunday, I usually meet up for coffee with Deanna and Cassidy at the Coffee Bean, the best coffee shop in Bracken Ridge. It's like our little ritual. We get to catch up and gossip and complain to Cassidy about how single life sucks.

I pull up outside the cafe, grabbing my purse from the seat next to me and climb out.

I'm about to enter the cafe when something catches my attention.

Gears walks down the street toward a car parked a few doors away. I watch as an old woman walks next to him, chatting away as he carries her bags. It's such an anomaly that I stop and stare, backing off into the alley slightly so I'm not seen.

This must be his grandma, the woman who raised him? When he told me about his mom, I didn't know what to say. I've never heard a story like that before, and it was clear when he told me that she'd been murdered, that he didn't want to go into it further.

It was such a vulnerable moment, and unexpected. I can't imagine Gears as a little boy without his mom. How hard that must have been for him..

He's someone I can't figure out. One minute, he's rough and rugged, ready to do anything he wants to me. The next, he's carrying groceries and being all sweet and helpful.

He's wearing his usual jeans, boots, and cut, with a short-sleeved black Henley underneath. His hair shines golden in the light, tied back, so I get to see all of his face. He's clean shaven and Lord have mercy if he doesn't light my ovaries on fire.

When they stop at the car, he loads the bags inside. She's still talking to him and he listens intently, saying something back as he closes the trunk. When he gets to her side, he takes her purse and opens her car door, helping her inside. He sets her purse down on her lap as she beams up at him, her face lighting up as he secures her seatbelt, and finally, he shuts the door and goes around to the driver's side. All the while, I stay out of sight.

I don't know what it is about the moment that has me reeling.

I keep watching until he pulls out onto the main street, driving her Toyota Rav 4 as they disappear into the distance.

So, he's a gorgeous, sexy badass who can cook, and he's also a really sweet guy who dotes on his grandma?

He continues to surprise me on all levels.

Seeing him with his grandma put a lump in my throat. The way he was almost…soft, and Gears isn't a soft man by any means. The way she smiled when he strapped her in the car.

This man confounds me completely.

I straighten my spine and make my way into the cafe, wondering what the hell I'm going to do with him. After my little stunt, I've yet to learn what Gears is going to do next. He's unpredictable, and on many levels, so am I. Had I been completely sober, would I have sneaked into his room and blown him? Probably not. Drunk me, however, certainly isn't regretting anything.

I look around for Deanna, slightly shocked when I see a man standing at the table talking to her. With his back to me, I can read his cut: New Orleans Rebels MC. I know who it is right away.

Cash. His salt and pepper hair, cut shorter since the last time he was here, frames his handsome face. His strong arms, covered in tattoos, gripping the back of the chair as he leans. And if I didn't already know about Deanna's crush, I'd definitely be able to tell from the way she's beaming up at him. Deanna beams at nobody.

I smile to myself as I approach the table, and just as I get there, he turns.

He straightens, still gripping the chair with white knuckles, his face slightly tanned. I can see the attraction. He's larger than life.

"Amelia," he says in a low, gravelly voice. I'm surprised he remembers my name.

"Hi, Cash, it's been a while."

He moves, gesturing for me to sit in the chair he's holding. "I was just passin' through."

"All the way from New Orleans?" I question, giving Deanna a look. "Long way to come for coffee."

He regards me for a moment, but I manage to keep my face unassuming.

"Had some business to take care of, got family in Phoenix. I always like to stop in and see Hutch and the boys," he explains, not that he owes me any explanation.

I take a seat as Deanna and my eyes meet across the table. She's slightly flushed in the cheeks. As her bestie, it's my job to notice these things.

"He's been staying with Mom and Dad for a few nights," Deanna pipes up.

"Your Dad kinda insisted," he says to Deanna, palming the back of his neck. "Wouldn't hear of me booking a hotel room."

"Great, so you've enjoyed Mom's burnt pot roast as well as her nagging all weekend," she goes on.

They both laugh.

Woah.

Okay.

I mean, obviously, I know about her little crush, something he may be aware of too, but isn't acting on. However, the energy going on here is off the charts.

Watching as he shakes his head, I give Deanna a look, which she completely ignores.

"Well, I'll let you ladies enjoy your brunch," he drawls, glancing back at me.

"Are you coming to the barbecue tonight at the club?" Deanna asks casually, before he leaves.

He really does have nice arms...

"Wouldn't miss it for the world." He gives her a wink.

I smile, then say, "You're quite welcome to join us. We'll try to keep the single-lady complaints to a bare minimum."

He rubs his chin. "Surely there's no shortage of worthy men in this town?" He looks genuinely perplexed.

Deanna and I both snort.

"You've no idea," I say. "The ratio of available men to women are one to three, and that's including the dicks we wouldn't touch with a ten-foot pole."

"She's right. The men in this town are more into hog calling and tractor maintenance. That's if they're not part of club," Deanna quips. "And we don't date members of the club."

"I think the men in this town are fuckin' idiots, then." He gives us a salute. "I got some stuff to take care of. I'll see you ladies later."

"Bye, Cash," Deanna replies in a voice I've never heard before.

"See ya," I echo, as he turns and heads over to the counter, retrieving his takeaway coffee.

I kick Deanna under the table. "Ow!" she groans. "What was that for?"

"For God's sake, talk about fuck-me eyes."

"Shh, he's still within earshot!"

He gives us a chin lift as he passes by the front window with his coffee in hand.

When he's safely disappeared, I start to laugh. "Oh my God, you've got it bad!"

"No shit. It's not my fault my vagina goes into overdrive whenever he's around. Don't blame me, blame my hormones."

I snort. "Seriously, I don't think crushing on your dad's

best friend is a good idea. It's not like anything is going to happen, right?"

If I know Deanna, then I know she'll have something cooking.

She tries, and fails, to compose herself. "Of course it isn't. He doesn't even know I exist, aside from being Hutch's kid. Or if he does, he's definitely not acting on anything."

"You can't blame the guy."

"It's not like he knew me as a child or I grew up around him," she goes on. "That would be weird. We met for the first time when I was in high school, and I wasn't into hot older guys back then."

"So, what are you going to do?"

"Nothing." She shrugs. "Which isn't the worst part."

I grab a menu and idly scour it, even though I know what I'm going to order. "What's the worst part?"

"The fact I have to use B.O.B. tonight instead of Cash's dick."

I shake my head. "If only he could hear your dirty mouth." I snicker.

She narrows her eyes, as if just remembering something. "Where did you get to last night?"

Oh shit.

"What do you mean?" I keep my eyes on the menu.

"You left for a while, then came back, then left again. Did you hook up with someone?"

"At the club?" I ask, astonished.

I don't want to lie to her...

She leans over on the table. "I smell trouble, Amelia."

I swallow hard. "Uh, I got a ride home with Kennedy and Bones…"

"Before that."

I shut the menu and look up at her. "*Fuck*," I mutter. I

135

can't keep it any longer from my best friend. "Fine. But you have to pinkie swear you won't say a word. Someone's life could literally be on the line."

Her eyes go wide as she immediately offers me her pinkie. "I'll take it to the grave."

We twist our pinkies, and I let out a deep sigh. "I sucked Gears off in his room upstairs."

She stares at me for an uncomfortably long time, then, "You did what?"

"Please don't judge me," I whisper-shout, looking around. "And when Cassidy gets here, change the subject."

"What the hell?"

"I know."

"Explain."

"He has a nice dick." I hope she'll buy it.

She blinks rapidly a few times. "Gears is a *prospect.*"

"I know that."

"You're a club sister."

"I know that, too."

"That's so fucking hot!"

I let out a sigh of relief as I sag back in the chair, unaware until now, that I needed to get this off my chest.

"Thank Christ, because I can't keep this to myself any longer."

"How long has this being going on?"

"Not long…we've been kinda…*sexting.*" I can't bring myself to tell her what we've really been up to.

"Oh my God!"

"Yep."

"Like, dick pics?"

I nod.

"What else?" she presses. "I want all the gory details."

"Just dirty stuff, and yes, before you ask, he's huge."

She sits back, regarding me with a proud expression. "I never picked you to go for a younger man."

"I thought you'd be way more judgy, being he's a prospect."

"You're just fucking, though, right? It's not like it's going anywhere."

I shake my head. "No, we haven't done it. I just crept up to his room and, well, you know the rest. He likes to think he has the upper hand, and I wanted to reel him back in."

"I'm surprised he let you leave without screwing you."

"He tripped as I ran out and now, I feel kinda bad."

She shakes her head, amusement crossing her tone. "God, Ameila, and they call me a dark horse. You take the cake, hands down."

"I'm not so sure it's something to be proud of. I mean, he'll get into a lot of trouble, and so will I…"

"I won't say anything."

"I didn't mean that, I just meant, if my brother's catch on, he'll be kicked out of the club. I can't let that happen."

"But you can't walk away either?"

Not yet.

"I don't know," I admit. "I really didn't plan any of this, and he's younger than me…"

"Wait, you don't have…*feelings* for him, do you?"

I snort. "No." That's a lie. "I barely know him."

I don't know if she believes me, but Cassidy walks in and waves over to us just in time.

"Not a word," I mutter.

"My lips are sealed," she replies, smiling at Cass. "Which is more than I can say for yours."

I give her another kick under the table.

It seems I can't escape thinking about Gears any place I go.

GEARS

THE BARBECUE IS LIKE TORTURE. ESPECIALLY BECAUSE Amelia shows up.

I can't talk to her or say anything, especially since I'm doing prospect jobs.

Cash, the Prez of the New Orleans chapter shows up and Hutch has the grill going full throttle as the two mix and catch up.

I take the opportunity to go out back, check the kegs, and clean up. Seeing Amelia, in a dress no less, is driving me insane. I need a self-imposed time-out before I rip her off the bench, throw her over my shoulder, and ravage her on the nearest available surface.

Just fuckin' cool it.

A chick has never had me this worked up, not ever.

But her sneaking upstairs to blow me, then taking off before I could return the favor…well, that's just not gonna cut it.

I've actually contemplated whether a near and sudden death would be worth it, just to be with her for a night, and I know the answer is yes, because I'm that fuckin' crazy.

I know I have to put a lid on this.

But it's all I think about.

I choose to work a lot because I need the scratch. My grandma's place is a lot to maintain, but I do it out of love. I can never give her back what she's given me. We didn't have much money, but she made up for that with the love and attention she gave me when every other adult in my life failed.

I close my eyes, trying to shake it off. Lately, I've been thinking about my mom a lot, and I know it's because the time is looming. The time to seek revenge and justice for her brutal killing. A murder over a drug debt of only a few hundred bucks.

I can't go on living this charade forever, though it's been good while it lasted.

"Got a job in Phoenix tomorrow," Brock says, coming up behind me as I wrestle with a keg.

I turn to face him. "All right."

"Can get Roxy to cover your shift. Bones and I will be in Mesa, so need you to take the truck with Nitro."

"Gotcha."

I hook the keg up, and when I turn again, he's still standing there.

I might be getting paranoid as he watches me.

"Hutch says you're a valuable asset to the club with keepin' the Burger Joint on its feet."

I shrug. "Happy to help."

"I'm gonna recommend that you get patched in. How'd you feel about that?"

I glance at him, surprised. I can't help the shit-eating grin that spreads across my face.

"For real?"

He crosses his arms over his chest. "For real."

I run a hand through my hair. "Fuckin' awesome."

He points at me. "Gotta bring it up at the table. Don't be surprised if some of the committee don't think you're ready. I'll pitch for you, though."

Why's he being all nice to me? This isn't like Brock.

"Thanks, man."

He gives me a chin lift. "Can see you're good for the club. No point keepin' you prospectin' when you can clearly do more."

My throat runs dry. *Loyalty.* It's all that keeps me going.

I don't want to ever disappoint my club…

"Well, haven't poisoned anyone on the grill yet." I shrug, trying to play it off.

"Takes a lot of guts to pull that off. After all the shit that went down with Jack, this just cements the fact you should be patched in." He pats me hard on the shoulder. Brock's a big man, almost as big as Steel, and I dread to think what the end of that fist feels like. He hasn't quite gotten to beating me up yet, though I'm sure that'll happen if what I'm doing to Amelia ever comes to light.

"Appreciate it."

"Who taught you how to cook?"

"My grandma."

"You got any family, Gears?" It's the first time anyone in the club, aside from Hutch, has ever asked me anything about myself.

I shake my head. "Nah, just me and Grams."

"Your mama?"

I swallow hard. I don't wanna tell him about her being murdered, but I also don't wanna lie. "She died when I was six."

"Sorry to hear that. Must've been tough."

I don't meet his eyes. "I don't remember much about her. Probably better that way."

He gives me another look, then takes off. "I'll text you the address for tomorrow."

I'm a fuckin' pussy.

Fessing up is out of the question. As much as I don't like to lie, this can never come to light.

At least getting patched in will be something I can say I've achieved, not that anyone except my own ego will appreciate it.

But, being patched in changes everything.

Maybe I need to rethink my strategy? Maybe I can do both…

I don't want to tie myself in knots, so I shut the thought down. It's too much to think about.

I've already made my decision, and I have to stick to it.

I head back out to the bar and run right into Amelia.

I go one way, and so does she. I try to go around her, and we crash again.

She smiles, laughing as we try to get around each other.

"Fuck," I mutter.

"Sorry, Gears," she says, her voice sultry and soft and all I can think about when I glance at her lips is how they were wrapped around my cock last night, playing with my piercings.

"You don't seem very sorry," I grit out, just barely reining myself in from touching her.

"That's because I'm not," she whispers.

I glance around to see everyone is still outside. "You wear that skirt for me?"

She nods, heading behind the bar.

"You got panties on?"

She shakes her head, and I groan.

My eyes stay fixed on her ass as she walks toward the mixers, and I try hard to keep my feet planted on the ground. "You need a hand with that?"

She looks over her shoulder and gives me another nod, biting down on her bottom lip.

I head behind the bar, having another look around me. "What did I say about teasin' me?"

"Well, it seems to turn you on," she whispers, grabbing a couple of glasses and filling them with soda.

I get a tray and load some more glasses onto it, ready to refill with beer.

"*You* turn me on," I growl, keeping my distance so I'm close but still not touching. "And what you did last night, that can't be forgiven."

She looks up from under her lashes. "Does that mean I need to be punished?"

Fuck me if she doesn't turn and bend over, pretending to reach something in the bottom fridge as her skirt rides up.

I move behind her, running a hand up her ass, under her skirt. Glancing around to make sure we're still not seen, I lean over to her ear. "Can't wait anymore," I say. "Need your pussy, your mouth, and your ass."

"Then take it," she breathes, relaxing back into my touch.

I'm so hard.

"Meet me. I'll come to yours…" *What am I saying?*

Fuck it.

This has gone on too long.

"That's a bad idea."

I grip her hips harder. "I need it, and so do you. Sick of sneaking around. If we're gonna get caught, might as well make it worth it."

"Famous last words."

I squeeze her ass again, looking down as I see her bare ass, out on display. "Don't be a bad girl and forget panties again, Amelia, or I'll spank this ass until it's glowing red."

Moving off her, I begin to fill up the glasses. My throat is dry, my cock is hard, and I have a need to claim this woman that rushes through my blood. At this this point, there is nothing I can do to stop it, and I don't want to.

Even after the moment I just had with Brock. I earned his respect, and though that cuts deep, this is even stronger than that.

I need Amelia's comfort. I need her joy. Her pleasure. Her very essence. I need it, and I'm gonna take it.

I'm going to hell anyway, so what's the fuckin' difference?

"When?" she asks, straightening herself out.

"I'll tell you when."

She gives me a look that goes straight to my dick. "Gonna keep me waiting?" she muses.

"It'll be worth it."

"There you go again, making promises."

"Trust me, *sugar,* I don't make promises I can't keep."

She snorts a laugh, then, giving me one last look, she grabs her drinks and takes off with them, her sassy hips swaying as I watch her leave.

Jesus Christ. She'll be the death of me.

Even I know there can only be so much tension before we both combust.

And that's gonna be soon, mark my words.

It's late when she messages, asking if I'm online.

Since Sunday is usually my one night off, I had a few drinks with the prospects and shot some pool, something we don't get to do a lot of these days. After helping clean up after the barbecue, I'm beat. Even though I want to run to Amelia's arms, I know the club still comes first.

Me: You have something in mind?
Amelia: I just wanted to see your face.

I stare at the message. *She just wanted to see my face?*

It's not what I was expecting. I don't even joke about my dick making a special appearance.

Me: What's wrong?
Amelia: Nothing. I want to see you.

I hit the FaceTime app on my phone and she picks up within a couple of rings.

As soon as her face appears on the screen, I release a breath I didn't realize I was holding.

"Hey," I say. "You good?"

The light is quite dim as I try to see any signs of her distress.

"I'm fine."

I lie back on the couch with one arm behind my head. We're both fully clothed, and though it sounds ridiculous, it feels strangely intimate.

This is just about sex? Please. As much as I try, my thoughts, as usual, go whichever way they want to.

"My face comfortin'?" I joke.

She smiles softly. "Something like that."

"I'm sorry it's late," I go on.

"I texted you, remember?"

"I meant, for me to come over…" I don't want her to forget her promise; I haven't forgotten mine. *Why am I stalling? Why didn't I go over there the minute I got off work?*

Maybe I want this to be kind of special, not just a quick *wham, bam, thank you, ma'am.*

Am I fuckin' fucked?

Maybe a secret part of me wants to drag this out for as long as possible, 'cause it'll be worth it. I know it will. Plus, I don't wanna come to her exhausted and reeking of beer, or fuckin' burgers, after a long day.

"It's okay. I know you had shit to do."

I stare at her. She's being strangely compliable. "Amelia, is everything okay? I know we don't know much about each other, but you know you can tell me anything."

She looks at me like she sees right into my soul. "I know you really do mean that," she breathes, like she's trying out the words for the first time.

"I do mean it. I'm here…if you need me…" *What the fuck am I saying?*

She smiles again. "Thank you."

I guess she doesn't want to talk about it.

"What did you do for the rest of the night?"

She shrugs. "I caught up with Sienna and Lucy for a little bit. We're organizing a girls' weekend away, should be fun."

When did this turn into a 'friendship' thing? I don't do fuckin' friendships… Then again, I did just offer for her to tell my anything…shit.

"Cool."

"Gears?"

"Yeah, babe."

"Do you think I'm beautiful?"

I frown. Why doesn't she know this already? "You know I do." She shifts the camera as I continue to watch her. "Why do you ask?"

"I just wanted to hear you say it."

"You're beautiful, Amelia. Everything about you is like a fuckin' angel."

"You don't have to just say it…"

"Mean it. You're too good for me, we both know that, but there's something about you that I can't put my finger on."

"The fact you can't have me?"

"Who says I can't?"

"You know who, and it sucks."

"You suck better." I try to be funny, but her smile doesn't reach her eyes. She's troubled, and I don't know why, but a nagging part of me needs to know.

"I shouldn't have done that," she admits.

"What? Suck me off?"

"Yes, it was reckless."

"Isn't that the whole part of the appeal? We both know we can't, and we both badly want it. Opposites attract, and all that shit."

"Is that why it feels so good?"

I want to wrap my arms around her and hold her tight. *Fuck.* Not that again...those...*feelings.*

They pop up out of nowhere, making me want to be better, do better.

It's my own fault; I should've run when I had the chance.

"Well, the thrill of getting caught is a big turn on."

She looks down at the camera again. "You like it, don't you?"

"You know it."

"Do you want to see me naked, Gears?"

Fuck yeah.

"After you tell me what's wrong," I say.

"I told you, I'm fine."

"I can tell you're not by your face, Amelia. Your eyes give you away. You can't hide from me, remember that."

"Why are you so sweet?" she asks, confounding me once more.

"What?"

"I saw you, in the street, with your grandma—at least I assume it was her. It was outside the Coffee Bean."

"I help her get her groceries on Sundays."

"That's just it," she goes on, palming her forehead.

147

"You're going to get in trouble, and then it'll be all my fault."

"Because I help my grandma on Sundays?"

"No, because deep down, you're an incredibly decent guy, and I don't want to ruin your life."

I take a long moment and choose my words carefully. "You could never ruin my life. Even if something bad happens, it will have been worth it."

"But we haven't even had sex yet." I like how she said *yet.*

I chuckle. "That's true, but would you believe me if I said that it isn't the only thing that interests me about you?"

"Do you mean that, or are you just trying to get into my panties?"

I sit up slightly. "If I were going to *just* do that, wouldn't I have done it already?"

"Maybe."

"Maybe?"

"We have a connection, Gears, you feel it. I know I'm not just imagining things."

I let out my breath slowly, trying to calm myself, because I know she's right. "I know, but we can't act on it. I shouldn't even be talkin' to you, much less seein' you naked on camera and touchin' you when I shouldn't."

"And we both know we can't hold out anymore. We won't get caught, Gears. We'll be careful."

"I saw your brother tonight. He wants me patched in."

She sits up straighter, her eyes lighting up. "For real?"

I nod. I can see the cogs in her head turning, and this would be a perfect scenario, even if I would get a beating for it. But I know what I have to do, and in the long run, it won't be fair on her. I'll hurt her without meaning to.

I have nothing to offer a woman like Amelia Altman. I'm not a dumb fuck.

"Yeah, so there's that."

"So you'd be a patched member, Gears. Things would be different."

"Maybe."

"There's no maybe about it. Brock and Axton may not be happy about it, but as a patched member..."

I look up at her again. "As a patched member, what?" I know what she was going to say, but I'm not in a position to claim her as my ol' lady.

She closes her mouth.

"Amelia," I breathe.

"I get it. Even then, right, Gears?"

"Don't be like that."

"So we'd still sneak around because you wouldn't want to defy my brothers? Or the stupid club? How many times do I have to tell you? They won't be ruling my life. I won't let them. I'm a grown woman, who is quite capable of making her own decisions, and I can invite whomever I choose into my bed."

I love this feisty side in her that comes out every now and again. It makes my heart soar.

I want to tell her. I want to open up to her, explain my reasons...but in order to do that, it puts my whole plan in jeopardy. And I can't have that.

I will also never endanger her, and the less she knows, the better.

"You know I want you," I begin.

"Yes, but I'm just another bimbo to you, right? Someone to get off with because it's easy, and once you're patched in, that'll be it. You'll have all the sweet butts throwing themselves at you, which is really what you want."

That's not it at all.

149

"You're so far from the truth, it's not even funny."

"Really? I'm sure at twenty-one, you're not even going to look at another woman."

"What is this really about?"

"It's not about anything, clearly."

"Clearly, it is."

We have a stare down, and I almost think she's going to hang up on me. Instead, she snorts. "Fine. I'm good enough to fuck in secret. Hell, I'm good enough to watch you jerk yourself off on a goddamn camera, but heaven forbid if the stupid club finds out."

"You know the rules better than anyone."

"What about fuck the rules?"

"It's easy to say that when you won't be the one losing your livelihood." It comes out harsher than I meant it to, but if I lose my job, Grams loses her home, and that can't happen. I've made provisions, but I'm not at my goal yet. I need more time...

"I should go."

"Please don't," I find myself saying. "I didn't mean that how it came out. I just don't want to see that frown on your face, and when I do, I want to help."

"You can't help, Gears, it's not your job anyway."

Oh, but fuck, I wish it were. Her words slice me like nothing else. *I'm not good enough.*

"As part of this MC, it's my job to protect you..."

"Don't pull that club shit on me. Not you, Gears. I've been hearing it for far too long."

I can never say or do anything right. Should've stuck to getting my dick wet and not giving a shit. If only that's who I was, but I'm not.

She shakes her head, sadness falling over her face.

"What can I say to make it better when I don't know what it is I've done?"

"It's not you," she says.

I snort. "It's not you, it's me, right? So, you are actually mad at me, but won't tell me why? It ain't because of the sweet butts or the club, it's to do with you."

"I said I wasn't mad, didn't I?" The Altman temper rears its head. "So just drop it!"

I palm the back of my neck. "Amel—" The connection cuts out.

She hung up on me. I try to connect again, but it goes straight to voicemail.

Fuck.

I never knew what it was like, until this moment, to be at a total loss. It may not be my job, as she so eloquently put it, but I'll be damned if she's gonna toss me away.

I'm not done with her yet, and judging by how upset she was, she may be done with me.

14

AMELIA

I DON'T KNOW WHAT I'M DOING, OR WHY I PICKED A FIGHT with Gears. It's the last thing I wanted to do.

Yet, hearing him say the club came first, I don't know why, but it just shot a pain straight to my heart where I have no reason to feel anything.

I know the drill. I know the rules. I know it better than most. But something inside me just snapped.

I'm tired of playing by the rules. It's one of the reasons I've been cam-girling with Gears in the first place.

He's exciting. He's confident. And he likes me just as I am. Not a little bit thinner, or with bigger breasts, or a mouth that shuts up and only speaks when spoken to. Like my past boyfriends and disastrous relationships.

Then I remember *him.*

David Logan.

The guy I had a crush on in my freshman year of college.

The man who took everything from me.

The very person who haunts my dreams and taught me never to trust.

I had a crush on him forever, and he knew it. All the girls were after him, but he took a liking to me. And I lapped it up. I thought he was so sweet, but looking back now, I realize it was all a mask. He was from a broken family, arriving on a scholarship that he worked hard for, and he charmed his way to being the most popular boy in school.

Until the night we went to a frat party. We were fooling around, and though I'd been with one guy before, I wasn't experienced. I wanted him to like me, but things were moving too fast. I asked him to stop, and he didn't.

I couldn't push him off, so he just kept going.

David Logan raped me.

And when he was done, he told me that I shouldn't be such a cock tease when I was asking for it all along.

I sat there afterward, unable to move, speak, or do anything.

I never reported him.

I switched schools because I couldn't face him, or the shame of what had happened to me.

Not even my parents knew, and definitely not Brock. He would've killed him and ended up in jail along with Axton. I couldn't let him ruin his life.

So, David got away with it, and I let him. All because I was too scared to report it.

I suppose in a way he taught me how to never trust a man ever again, except my brothers and father, but even they don't know what's best for me. They only think they do.

All the protection in the world, and it happened at a frat party with people in the very next room.

I partied hard for a couple of years after. I drank a lot to numb the pain, all while hiding it from my parents. My friends didn't notice anything, except Deanna. She's always been a good friend.

She encouraged me to report what David did, but I just couldn't go through with it. In any case, we'd been underage drinking, and making out, and I thought nobody would believe me.

For a lot of years, I blamed myself by believing I really was a cock tease. Lately, those feelings of self-hatred have been raising their ugly head, and as much as I try, I know that a part of me is broken and may never be repaired.

It's taken me a long time to ever be comfortable in my own skin, with my body, with sex…not that there's been much of that, since I was only with my last boyfriend for a year. And it was nothing to write home about.

I guess those insecurities never really went away. Yet, when I think about Gears and how he makes me feel, I realize I've clung to him.

Enjoying his praise when I do something he likes.

Loving his dirty words, even though I don't want to.

I don't want to feel ashamed about sex or see it as being shameful, and with him, it's never that. With him, it feels right.

It's why I got mad.

Imagining him patched in and enjoying all the samplings the club has to offer. If I'm being truthful, I don't want him to want anyone else, which is completely ridiculous. He owes me nothing. But I feel a surge of jealousy the second I think about those sweet butts who were all over him on his birthday.

It seems Gears isn't the only one with a jealous side.

A whole day goes by, and I can see I've had several missed calls from him, which I've ignored. I don't know why, maybe I'm just too chicken to hear what he has to say.

He's also texted me too.

Gears: Amelia, don't hide from me.

And…

Gears: I can fix this.

And…

Gears: I want you.

I swallow hard at his words. *Is it so wrong to be dependent on his every whim?*

I know it's a dangerous game, one that he's not even aware that I'm playing, but I *need* him. No matter where that leaves us, I want to be in his arms.

I want to be the only woman he looks at.

And if I'm honest, the only one he fucks.

I don't see him until two days later at the club, and everyone is around, so we can't speak to each other. We only shoot each other glances every now and again while keeping our expressions neutral.

Then the next day I see him at the Coffee Bean picking up dinner, but Brock is with him.

Our eyes meet and I look away, unable to take his scrutiny. I haven't even replied to his texts.

I don't know how Brock doesn't notice the tension between us. It's not like him, but then again, he's got a lot on his plate and he and Angel are trying for another kid.

Rawlings and Ethan Wolf are with him. Brock holds the baby, who's thankfully sleeping, as Rawlings spots me and runs in my direction. "Hey, Aunty Amelia," she chimes, squeezing me around the middle as we hug.

"Hey, kiddo, what are you guys doing here?"

"Mom had to work and Dad promised I could get a hot chocolate, and Ethan pooped his diaper."

I roll my lips as Brock gives me a distasteful look. "I get all the good jobs," he mutters.

Brock is a good dad, despite his grumpy appearance. There's nothing sweeter than seeing my larger-than-life brother, covered in tats with his Rebels cut on, holding a baby in his arms, to raise an eyebrow or two.

Ethan wolf is eighteen months old and is usually a little firecracker cracker. Looks like someone wore him out today.

"You must've been a good girl," I say, as Gears hovers behind Brock, looking uncomfortable.

"Yeah, but I'm not allowed to tell Mom I had hot chocolate and pie before dinner time. We're supposed to be on a health kick. Right, Dad?"

"Yup, that's why we have pizza on Thursday night while Mom is at work." He gives her a wink, and she pretends to zip her mouth.

Father of the year.

Angel runs the tattoo and piercing parlor in Bracken Ridge. Now that she has the baby, she only works a few days a week, leaving Brock in charge. Which is when all hell breaks loose.

"Did you walk?" Brock asks. "Didn't see your car out front."

"Yeah." I glance at Gears. "Thought I'd get some fresh air after being cooped up inside all day."

"Gears can give you a ride in the van," he says, and my eyes go slightly round. "He's headed past the office and it's gettin' dark."

"That's okay, I'm just going to walk home," I reply. I do not want to be alone in the van with him. I need to think about what I'm going to say and now isn't the right time.

"Gears will drive you home," Brock says again, shoving the pacifier back into Ethan's mouth when he starts to wake up and garble.

There is literally no point in arguing.

The server calls their order.

"See you tomorrow, Gears. Don't be late," he says,

passing Rawlings her hot chocolate while she jumps up and down with glee. Gears gives him a nod.

"Bye, Rawlings," I call out to her, and she gives me a wave while she skips after Brock.

Once he's outside and they're going toward Brock's truck, I look up at him. "Well, this is nice and awkward," I say, shifting from one foot to the other.

"You haven't returned my texts."

"I'm sorry. I didn't know what to say."

"How about, *I'm alive and well and haven't been placed on the side of a milk carton.*"

I take a deep breath. "That's a little dramatic."

"We're done, I get it, but I still gotta drive you home," he says as the attendant passes him his snack.

"You really don't have to do that."

"I actually do, which you well know."

"I've got two feet."

He comes closer to me, inches away from my face. "Get in that fuckin' van, Amelia, or so help me God…" His voice is low and growly…and it does things to me that it shouldn't.

"Keep your hair on," I huff, pushing past him toward the door.

He follows behind as I spot the van right outside.

I climb in and he goes around to the driver's side, climbs in, and starts the engine.

We say nothing. Not one single word as we drive the ten minutes to my apartment.

It feels like the longest ten minutes of my entire life.

I stare out of the window, wondering what the hell to say as darkness almost falls.

When he stops the van in the lot out front, he keeps the engine running. I shift uncomfortably to unbuckle my seat belt as he stares straight ahead.

"Are you giving me the silent treatment?" I ask when I can't take it any longer.

He doesn't even look at me. "If anythin', *sugar*, I think it's you who's been givin' me the silent treatment."

The intense look he gives me, like he's really pissed I didn't call or text him, has my insides burning. I don't think. I just launch myself at him, unable to contain it any longer.

I kiss him, urgently, a groan leaving my mouth when he grips my face and kisses me back with just as much desperation.

It's frantic. Hot. And so damn sexy.

His lips are soft and welcoming, his tongue meeting mine as the leather seat crunches under my eager movements.

I push my hand against his chest as his hands move to my waist and he hauls me off my seat, rucking my skirt up so I can straddle across his lap. His body is rock solid, his cock hard as I press my pussy into him. As he growls low in his throat, I feel slickness between my legs.

I need him to touch me.

"Babe," he manages, breathless, as our kissing gets more and more heated by the second. "Gonna fuck you…"

I groan, every cell and nerve ending in my body on fire for him. "I want it," I reply, reaching one hand down to massage his cock.

He hisses, bucking as he watches my hand fondling him. "But not here, Amelia. We're in full view of the neighbors."

I begin to kiss his jaw, his neck, biting down gently on his pulse point as he makes the most delicious sounds I've ever heard a man make.

"I don't care," I pant.

He reaches his hand between my legs, cursing as he

feels my sodden panties, then slips his hand under the fabric and kisses me again, all tongue. I begin to undo my blouse, his eyes flicking down as he runs his fingers through my folds.

"Need your pussy, babe," he mutters. "Need your tight little pussy ridin' my cock."

He swirls his fingertips over my clit as I throw my head back, my blouse wide open, my tits in his face as he brings his mouth down to my nipple, covering the thin fabric with his lips as he sucks. I come hard with a choked scream, and just as I do, he inserts two fingers, moving them in and out as my orgasm goes on and on.

"Need this pussy wet for my cock," he whispers in my ear.

"It's wet, Gears!" I cry. "So fucking wet."

He chuckles. "I've got piercings that your tight little hole needs all the lube it can get, you got me?"

"I need your cock," I say, squeezing it again. "Let's get inside."

He's clearly the only one thinking rationally. "My place," he says, moving his mouth to my other nipple. "If Brock drives past this way and sees the van here…"

"How fast can you drive?" I pant.

He slides his fingers out of me, kissing me one last time, and says, "Buckle up, *sugar,* you're about to find out."

As it turns out, he drives pretty damn fast.

We sneak in the back door of the Stone Crow and up to his apartment, barely making it inside with my blouse still wide open and my skirt halfway up my ass.

Then we're only for each other.

He stalks toward me, cupping my face as he kisses me again, more roughly this time.

"Need to taste your pussy," he mumbles, his hands moving down to cup my breasts.

My hands are already fiddling with his belt buckle and he rips his cut and his shirt off, tossing them both onto the floor as we stumble toward the bed.

I strip my blouse off and unclip my bra as he pulls his boots and socks off. Then I'm helping him shrug down his jeans, needing to see all of him. His cock bobs free and I stare down at it, my pussy throbbing and mouth salivating at the sight. I want everything and anything with him right in this moment.

"Are you my dirty little slut, Amelia?"

My eyes meet his again. "Yes," I whisper, my hand reaching for his cock as he groans. "Ever since I sucked your cock on your birthday, I've wanted more."

"Have you touched your pussy, thinkin' about me?"

I nod.

"With your dildo, Amelia?"

"Yes," I splutter, feeling his hard length and his piercings. He looks down when I begin to explore with my fingertips.

"Fuck," he groans.

Cupping my tits, he then pushes me down onto the bed, riding my skirt up as he straddles across me, his head tipping down to suck a nipple into his mouth.

"Tell me what you want, Amelia."

I'm red, flustered, and so damn hot. I can't contain how much lust I feel for him. My senses are in overdrive.

"I want you to fuck me with your tongue."

He grins, moving his mouth to my other nipple, he sucks, licks, and pulls it with his mouth as my hands grip his hair and I moan. My pussy is begging for another release. He works his way down my body, peeling my heels off and throwing them aside, then reaches under my skirt and pulls my panties off. Rucking my skirt up to my waist, he begins kissing my stomach, the tops of my thighs, my inner thighs, everywhere except where I want him to.

"Spread your legs for me, Amelia," he says, his voice deeper and raspy. I do so, and he groans, spreading me wide with one hand. I feel his breath against my core as I squeeze my eyes shut.

Then, his tongue swipes through my folds as I buck off the bed. He chuckles, holding me down at the hips, my hands gripping his hair tighter.

"I need to come, Gears," I pant.

"You'll come when I say you can come." He swipes his tongue again, and this time it hits my clit.

I make a strangled noise that doesn't even sound human.

"Please," I beg. *"Please, Gears…"*

He starts to swirl around and around my clit, and I see stars. I ride his face as I come again, his name moaned on a breath over and over again. He doesn't stop there, though. He lives up to his promise and begins to eat me out, his tongue working frantically as I open my eyes and glance down. Moving up to my elbows, he glances up at me. His face buried between my legs is something I will never forget, and when his tongue starts to plough into my hole, I throw my head back and come again as he fucks me with it.

When I finish, he crawls over the top of my body, his hard, angry cock bobbing at my thigh as I grip his ass. He brings his mouth to mine and kisses me, his tongue in my mouth, replicating what he just did, making my thighs clench.

He pulls back. "See how good you taste," he whispers. "Do you want my cock now, *sugar?*"

I nod in a daze, unable to form words.

Grinning, he climbs off the bed and rips my skirt all the

way off, then goes to his discarded jeans and comes back with a condom. I watch as he rips the packet open and rolls it on his cock. He's huge. I can see why he needed to limber me up.

Coming over the top of me again, he holds his cock at the base and teases me with the tip, sliding through my slick pussy as we both groan. Gripping his ass tighter, I encourage him as he moves to my entrance.

He starts slow, and I know it's because he's afraid of hurting me, edging in as he moves his hips back and forth, sliding in a little bit more every time. I feel his piercings rubbing my walls as I squeeze his cock. It feels so good already.

"Gears," I moan.

"This okay, baby?"

I nod, our eyes meeting as he stares down at me. The look in his eyes…fuck me, what is that? He looks at me like I'm the most precious thing in the world.

"It feels so good, Gears. Don't be afraid of hurting me, I want all of you."

I move my hips toward him, and with one thrust, he's all the way in. He stills as we both groan at the feeling, letting me adjust to his size. I feel so damn full. We're so fucking close; it's amazing.

Hissing, he pulls out slowly all the way, then slides back in just as slow.

The sensation sends me to heaven.

"This sweet pussy," he breathes. "This pussy is mine, Amelia. Say it."

"This pussy is yours, Gears."

"Good girl. So tight, so fuckin' tight, baby."

I smile at him, loving how he makes me feel. He slides in and out, his pace maddeningly slow, but I feel every single inch of his monster cock as the ripples of his piercings rub my walls and heighten every sense I have.

I wrap my legs around him as he moves up so his hands are planted on either side of my head. Running a hand down his torso, I marvel at his tanned skin, how ripped he is, how he moves his hips…

He increases his pace, his cock thrusting in and out with purpose, hitting the very end of me so I feel it everywhere. Grabbing my hips, he tilts them, and as soon as he does that, my orgasm builds so much faster…he's hitting my clit and my G-spot…and I start to quiver, whimpering and moaning beyond my control. The bed rocks as we fuck harder and harder.

"Gears!" I cry. "Oh God, Gears!"

"Yeah, baby, that's it, take my cock like a good girl. Fuck, your pussy looks so good swallowing my cock."

I orgasm harder than I ever have as he fucks me into the mattress, my head spinning as his thrusts begin to stutter. I know he's close. Then, he stills, calling my name as I watch him come. It's the most beautiful thing I've ever seen. Way better than on the end of a camera.

He's so sexy, his body is insane, and I want him all over again.

He collapses down on top of me as I wrap my limbs around him, his breathing just as heavy as mine.

"Gears," I pant.

"Yeah, baby?"

"I need that all over again, please."

He chuckles into the duvet, then moves his mouth to mine. "Oh that's a given, *sugar,* and now that I've got you, I might not ever let you go."

15

GEARS

<small>HER LIPS ON MY BODY.</small>

Her hands everywhere.

Our silhouettes on the wall.

She's ruined me.

Pulling her to me, she straddles my lap. I don't give her a break; I'm ready again. This time, I want it to last a lot longer.

I sit up so our bodies are pressed together, cupping her face as we kiss. Her arms wrap around me and my heart hammers in my chest. Sex permeates the air, along with the sweet scent of her perfume, and it's intoxicating.

I've never felt like this before.

It's not just the sex, even though her body is amazing and we fit together so well. It's the feeling.

And it's a feeling I can't shake.

"You're beautiful," I tell her in between kisses.

"Mmm," she murmurs, her hands in my hair.

I'm wild with her, way more than with the other women I've been with. I never go down on chicks, for one, but with her, I have to have every inch of her body, and her ass is next.

I smack it as she groans.

"That tight little pussy fits my cock so well."

"Mmhmm."

I chuckle.

"What?" she breathes.

I shake it off.

"What?" she insists.

"You're a bad influence."

She balks. "I'm a bad influence?"

I squeeze her ass cheek. "Yup, you jumped me, remember."

"I couldn't help it. I don't know what came over me."

"We have a connection, like you said, no point denying it." I kiss her softer, then add, "If you ever do that to me again, I'll tie your hands behind your back and use your body as I see fit, takin' turns at fuckin' your face and your pussy, got me?"

She stares at me. "Holy shit."

I grin. "Didn't hear you say yes, *sugar.*"

"How'd you learn to talk like that?"

"Practice." I laugh.

"You talk like that to all the girls you bone?"

"Not allowed to bone women at the club, remember."

"Out of the club?"

"Nosy little thing, aren't you? And the answer is no, I'm not dirty like I am with you. For some reason, you bring it out in me."

She looks pleased with that answer. "What do you want to do with me next?"

I kiss her chastely. "Whatever I want."

She yelps as I squeeze both her ass cheeks and then, moving one hand to the base of my cock, I lower her down as she sinks onto me. We both groan at the same time.

"Fillin' your pussy, just like I promised," I growl, looking down at where we're joined.

"You certainly know how to move." She sighs, gripping my shoulders as I lift her hips up and she sinks down slowly again.

"Not just a pretty face."

I run my hands up her back, feeling her soft skin, then cup her ass cheeks again as we move into a steady rhythm. Having her here, on top of me, beneath me, *everywhere*, it feels surreal.

She's been on the other end of a camera for so long, so close, but also just out of reach. Now she's in my arms and it feels like the best place in the world. Like I can do anything.

I've never experienced it before.

She throws her head back as I kiss and suck on her neck, not even giving a fuck that I'll leave marks. The truth is, I want to mark her, make her mine, let her know who she belongs to.

And there I go again, getting way ahead of myself.

We're tangled around each other as I thread my hands into her hair.

"You're *mine*, Amelia," I growl.

"Yours," she cries, bringing her eyes back to face me. "Yours, Gears."

I flip her over suddenly, making her yelp as I pull out.

Gripping her hips, I flip her over again, so she's face down on the bed. I run my hands up her ass, her curves so fuckin' sexy that I take a moment to appreciate them.

"Up on your knees," I tell her, watching as she obeys without a fuss.

"Are you gonna be my good little girl, or a dirty little

slut who didn't wear her panties at the office, then teased me about it."

She wiggles her ass in response.

"Use your words, Amelia."

"I'm your dirty little slut," she breathes. Hearing her say it makes my cock swell.

I spank her ass hard on one cheek, then the other as she yelps again. Watching her pale skin turn pink just about has my cock leaking, but I manage to contain it.

I lean down and kiss her ass cheeks where I smacked her. "Spread your legs wider," I tell her.

She does as I say, and I bend down to lick her out, making her squirm as she pushes her pussy back against my face. *I'll never get enough of her. Could any man?*

I lick, suck, and fuck her from behind with my tongue as she bends down on her elbows to give me better access. She starts to come, and as she does, I press her clit hard with my fingers while my tongue surges in and out; she cries out. Her moans and screams make my dick so damn hard.

Nope. I'll never tire of her.

"You taste so fuckin' good when you come," I mutter, moving behind her, kissing her ass cheeks again as I rub my fingers through her folds all the way back to her puckered hole. "You done this before?" I tap her asshole.

"No," she murmurs. "Won't it hurt?"

I brush her hair over one shoulder and bite down gently. "With my cock, yes. Piercings and anal don't work so well, but we can build up to that…"

Swirling her slickness over her ass, I run my other palm up her back, enjoying the feel of her skin. I continue to play with her as she pants, and every now and again, she presses her ass back slightly, as if encouraging me.

My cock is at full mast and ready to blow again,

hanging heavily as it bobs against her thigh. With every single touch, I'm fighting hard to hold on, especially in this position where I can see everything.

"I want it, Gears," she whispers.

I know she does. Every single touch I give her, she responds to. Taking it slow, I ease the tip of my finger into her hole, repeating the process until I'm up to the first knuckle.

"Gonna feel strange, baby," I say, "but it'll feel so good when you come."

A shudder goes through her body as I keep working her ass, my other hand brushing between her legs to her pussy. She's so wet from her last climax, she's literally dripping, her arousal coating her thighs. I could spend eternity here.

I insert a finger into her pussy, then two, my other hand still working in and out of her ass.

"Oh God," she cries.

"Relax." I chuckle as I feel her hole grip my finger. "It'll hurt less if you trust me. I won't hurt you."

She unclenches, and I work in and out, spreading her slickness, marveling at the fact I don't need lube. She's got enough of it. Once I have my next knuckle deep, she sits back, taking me farther. My fingers inside her pussy curve as I massage her G-spot, knowing every sensation she's feeling is heightened.

"Come for me, my beautiful little slut," I growl in her ear, and she lets go.

Her orgasm echoes around the room as I move my finger the whole way in and out, riding her through it as she cries out, her hand darting between her legs to rub her clit.

I don't think I've ever heard such animalistic noises coming out of woman's mouth before. It makes me want to pound my chest like a caveman and ride her rough and fast.

Pulling out, I smack her ass and place another kiss on the reddened skin. Then I'm rolling on another wrap and coming right back up behind her. Cock in hand, I shove it hard inside her pussy, groaning in relief at the feel of her. She cries out, her hands gripping the sheets below us. As I start to move, sliding my cock in and out, my teeth grit with every sensation.

I give it to her, thrusting as I hit the end of her, knowing she's still sensitive from the last orgasm.

"Tell me, baby, tell me how good it is," I growl in her ear.

"It's sooooo good, Gears, ooooh, oh, oh…"

I chuckle, my balls slapping against her mound as I move faster, my cock ready to explode. Every vein, every single nerve in my cock is being strangled by her pussy.

The bed starts to rock, and I know I can't hold off much longer, especially when she starts to come again. I bang her harder, moving up to my knees as I grab her ass cheeks and give it to her. She moves her ass back onto me, milking me as I shoot my load, stilling as I cry out her name on a strangled moan.

"Fuck," I mutter. "Fuck, Amelia."

I slide out, and scoot beside her to pull her with me, into my arms.

She pants, trying to catch her breath as we lie tangled together.

"That was amazing," she breathes. "Once I got used to the sensation."

"We can get some toys," I mumble into her hair.

She snorts a laugh. "Like a butt plug?"

"Exactly."

She stills, "Oh."

"You'd look fuckin' amazing with a butt plug in your ass." I reach down and pull the condom off, tie the end, and drop it on the side table to dispose of later.

"I didn't think I'd like it."

"Most people don't."

She hesitates, then asks, "Would you like it?"

I kiss her head. "I'd let you do anything to me."

She snuggles into my side as I reach to pull the comforter over us.

"You would?"

"If it pleased you, yes." I feel her smile against my skin. "You like that idea, don't you?"

"Pleasing me, or letting me fuck your ass with a butt plug?"

I snort a laugh. "Both. Told you before, with you, I'm up for anythin'. And before you go gettin' all nosy, no, I haven't had my ass reamed before."

She giggles this time, kissing my skin. "First time for everything."

I pull her closer. "I like havin' you close, Amelia."

"I know," she sighs. "Me too."

"I don't know where this leaves us."

"We can fuck in secret," she says quickly. "Nobody has to know, until you're patched in…that's if…you want to do this again."

I turn to her as she looks up at me. "I told you before, this pussy is mine. If another man so much as looks your way, so help me God."

She rolls her lips and fights a smile. "Possessive ass."

"Dirty slut."

A grin splits her face. "It's a good thing I don't take offense to your nicknames."

"You like it, and I think you like bein' my dirty little secret, don't you, *sugar?*"

She can't deny it; she gets so hot and horny every time I talk dirty to her.

"I like it when you do it."

"Glad to hear it."

"But you know, my vagina is going to need a little break after all of that."

I chuckle, enjoying this moment of closeness. It's a rarity for me, as I don't do pillow talk. "You think I'm finished with you already?"

She puts her arm over my chest and squeezes me. "I have to get going soon."

I balk. "No chance in hell."

"Gears, I can't sleep here."

"Like fuck you can't. I've got tonight off, and you're not goin' anywhere."

"Can we at least take a shower?"

"Yes, but only if I get to fuck you in it."

She laughs softly. "You have a one-track mind, did anyone ever tell you that?"

"Like I said, *sugar,* there're a lot of firsts when it comes to you."

Later, we shower together, and just like I envisioned; we can't keep our hands off one another. Especially when she goes down on her knees and starts to suck me off.

"Does this thing ever go down?" She laughs, running her tongue over my piercings.

"Around you? No, and that's a disaster, especially when I'm at the club."

She runs her tongue all the way down my cock as I grip her hair in one hand, bobbing her head until I'm fucking her mouth.

"I did tell you," I grunt, as she takes all of me. "That I'll fuck your mouth, pussy, and now your ass if you do bad shit again, like not wear panties."

I'm gonna blow if she keeps this up, though. I wanna be inside her again.

"Gotta get a wrap," I mumble. "Need your pussy."

"Just pull out," she breathes, licking my tip, teasing me.

I haul her by the armpits as she squeals, then push her against the wall.

"I'm clean," I growl in her ear, moving down to kiss her pulse point and neck. I suck hard, knowing I've already left a mark, and I'm gonna leave a few more. Fuck what anybody else thinks when they see it. She can explain if she wants to.

"It's okay," she cries. "Just get inside me."

I chuckle as I grab her by the hips and lift her, pressing her against the wall as she wraps her legs around me. Moving my cock to her pussy, I slide right in.

"Dreamed of this," I grunt, thrusting deep. "Fucked my palm more times than I care to remember wishing it was you."

She scratches my back in response, her hands trailing down to my ass where she squeezes, and I quicken my pace.

Feeling her walls clenching around me, with nothing between us, it sends me over the edge. She tumbles quickly too as I reach down and suck her nipple, riding her through it, then I let go, grabbing my dick and spurting my cum all over her stomach.

She glances down, watching me as I pant hard, watching too.

"Feels so good with nothin' between us," I pant once I'm completely empty.

"Does that stuff ever run out?" She laughs.

I look up at her and I can't help the shit-eating grin that splits across my face. I press my lips to hers. "There are some perks to being young."

"What, that you can legally drink now?"

"I think it's hot that you're older than me."

"I think it's hot that you want me to peg you."

I burst out laughing. "I don't know about peggin', babe, but my body is yours. I'm not afraid to experiment."

She wraps her arms around my neck, in no hurry to leave, and we kiss, letting the warm spray cast over us until all the hot water runs out.

I step out, pass her a towel, and try not to fight the feeling of how normal this all feels.

I've never showered with a woman before.

Just as I'm getting dry, I hear a knock at the door.

I never have visitors up here, and Roxy, who lives across the hall, is on shift tonight. I really hope it isn't anyone from the club, coming to see if I can fill in.

I wrap a towel around my waist.

"Wait here," I tell Amelia. She nods as I shut the bathroom door and go toward the door.

"Hey, brother," Axton says as my eyes go wide.

I was not expecting that.

"Hi, Ax, what's up?"

"Sorry to bother. I wanted to come by and grab that air fryer I left in the kitchenette. Been meanin' to pick up, and saw the van out back."

Tonight?

Of all the fuckin' people to be knocking on my door...

I palm the back of my head. "I, uh, I took it downstairs, left it in Stevie's office," I reply. "I know how much you love that thing."

I hope he doesn't notice the rumpled sheets and Amelia's clothes strewn around the room, including her bra flung across the end of the bed. Then, just as I think it, he glances over my shoulder at the mess. Noticing how I'm dressed, he clears his throat and runs a hand through his hair. "Shit, you've got company. Sorry, man."

He's also the only one who's polite to me, but then he's only just been patched in himself.

It's not like I can deny it. "That's all right." I feel the color draining from my face, thinking that somehow he'll know those are his sister's clothes and I'm about two seconds away from having my face rearranged.

He lowers his tone. "Didn't know you were seein' anyone."

I run a hand over my face. *Okay, Axton, time to fuck off now.* "I'm not."

He gives me a knowing look, then turning to leave, he gives me a sly grin over his shoulder. "Fuckin' pretty boy."

I give him a chin lift. "Got me there."

"Have a good night," he calls out as I shut the door and lock it, just to be sure.

My heart races in my chest like a runaway freight train without any brakes.

I thought we were busted.

And what's worse...I didn't give two fucks.

Amelia Altman is mine, and if Axton and Brock want to bury me out in the desert or feed me to the coyotes, then so be it.

It's not the club holding me to this earth anymore, like I thought it was, makin' me want to be better, makin' me want to do better; it's her. It's always been her.

And that is a fuckin' problem.

16

AMELIA

THE SECOND I HEAR MY BROTHER'S VOICE, I GO INTO A panic.

I know Axton would be a little more understanding than Brock if we got found out, but not much more. Both of my brothers are ridiculous when it comes to being overbearing.

What makes matters worse is that I have to hide out in the bathroom, like I'm ashamed of myself, until he's gone.

When I hear the door close, Gears appears at the bathroom door as I stand there in a towel, my feet rooted to the floor.

"That was close," he says, brushing a hand through his wet hair.

"Sure was," I reply. "Did he suspect anything?"

"He saw your clothes."

I slap a hand over my mouth. "He did?"

"Yep, but he didn't know they belong to you, thank Christ."

"Busted before we even got to snuggle," I say, feeling very brave.

He holds out his hand for me, and I take it as he leads me back into the main room, over to the bed.

I glance around, seeing our clothes strewn around the room, and Gears's wallet open on the side table with condoms hanging out of it.

I cringe. "Crap."

"You can imagine the joy on my face when I opened the door to see him standing there."

"What were you saying about that being a close call?" I can't help but laugh.

"I'm glad you find it so funny. It could've been my body parts buried out in the desert."

"Coyote food?"

"Exactly."

"It's probably better if you come to my place, but don't come in the van, or leave your motorcycle."

"Gettin' demandin'."

I prod him in the chest. "That's if you want to see me again?"

He rubs his nose with mine. "What do you think?"

Pulling his towel off, I let it drop to the floor by our feet.

"I think you could start using that mouth for something far more productive."

"Decided to stay, then?" He pushes me back onto the bed.

"Since Axton is lurking close, I guess I have no other option."

"Right," he snickers.

"Anyone would think you're happy about that?"

I scoot back on the bed as he rips my towel off. "Just happy to still have my balls."

Reaching between his legs, I cup him. "You certainly do."

We spend the rest of the night tangled around each other, like we never want the night to end because we don't know what morning will bring. In a way, we don't.

But none of that matters. Not when I'm with him.

"You screwed Gears, didn't you?" Deanna scrutinizes my face as I flop down onto her couch.

My eyes open quickly. "Why do you say that?" I did a good job of covering all the hickies he gave me. Luckily, it's cold out and I can get away with wearing scarves.

She eyes me suspiciously. "You have that freshly fucked glow about you that can't be mistaken for anything else."

"How observant of you."

"So that's a yes?"

I put my arm over my face as she stands and waits for my reply.

"It just sorta…kinda…*happened*. Brock said for him to give me a ride home. We didn't talk because he was still mad at me for ghosting him after that whole sucking him off thing on his birthday, then one thing led to another…" There's a long pause of silence, and I peek out from under my arm. "What?"

"When was this?"

"Last night."

"And you didn't call or text me to tell me everything?"

"I couldn't, I was with him."

She plops down on the couch next to me. "You mean to say that you stayed the night?"

I cover my eyes again. "Yes, well, Axton came up to the apartment, if you can believe it, so it was too risky to leave, in case he was still down in the bar."

"So? What was it like?"

"Ugh, amazing."

"What about his cock?"

"That's amazing, too."

"Use your describing words, Amelia, for God's sake."

"He's a monster, big and thick, and he goes all night."

She snorts. "Holy fuck. That's just great."

"For me it was."

"He's young, of course, he can go all night."

"You've no idea. He couldn't keep his hands off me."

"Did he go down on you?"

I sigh. "Yup, and he's good at that, too."

"Ugh, this is so unfair! I'm sexually frustrated enough."

"Well, I'm sorry, but you did ask."

"You and Gears, I'd never have picked it in a million years."

Why I was ever afraid to tell Deanna is beyond me. She's been asking me ever since I told her about me blowing Gears off if we'd seen each other again.

"Well, me either, it all happened the night he helped fix my car."

"He'll be patched in soon."

"Like that means anything."

"You're right, but you have to start standing up for yourself. I've been telling you that for years."

"You don't have two brothers and an ex-military father," I groan.

"Yeah, worse, I have Richie Hutchinson."

I peek at her again. "Which is why you can't fuck Cash."

Her eyes go wide. "Yes, and also the reason that my B.O.B needed recharging after the night of the barbecue."

I slap my forehead. "You wore the thing out?"

"Have you seen that man?"

The doorbell rings and I sit up. Ever since Axton came

up to his old apartment, I've been jumpy. "Who's coming over?"

"Relax, it's Lily," she says. "We're going over some of Gunner's photos for the new shoot he did for Ryder Magazine."

"God, is he still taking his clothes off for a living?"

Gunner is one of the prettiest men you'll ever see, and he also happens to be super sweet. He's nice to all the girls in the club, unlike some of the brothers.

"Yes, and he's making a shitload of money."

I flop back down again as Deanna goes to answer the door.

"Hey Lil," Deanna says, as they hug. "It's been a minute."

"I'm sorry, it's been so busy at the salon," she groans as Deanna lets her in. "Hey, Amelia."

I open my eyes. "Hi, Lily."

"Why are you looking like you just got run over by a bus?"

"I had a long week and a late night," I reply, not that I'll tell her the real reason I barely got any sleep. And it isn't as if being in Gears's arms isn't comfortable, because it is, but we were too busy being all over each other. "And I was just giving Deanna some advice."

"About what?"

"Fucking Cash," I reply.

"Amelia!"

Lily laughs. "Come on, Deanna, it's not like it's a secret. I was with you in New Orleans, remember."

She sits back down on the couch. "Yeah, and it isn't like Cash is remotely aware I even exist. I'm half his age, and he has sweet butts lining up around the corner. I remember how they all flaunted their asses around at the club, hoping to get his attention, hanging on to his every word."

"Wait, is he really, like, fifty years old?" she asks.

I glance at Lily. "Pretty hot right?"

"Totally," she agrees.

"Yeah, and totally not happening," Deanna sighs.

"Hutch may have a few things to say about that," I chime. "I mean, they've been friends since before you were born."

"Ugh, don't remind me," she groans.

"How are things with you and Guns?" I ask Lily.

She beams. "Never better. He's been driving me crazy at the salon, though. He does ear and belly button piercings one day a week, and I swear to God, if I get one more horny teenager hitting on my man…"

"It's not as if you have anything to worry about," Deanna adds. "You tamed the wild beast, and not before time."

Gunner used to be the resident fuck boy of the club, and Lily was off-limits because she's Steel's sister. Plus, she'd had a crush on him since she was a girl that he never knew about.

She's been good for him, and he's been good for her. They both deserve to be happy.

"That, and I did tell Gunner that if he ever cheated on me, I'd have his balls in a vice." Lily laughs.

"Listening to all of this?" Deanna throws at me.

I give her daggers, then smile sweetly at Lily when her eyes flick to mine.

"You do need to get out more, Amelia," Lily agrees. "Maybe we could all have a girls' night out? Check out the local talent, strictly for you girls, of course."

"Like there're any hot guys in Bracken Ridge," I snort. *Albeit one.*

"Yeah, and Cash went and took his dick all the way back to New Orleans," Deanna moans.

"Listen to the pair of you," Lily says, shaking her head

as she looks at us both. "Leave it to me. I heard Magic Men are coming to Bracken Ridge next weekend. I could get us tickets."

I burst out laughing as Deanna bounces up and down on the couch, clapping.

"How did I not know about this?" Deanna gasps. "Magic Men?"

"Yup, and they go fully naked."

I don't know if it's just me in general, or maybe all the hot sex I had last night, but not even the thought of multiple naked men can entice me to want to leave Gears's side.

I know it sounds sappy, and I'm probably in over my head, but he's the only man that does it for me, or at least, that's how it feels.

Though, just like I thought, my vagina is certainly paying the price this morning. The man never goes down.

The way he held me….and when I woke up in the night to go pee, as I got back to bed, he'd rolled over to my side and had his arm spread out across my side of the bed. I slid back in under it, snuggling under the covers, and we spooned. *Fucking spooned.*

His scent…I can't even describe it. But it's damn hot, just like the rest of him.

I have to admit, even though I shouldn't, almost being caught by Axton had the blood pumping in my ears.

The danger. The excitement. The forbidden.

Everything with Gears is completely off limits, yet I've never felt so alive.

Maybe I am just basking in the afterglow of the best sex of my life, that must be it.

It's exhilarating, knowing he's nuts about me in private, but when we're in public, we have to keep it under wraps. Then there's his body, and not just his cock, which is a pretty appealing package. His chest, shoulders, ripped abs, tight ass, his gorgeous face, and those eyes…visions of him on top of me, staring down while he rode me hard, calling me his good girl, after being his little slut for the duration, it sends heat right through me.

As if she knows I'm having flashbacks, Deanna waves a hand in front of my face.

"Earth to Amelia."

"Sorry," I say, clearing my throat. "Like I said, I had a long week and a bad night's sleep."

"I just asked if you'd be in on the girls' night?"

Why do I immediately think that Gears wouldn't be happy about that?

"Sure." I nod. "Sounds good."

Lily laughs. "Leave it to me, and if I can't get tickets, then we can still do something else. Maybe have dinner, *not* at the Burger Joint, but at a proper restaurant, and cocktails or a movie night…Magic Mike marathon?"

I chuckle. "You really have magic men on the brain, Lil. You also know if you do get tickets, you can't tell the boys. They'll freak."

"I don't know why men get so self-righteous,"

Lily huffs. "Like we're not grown women who can't look after ourselves and make our own decisions. They reap the benefits anyway. When I come home horny as fuck, Gunner won't be complaining."

"Gunner would be the only one to even consider letting you get tickets," Deanna agrees. "Hell, he'd probably wanna be in the show.

We all laugh. "As for the rest of us," I sigh. "We have to put up with overbearing brothers, dads, oh, and men who aren't our brothers, they only think they are."

"It's only because they care," Lily says, then to Deanna.

"Do you really think your dad would be cool with you and Cash?"

She slinks back against the couch. "Absolutely not. He'd make mincemeat out of his face." She slaps a hand over her forehead. "It's not gonna happen."

"Wait!" I say, sitting upright like an idea literally just hit me in the face. "At the barbecue, I heard Cash saying he's looking to do a full revamp of the clubhouse, like literally redecorate the whole club."

Deanna turns her head to me. "He did?"

I clap my hands together as my and Lily's eyes meet. "I mean, it's perfect."

"What's perfect?"

"You could do it!" Lily and I chime in unison.

She glances between us, then a small smile appears on her lips. "I wonder why he didn't mention it at dinner, then again, traveling to New Orleans for a job is a little crazy."

"It's worth finding out," Lily agrees. "And you'd be staying down there a while. That club is huge; it'd be a six month job at least."

Deanna snorts a laugh. "That won't be good for a business I'm trying to set up and make a name for myself here."

"You said yourself," I remind her, "that you'd probably have to move to the city to make things really take off."

I can see the wheels turning in her brain as she considers it.

"I guess…"

I've never seen Deanna second guess herself. She's spontaneous, she just does things, usually without giving it too much thought. She has a confidence I've always admired, and she's always been able to go for what she wanted without giving a shit what anyone else thought.

"We shouldn't be encouraging her," I say to Lily.

"We so should! Cash is hotter than most men half his

age," she replies with a shrug. "Just don't let your dad find out."

"That is not helping," Deanna moans. "The best thing I can do is stay away from that man."

"We disagree," we say in unison, both laughing again, giving each other a high-five.

"Were you guys separated at birth?" Deanna shakes her head at our cackling.

"God, I hope not," I groan. "Because then I'd have Steel as a brother as well."

Lily snorts. "Trust me, that's a whole shitshow right there."

"Tell me about it. How am I ever supposed to find a man with Axton and Brock breathing down my neck?"

"You get creative?" Lily shrugs. "They don't need to know *everything* you do."

I glance at Deanna as a small smile tugs at her lips.

There aren't any truer words spoken.

Gears and I can do this. Anyway, *it's just sex*.

I keep telling myself that over and over, because even though I know I shouldn't, I feel like I'm falling head over heels for the one man I can't have.

Chapter 17- *Gears*

The Burger Joint is busy the following night, and I don't clock off until after eleven.

I made the mistake of fooling around with some dessert ideas and now Kirsty and Roxy want them made into little takeaway boxes.

"I don't know who taught you to cook," Roxy had said earlier that night when she sampled my fudge brownies. "But these are delicious."

I started off with something easy, like ice cream sundaes, and Hutch installed a large freezer. During the day, when I've had some spare time, I've been experimenting with carrot cake, one of my grandma's favorites, and when I tried the fudge brownies, the girls seemed to like them.

"He's a natural." Kirsty beamed at me. The place has been packed every night we're open, so she's got plenty to be happy about.

I told them I liked creating and that I'd had a good teacher. I even box up a few slices of carrot cake for Grams. If she approves, I'll put it on the menu.

The boys came in for ice cream sundaes and ended up raiding the ice cream freezer. Least I've got Kirsty here to kick them all out when they get in the way. Watching that woman tell them off is hilarious.

Later, when I'm alone in the kitchen, having sent the kitchen staff home, Amelia knocks at the back door.

I know it's risky, but I had to see her, and I want her to sample some of the things I've been making.

When I open the door, she throws her arms around my neck, and we're kissing before I even get her safely inside.

"Woah," I say when we finally break away. "Somebody is happy to see me."

She peers over my shoulder. "When you said you had something in mind for dessert, I thought that was code for...*me.*"

I chuckle, pulling the door closed behind us and locking it, then I pull her to me, cup her face and kiss her hard, grinding my already hard cock into her stomach.

She murmurs as I take my sweet time, enjoying every second of it.

"It smells delicious in here," she says, as I pull her by the hand over to my workbench. "You've been cooking up a storm."

I've laid out all the desserts I've made for her to try on little white saucers. She smiles, and I'm relieved she looks pleased.

"Your tasting plates await." I gesture grandly at the offerings.

"You did all this for me?"

"Yep, then when you tell me which one you like best, I'll thank you properly."

She gives me a cheeky, suggestive look, moving to the bench as I come behind her. Caging her in, I press my body into hers.

"I kinda like the idea of you all covered in flour, smelling like s'mores and ice cream while you do me," she murmurs as I bring my mouth to her neck and kiss her.

I hold her hips with both hands, then run a palm over her ass while I scoop a spoonful of carrot cake with my other hand, bringing it up to her mouth.

"You're going to feed me too?"

I nip her ear with my teeth. "My cock can't be the only thing you enjoy having in your mouth, *sugar.*"

She nudges her ass back into my cock, and I almost contemplate forgetting about this whole thing and just fucking her over the bench with her face pressing against the stainless steel and her skirt up around her hips.

I crack my neck as the spoon goes into her mouth.

"Mmm," she says, and I watch her clean the spoon, licking the cream frosting off as I fight my carnal urges.

"You're an expert with that tongue, Amelia."

I move to the second plate, the one with the fudge brownie. "I love chocolate," she tells me.

"You're gonna love this then. We served it with hot fudge sauce and ice cream. This is the last piece."

"You saved it for me," she sing-songs. I think I like playful Amelia, it's a hell of a change from the little spitfire I'm so used to. Though, she can be a spitfire anytime in the bedroom, I like her panting and ready for me.

"Seein' as you seem to think this is all just about sex," I tell her, scooping up the brownie, making sure to get some of the sauce I drizzled around the plate.

As soon as I say it, I regret it. This is supposed to be just about sex. I'm not supposed to be leading her on, making her think we may have a future, or fuck, I don't know, something more than just being physical. But the selfish asshole in me wants it all.

It's not like she's going to have a real future with me anyway. We both know Amelia is going places I simply won't.

I can make fancy cakes and burgers, big fuckin' whoop. She's gonna need more, and she deserves more. Small-town life won't be enough for her.

I take the spoon up to her mouth, watching her lips suck, and I grip her hip even harder.

"Want to rub that chocolate sauce on your nipples and lick it all off," I growl, nipping her ear. "Make you beg me to fuck you over this bench."

She groans and reaches back, grabbing my ass with one hand and gripping the bench with the other. Arching her back, she licks the sauce from her lip.

As I rub my dick against her ass, I try to keep it together. I swipe my thumb over her bottom lip, catching the sauce as she sucks it off my thumb.

"*Fuck,*" I hiss.

I like this game.

I reach down, rucking her skirt up with one hand, as I take a brutal stab of the cream sponge, my patience for her body running thin. Just as I'm about to move the spoon to her mouth, I stop.

"You're not wearin' panties, are you, Amelia?" my hand, feeling the smoothness of her skin on her outer thigh, tells me there's no fabric there, and as I pull her skirt up higher, I see her bare ass.

She shakes her head, reaching for my wrist as she brings the spoon to her lips. She slides the cake into her mouth, licking cream from her bottom lip. Grabbing her ass, I give it a squeeze.

"What did I tell you about not wearin' panties?"

"I thought you meant only when I was at work," she says, her mouth full, and her tone innocent. But I know better.

I move my mouth to her neck and bite down hard. She squeals, pushing her ass farther into me as I fondle her, working the other side of her skirt up so both her cheeks are out on display. When I glance down, I almost lose it. She's so fuckin' beautiful.

I smack her ass cheek once, hard. She doesn't even flinch.

"You know what I told you." I smack the other one. A noise leaves her mouth that I only ever want to hear when I'm doing this to her. "And you didn't listen."

As I smack her again, once on each cheek, I enjoy the sight of her skin already getting pink. I bend down, and kiss where I smacked, making her squirm and whisper my name.

Standing back up, I move my hands to her tits and cup them, squeezing as she grinds against me.

"I like defying you," she breathes.

"I can see that."

"I like it when you punish me."

I pull on both her nipples and she cries out.

"Such a bad little slut," I tell her. "Walkin' around here with no panties on. I bet you only came over here to taste my dick, didn't you, Amelia?"

She shakes her head.

I move my hand around the front of her pussy and smack her lightly between the legs. "Tell the truth." I can feel how wet she is, but I won't touch her there. I want her to beg me for it.

"No!" she cries.

I shake my head, pulling the hem of her sweater and the top underneath, then rip it right off over her head, throwing it down on the ground. She's standing in just her bra, with the skirt up around her waist. It's such a sexy sight, I groan as I look her over. Her bra is black and has see-through cups, and I love the thought of her putting this on with me in mind. Pulling the cups down, I let her tits pop out as I tweak her nipples and nibble on her neck.

"Every time you lie to me, I'm going to deny you your pleasure, and trust me when I say, I've got nowhere else to go, baby. I can do this all night."

"*Touch me,*" she whispers, grabbing my wrist, trying to move it down to her pussy.

"Dirty little girl," I chastise. "Spread your legs." She does as I say and I go down to my knees. "Bend over farther, and stick your ass out." She complies again, and I marvel at the sight of her bare in front of me.

Leaning down, I blow on her pussy and she shudders. My gaze drifts lower to see her arousal coating her inner thighs.

"Look how fuckin' wet you are for me," I growl, gripping her ass cheeks. "You're such a bad girl, Amelia. Bad girls get punished." I want to fuck her with my tongue so badly, but this is about making her wait and telling me what she wants me to do.

"Gears," she cries when I stand, still not touching her where she wants it most. Her hands have moved to her tits. She cups them one at a time and plays with her nipples, growing more eager by the second. "I need it."

"What do you need, *sugar?*"

"Your mouth on me."

"Where?"

"My pussy."

"Where else?"

"My ass."

I grin, moving my hands over hers, taking over as I strum her nipples. Her head flops back on my shoulder with a moan from deep in her chest. My dick is so hard that it may bust through my pants. It'd be so easy to fuck her hard and fast, just like she wants, but this is so much more fun.

"You've been thinkin' about me, haven't you?"

She nods.

"You've been having dreams about my cock."

She nods again.

"You want it all day, every day, don't you, baby?"

"Uh huh."

My grin can only grow at her responses. Moving my hand around to her pussy, I swipe my fingers through once and she almost combusts. "So fuckin' wet for me."

I plant a chaste kiss on her head before I move back down to my knees. Parting her ass cheeks, I swipe my tongue through her folds. "If you come," I tell her, "before I tell you to, you won't get my cock."

"Oh, oh…" she murmurs as I move my tongue to her clit, circling it with the tip as she moans.

I spread her slickness all the way to her ass, then move my fingers to my mouth and suck on them. "You taste like heaven."

I lick her pussy, then her ass, back and forth, teasing her thoroughly. Her moans make me reach for my dick as I pull my work pants down and free my cock. It hangs heavily as I sheath it a couple of times with my palm.

Then, I spear her pussy with my tongue, and she cries out, grinding against me as I fuck her. Gripping her ass cheek, I circle her clit again and again, pushing her to the brink. I know she's holding on, trying not to come, and that turns me on so bad.

"Don't come," I whisper.

"Gears! *I can't stop!*"

I want her to, just so I can punish her.

"You'll come when I say you can," I growl, going back in as I let her have it. Two seconds later, she comes, calling out wildly, both her hands on the bench as she grinds against my face.

I've never seen anything so hot in all my life.

"Oh dear," I say mockingly, my voice thick with arousal. "You came, Amelia."

I keep riding her through it, until she's spent, then I stand. I grab her face, tilt her head, and push my tongue into her mouth. Hers meets mine with just as much passion, and as we're kissing, her hand reaches for my cock and fists me.

When I break away, I say, "Dirty little girl, you just want cock, don't you?"

She nods, drops to her knees, and starts to suck me off with such wild abandon, I groan loudly, hissing as she grips the base of my cock. I start thrusting, watching as she takes all of me, hollowing her cheeks as she swirls her tongue over my tip.

I know I'm not gonna last. We did too much teasing with the dessert, and now I just need my release.

"That's it," I murmur. "Take all of it, Amelia. Make me come."

She sucks harder as I thread my fingers into her hair, fucking her face as I start to unravel.

"Can't hold on," I grit out. "You gonna take my cum?"

She nods quickly, and I start to spurt, watching as she takes it, my cum spilling out of her mouth as I still, emptying myself with a loud groan.

Wiping her mouth with the back of her hand, she says, "I prefer the fudge brownie."

I chuckle, yanking her up as I bring her to my mouth, tasting myself on her lips as we kiss. "I think I prefer you without panties all the time."

She smiles, wrapping her arms around my neck, our bodies pushed together as I hold her.

"I could get used to this," she says.

I should feel a pang of regret. I should feel like the world's biggest asshole.

But I want her. And Amelia Altman is the one thing nobody can keep me from. I won't do it. Fuck the consequences, fuck what I have to do, she's *mine.*

"Yeah? Because if you think we're done, you're sadly mistaken, *sugar.*"

"Always tell me the truth," she says out of nowhere.

I nod. "Always."

"What's your real name?"

I hesitate. "Jake."

She smiles softly. "It suits you."

"It was my grandpa's name."

She cups my face, oblivious to the fact she's still standing half naked in the Burger Joint kitchen.

"It's a good name. How did you get your biker name?"

I smile. "I'm good at switchin' gears, I guess. Not just

mechanically, but anythin'. You can show me somethin' once, and I can do it."

"So are you some sort of genius?" she muses.

I smile against her lips. "If I were, I wouldn't be flippin' burgers, baby."

"Your mom would be proud of you."

I stop in my tracks. Of course, she's just being nice. She doesn't know about my mom and her problems.

"She was a junkie," I say in a low voice. "That's what got her killed."

That has her pausing for a moment. "What happened to the guy? Did they ever…"

"Yeah, he got locked up, but he's due for parole soon…" It slips out before I mean it to.

"He is?"

"Yeah."

"But you were…*six?* And you're twenty-one now, so he got…fifteen years?"

"Good behavior."

"He deserves the death penalty."

The hole in my chest doesn't seem as suffocating as it usually does when I think about him and what he took from me. It's only because Amelia makes everything better.

"He does. But I believe in karma."

Oh boy, do I.

She frowns. "Gears, you wouldn't…"

I kiss her chastely. "Let's get dressed and get out of here. I need to fuck you in a bed."

She nods and begins to pull down her skirt. It's like she knows not to push this issue with me. I can't go there. I can never ever go there.

And in the end, Amelia will hate me, but she'll get over it.

Someday, when all the dust has settled, she'll understand why. What I saw at age six, no kid should ever have to see. My mom may have been a junkie who couldn't take care of me, but she didn't deserve to be beaten to death. She didn't deserve the abuse given to her. She tried; that's all any of us are really doing. Trying to get through the maze of life, the best way we can.

It's only because of my grams that I've managed to keep on the straight and narrow. At one point in my life, she's all I had to live for. And I know it means leaving her too, but some things are just bigger than your heart and soul allows. Sometimes something has to give.

And I plan on giving that dick every painful, degrading, pitiful moment that he gave my mom. He just doesn't know it yet.

And it's why I can't stay.

I'm gonna kill him.

I'm gonna kill him with my own bare hands.

My face will be the last thing he sees before he takes his last breath.

Being here is my purgatory, and I know it can't last forever.

Nothing does.

Not even this.

AMELIA

I'LL NEVER LOOK AT A FUDGE BROWNIE THE SAME WAY again.

He's right. I did dress knowing he'd be mad at me for not wearing panties, and yes, I did go there hoping for sex, but what I got was so much more.

I mean, a dessert tasting plate? Could this man get any more divine?

And the moments when he spoke about his mom, he was so fractured, so still and quiet, but he didn't lie. I know it's a hard limit for him, the same way David is for me.

Even when we have dirty sex, it never feels dirty. Even when Gears calls me those dirty names when we're hot and heavy, it never feels like I'm really his slut. It feels like I'm something precious to him, something that he cherishes.

He's so gentle with me afterward, taking the time to hold me, touch me softly and talk. It's like he knows what I need, without actually knowing it.

We just fit.

I know we shouldn't, but we just do.

He makes me feel safe.

He doesn't just fuck me then leave, or make some excuse. It's like he doesn't want to leave. In fact, he stayed the night at my place after I drove us, keeping his promise of needing a bed to fuck me in.

It shouldn't feel like this, but we've gone way past *just sex*, whether he wants to admit it or not.

A part of me keeps hoping that once he's patched in, things will change. He'll have the option of claiming me, and we can be together. As much as my brothers won't like it, there's nothing they can do once he's a club member. I just need to hold on…but what if he doesn't want that? What if I'm just making this all up and he doesn't feel anything that I do? What if I'm making a huge mistake in assuming he's into it just as much as I am?

More to the point, why do I trust him when I barely know anything about him?

I mean, I know a lot of intimate things about him that I wouldn't know otherwise, but I don't know any simple stuff, like what food he enjoys or what he drinks or why the fuck he even cares about what dessert I like. He makes me feel things I never have with any other guy, and as much as I try to play it off as being lust, I know that it runs so much deeper. I know that with every moment I spend with him, those feelings get stronger.

"You're chipper," Kennedy says as I pass her in the hall after I arrive at the office. "Have a hot date last night?"

Why does everyone suddenly notice that I'm in a good mood lately?

I'm seriously starting to wonder if people thought I was a real bitch before I got involved with Gears, and why is everyone so fucking observant.

"I wish," I scoff. Best to play it off as something random so she doesn't get suspicious. I've always been a bad liar. "I ended up having drinks and pizza with Frankie and Sienna last night, and watched a movie. I haven't done that in ages."

And then Gears went down on me in the Burger Joint kitchen and I had the best orgasm of my life.

"Speaking of which, I thought I might stop by the Burger Joint after work and pick up some food, do you feel like grabbing a bite?"

Oh, the irony.

"I, uh, I'm not sure when I'll be done here. I've got a bit to catch up on."

"My treat." Kennedy beams. "You've been working your ass off since we moved, and as your boss, I'm putting my foot down. Plus, I hear Gears makes a killer fudge brownie."

Kill me now.

"How can I say no to a fudge brownie?" I reply, trying not to let the heat creep across my cheeks.

"Exactly. We'll go straight from work?"

I nod. "Sounds good."

This sneaking around thing is far more exciting than it should be. Especially when we get to the Burger Joint and find a table. It's not even seven o'clock and the place is packed. I see Gears through the small server window, with what looks like a million burgers lined up on the grill. How he does it all with just one other cook, I'll never know. Smiling to myself, we find a table.

We place our orders at the counter, and just as I take the table number, Gears looks up at me through the window. I keep my expression neutral, turning to walk back to the table.

About five minutes later, I get a text.

Gears: Excuse yourself and come in the back.

I bite my lip, shaking my head.

Me: I can't. Won't Kennedy get just a little bit suspicious?

He starts to reply.

Gears: I'm sure you can make something up...don't keep me waiting...

I take a sip of my soda while Kennedy sends a text.

"I might just go check out the dessert cabinet. Gears said there's a nice carrot cake. Would you like something?"

She looks up. "Maybe a fudge brownie to go?"

Thankful she doesn't want to come check out the cakes with me, I slip through to the kitchen, keeping my head low toward the small office where Gears keeps all the supplies and a small laptop for ordering.

I don't even get in the door before I feel his hands around me, pulling me to him.

"Took your time." His mouth finds mine as soon as those words leave his lips. We kiss as he lifts me, sitting me on the edge of the desk.

"Gears," I pant when I pull away. "We can't, not here."

"Just needed to see you."

He reaches his hand under the waistband of my work pants and smirks. "Good girl. You managed to wear panties today."

"I don't have long. I told Kennedy I'm checking out the desserts."

He smirks, giving me a lopsided grin. "We both know how that ended last time."

"Exactly, which is why I shouldn't even be in here."

He puts one finger over my lips. "I heard Lily was tryin' to get some tickets to Magic Men."

My eyes go slightly wide. "How did you hear that?"

He shakes his head, his lips curling up. "I hear everything."

"And you disapprove?"

"No, but I expect you to come to my place after and work out all that sexual frustration on me. And you know what'll happen if another man touches you."

I swallow hard. Every nerve in my body is on fire; I feel it all the way down to my toes.

He starts to unbutton my blouse.

"What?" I whisper.

He kisses me again. "I'll tie you up."

I roll my lips. "That's just an incentive." I slap his hand away after he gets two buttons undone.

"Not if I leave you there while you've thought about what you've done."

I bite down on my lip. Then, he reaches into the drawer and presses something into my hand. It's in a small bag.

"What's this?"

"A gift." He snickers.

I frown, opening the drawstring and peeking inside. My eyes just about bulge out of their sockets. I look up at him. "Is this what I think it is?"

He grins. "Yup. Do you like it?"

In the bag is a butt plug with what looks like a large, clear diamond shaped head at the end of it. My mouth goes dry. "It's, uh…unexpected."

He cups my face. "You want me to use it on you?"

I look down at it, then back at him. "Yes," I whisper, earning me another grin.

"Dirty little girl," he whispers back.

"Amelia!"

Gears and I both still as Brock's voice rings through the kitchen.

Holy shit.

We spring apart as I smooth my pants down and put the drawstring bag in my pocket just as Gears grabs a box of sauce from the shelf.

Two seconds later, Brock appears in the doorway.

My heart hammers in my chest as my eyes meet my brother's.

"Why don't you yell a bit louder," I say, annoyance in my tone. "I don't think the other side of town heard you."

"What are you doin' back here?" He eyes Gears with suspicion as he passes him.

Think, shit, think!

I grab the caramel syrup from the shelf in my periphery. "The barista ran out. I said I'd help out and get some more. Gears was showing me where it was kept." *Lame, fucking lame.*

He frowns.

From inside the kitchen, I hear Gears calling out more orders. *See, big brother, he's working. Nothing to see here.*

I'm sure my cheeks are flushed red, as if the adrenaline pumping through me isn't enough to make me combust.

"Why are you looking for me?" I add, since I can't get around him. Brock takes up all of the doorway.

"Was wonderin' if you could babysit the kids tomorrow night. Thought I'd surprise Angel with a night out."

I can't help but smile. "You know you can call me for shit like that."

"I was ordering dinner and saw Kennedy. She said you were back here."

Oh.

"Of course I can. What time?"

"Seven, don't wanna get back too late."

I fight a smile. "Sure thing. Got anything nice planned?"

"Dinner, and some sex in the back of my truck."

"Ew."

"Gotta fit shit in when you got an ol' lady you're tryin' to knock up."

"Double ew."

He scratches his chin.

"Well..." I shake the bottle at him. "I'd better get this back to the front or they'll wonder where I got to."

He moves so I can get by.

"Amelia?"

I turn. "Yeah?"

"Is everything okay?"

I swallow hard. "Everything's fine, Brock."

"Gears wasn't bein' a jerk?"

I want to choke on my tongue when I say, "No more than usual."

That seems to satisfy him as I stalk off with the bottle, passing by the grill as Gears looks up at me and we lock eyes for a moment. I leave the syrup under the counter near the coffee machine and order our dessert.

As I sit back down, Kennedy's rubbing her stomach. "I'm so full," she complains. "Hey, did Brock find you?"

"Oh yeah," I say, casually. "Gears had some new sponge cake he wanted me to try out. For a guy who used to work in a car yard, he's a pretty good cook."

"Bones said he's getting patched in, so that'll make Hutch happy. He'll be contributing to the club coffers and it's clear he can do a lot more than prospecting."

"He's definitely a hard worker, from what I can tell." *Especially with his mouth and tongue.*

She glances down at my blouse...*shit.*

"Anyway," I waffle on. "I'm beat, thanks for dinner. That really was a great burger. I may have to take a five-mile jog in the morning to work it off." I know I talk too much when I'm nervous.

"Thank you for dessert." She smiles, and I've no idea if she knows. She's got her lawyer face on. I guess that's better than her *you're busted* face.

Fuckity fuck.

Lawyers know everything. It's their job to spot when people are telling the truth and when they're being lying jerk faces.

This was too much. We shouldn't have risked it. I should've known that something would go wrong eventually. I mean, my brother almost caught us!

I take a deep breath.

It's both our faults for not being able to keep our hands off one another. Though Gears always seems genuinely interested in what I have to say, not just when he's peeling my clothes off. I've never been with a guy who cared that much before, or, if he's faking the niceties, he's really fucking good at it.

As we get up to leave, Brock wanders past our table with an armful of food.

"Kids can't get enough of Gears's brownies," he says, giving Kennedy an eye roll.

Another thing I won't be able to look at again in the same light.

Not that I'm complaining.

"I can imagine." Kennedy laughs.

He gives her a chin lift, then to me. "See you tomorrow night."

"I'll be there."

We follow him out and walk to our cars.

"See you in the morning," I say, but as I make my way over to my hatchback,

Kennedy turns to me. "Tell me to mind my own business," she says out of nowhere.

A lump forms in my throat as I wait.

"I just hope you know what you're doing."

My eyes go wide. "With what?" I stammer.

Her lips twitch. "Just be careful, Amelia. You're a big girl, but I don't want to see you get hurt."

I swallow hard. I don't say anything. I look down at my shoes, then back up at her.

I should never have gone into the goddamn kitchen.

There is no point denying it.

She knows.

She fucking knows.

"I know what I'm doing." But even as I say it, I don't know if the words are even true.

I don't know what's real anymore and what isn't.

I'm ready to leap into his arms and forget every bad thing that's ever happened to me before him, and if that's selfish of me, then so be it. He makes me feel good. About myself, about my life, about everything. And I hope in return I make him feel the same way. I think the shit-eating grin on his face every time I see him kinda tells me that I've accomplished that goal. How far his feelings go, I don't know. Maybe I don't want to. Maybe I want to live in this bubble, just for a little longer. It's safe here.

He's safe. He's like my happy place, and that is oh so wrong to put that on another person. It's not his job. I also know that it's a ticking time bomb, because it can't stay like that. I have my own demons to fight and my own battles to overcome. But is it so wrong to stay in this place of warmth just a little longer?

Emotion floods my vision.

"See you tomorrow," she says, giving me a small wave.

I nod, unable to speak.

I know I can trust Kennedy, but this is a complication.

Now two people know.

When I'm in the safety of my car and Kennedy has pulled out, I put my head in my hands.

I need to get a grip. If Kennedy can find out, Axton and Brock sure as shit can.

Maybe it's because I don't want it to end and I don't see

why it has to, not if we both want this.

If I confront him about my feelings, he might run the other way. I don't want to come across as needy just because we're good in bed together. Then I remember what he said about another man looking at me and that in itself must mean something. Surely?

Or is he just wanting me all to himself while we're fucking?

Confusion washes through me, and by the time I make it home, I'm more confused than ever.

I jump in the shower, trying to make sense of what the hell I'm doing.

When I get out, I see a text from Gears.

Gears: Hey, *sugar*, I'm off duty soon.

Is it wrong if I need him and he doesn't need to know exactly how much?

Me: Good, come over. I have a gift for you.

Gears: Can't wait.

When he arrives an hour later, he cups my face as the door closes behind him. He goes in to kiss me, then stops. "What's wrong?"

I shake my head. "Nothing."

I pull him to me. "Amelia."

He knows I've been crying, and why I've been crying is a mystery, even to me.

I'm not like this, not normally.

"I'm just tired, Gears, honestly."

"We don't have to…"

There he goes, making a mess of my heartstrings all over again. My composure is barely hanging on.

I kiss him. "I know, but I want to."

And just like that, as he walks me backwards toward the bed, he undoes it all.

And what's worse, I willingly let him.

18

GEARS

I PULL OUT, THEN PUSH BACK IN, GRIPPING HER HIPS AS I SINK my dick inside her tight pussy. Resting my weight on my hands, I stare down at her. Her beauty astounds me, shaking me to my very core.

I realize, somewhere, somehow, what we're doing fucking turned into something else. Like this, for example. I've never made love to a woman before, but this feels awfully close to it.

"That feels so good," she murmurs, her eyes closing, her heels digging into my ass as I rock my hips back and forth.

I'll never get sick of this; the closeness, how she feels at my mercy, how much I want to get even closer.

"You look so beautiful takin' me," I grunt, her tits jiggling as I thrust. "But you know what'll look even more beautiful?"

She shakes her head.

I grin, reaching for the butt plug on the side table. "This." I suck the metal knob on one end, so the jewel faces her. "This in your ass."

As I rock my hips again, she cries out. I tilt my hips

slightly, so I brush her clit, and that sends her over the edge, her moans turning me on as I ride her through it.

Pulling out, I flip her over and say, "Get on your knees."

She follows the order, wiggling her ass at me as I squeeze one cheek.

I coat the plug in lube and begin to work her back entrance, moving the cool metal through her folds and then back to her ass again.

"Relax, I won't hurt you," I tell her. "Grip the headboard."

She does as I say, and I edge the plug in gently, my cock hanging heavily, dying to be buried inside her.

"Gears..." she whispers.

"Is that okay, babe?"

She nods. "I like it... I need your cock. I need you inside me."

I grin. I wanna make her love it, and I know her next orgasm will be that much more intense with this inside her too to heighten everything.

She groans as I push it deeper, her knuckles holding on to the bed for dear life. I spank her ass once, and she cries out.

"What are you, Amelia?" I growl, nipping her ear.

"Yours," she cries.

I wasn't expecting that. It pleases me. "What else?"

She falters.

"What else, Amelia?" I tug the plug and run my other hand through her wet folds. She's close.

"Your dirty little slut," she whimpers.

I smile. "That's it, you're a dirty little girl who likes it in the ass."

"Take me," she cries. "I need to feel you."

I lean down and bite her ass cheek. "You'll feel me when I say so."

I tease her clit, moving the plug in and out, building her orgasm as she tips her head back and groans. I wish I could suck her pussy while she comes all over my face, but I need to be inside her. Now.

Reaching between my legs, I line up my cock, pushing in all the way as she moans loud for me. The plug is all the way in, and I keep it there as I move my cock, slowly at first.

"You want it like a good girl, or a bad girl, *sugar?"*

She hesitates, her groans going straight to my cock. "A bad girl," she murmurs. "Fuck me like I've been bad, Gears."

I smile, gripping her hips as I come up behind her and begin to fuck her hard. "You have been bad. I told you to wear panties and you didn't. Do you want other men seeing your cunt, Amelia?"

She groans at my dirty words. "No…no, I don't."

"Well, this is what bad, disobedient girls get." I rock into her, cupping her tits as she sticks her ass out farther. "Next time, my cock will be in your ass, not this cute little gem that you can barely even feel."

"I feel it," she moans. "Oh, oh…"

Reaching down, I tug the plug and she comes again, wailing my name like she's dying and it's her last wish. And it goes on, and on, and on.

I can't hold it. I pump into her one last time, then spurt my cum inside her. I curse her name, digging my hands into her hips as I still, and she pants like she can't get enough. Hell, we both can't get enough. We may actually die of fucking too much.

I collapse on top of her, into the mattress.

"Oh, Gears," she pants as I pull her hair back and kiss her neck.

"Yeah, baby?"

"That was so good."

I tap her ass. "Told ya."

"It feels so…strange, but in a good way."

"You'll get used to it."

I pull out and roll onto my back as she lies there, on her stomach, the diamond still sticking out of her ass, her cheeks pink from where I spanked her. I don't think I've ever seen anything so beautiful.

She turns her head to face me. "You're really good in bed."

I snort a laugh. "Thank you."

"You're welcome." Shifting closer, I kiss the side of her head before reaching down and pulling the butt plug out, tossing it on the side table. She gets up, goes into the bathroom to clean up, then returns and snuggles into my arms.

"I want you to tell me what got you so upset, Amelia. You know you can tell me anything."

She stays quiet.

"I don't like seein' you like that."

"I'm falling in love with you," she admits out of nowhere.

I feel my heart jolt in my chest. *She's in love with me?*

"You're…" I stammer, unable to say the words.

"Forget it," she mumbles, trying to turn away from me.

I pull her back, cradling her as we spoon, wrapping my arms around her. "Amelia, I fell in love with you the night I helped you with your car."

She goes still in my arms.

"I tried to fight it. I knew it was wrong, that I couldn't get involved, but I couldn't help it. I still can't. We shouldn't be doin' this while I'm a prospect, but I'm a greedy fucker."

She turns in my arms to face me. "You're in love with me?" she stammers out the words.

I cup her face with one hand. "I've never felt like this before, and that was before I ever touched you."

The faint lines between her eyes crease and I've no idea what she's thinking.

"Say something," I prompt when she looks down. "Don't leave me hangin' here, babe."

"We're so different."

"Know that."

"We shouldn't work."

"Know that too."

"We'll be in so much trouble with the club."

"Past the point of givin' a shit."

She strokes my face softly. "You've no idea how I feel about you, none at all, do you?"

I shake my head. "Not a mind reader, babe."

"If I tell you what was wrong, you have to promise to never say anything to anyone, especially not my brothers."

"You can tell me."

"I mean it. Tell me that, no matter what, it stays between us."

I make a crossing-my-heart notion with my pointer finger. Little does she know, I'll scour the ends of the earth before I let anyone get away with anything they've done to hurt her. But she doesn't have to know that.

An unreadable look crosses her face, then she takes a deep breath. "David, my college crush, raped me at a frat party my freshman year."

I stare at her. *What the ever living fuck?*

"Amelia?"

"He said if I told anyone, they wouldn't believe me, and it was my fault anyway for acting like a cock tease."

I pale.

All the shit we've done. The things I've said. I've been calling her a dirty slut…

I sit up. "Why didn't you tell me, before we…"

"I don't usually tell men I sleep with about my past, Gears. It's not a topic of conversation that I feel comfortable with sharing. It's been on my mind more lately, I think, because of what I've been feeling for you. You've made me feel normal again."

I run a hand through my hair. "I've called you some pretty fuckin' bad names!"

"You don't understand. I like it. No, I *love* it. When you're doing things to me and calling me names, it's not out of spite, or hatred, or contempt, I know you're giving me exactly what I want. I like you punishing me. Maybe that's sick, maybe there's something wrong with me, but I like it."

I shake my head. I'm beyond pissed, my blood boiling that someone could ever do that to her. I try to calm my breathing.

"I want to know his name, aside from just *David*."

"No, Gears. It's done. I've buried the past. It took me many years, but I'm finally at peace with what happened to me. And that's taken me a long time."

"Why didn't you ever go to the cops? If he's done it before, he could've done it again…"

"He did, to another girl later that year, then he moved away. She was too scared to go to the police, and begged me not to say anything because she'd deny it. I wish I had the courage back then to tell someone, but I didn't. I told Deanna, and that's it."

"So he gets away with it?"

"I know it's the coward's way out, but you've no idea what it's like, to have your liberties taken away, especially by a man that I liked so much. Hell, I thought I even loved him. Then he did that and acted like he'd done nothing wrong."

I'm already planning my revenge. She can say what she wants, but he doesn't deserve to be walking around like nothing happened.

I turn to her. "I'm sorry," I say softly, gripping her tighter. "I got rough with you, dirty with you, and I never would have done that if I'd known."

"There you go," she says, sitting up, pulling the duvet to cover herself. "He wins again because you would have treated me differently, like I'm some doll who may break, when I'm not. I have kinks, so what? We're not hurting anyone and, like I said, I like the punishment, and I like the praise that comes after too. Does that make me a sick person? Does it make me some kind of freak because it turns me on when I should be repulsed by it after what happened to me?"

I shake my head. "Of course not, but I don't really think you're a slut, Amelia. You know that, right?"

She huffs, getting annoyed. "Of course I know that! That's a real jerky thing to say, and it's kinda ruining the moment, to be honest."

"I'm not trying to be a jerk."

She runs a hand up my cheek. Feeling her warmth builds the ache in my chest, and all I want to do is hold her. Protect her. Keep her safe.

"I know that. But you don't have to feel weird that I like rough, dirty sex because of what happened to me. This isn't the same thing, and it's taken me a long time to come to terms with that and accept what I like instead of justifying it."

"As long as I'm not contributing to the trauma," I say, because it's true. "I never want to hurt you." I know how hard it was for me to stay on the straight and narrow after watching my mom get beaten to death. It had an impact on me that I'll never fully be able to get rid off…well, not until *he's* suffered. Which brings me back to the reason I should never have admitted I was in love with her...what the fuck am I supposed to do once I have to go and kill him? Just come back here and shack up with Amelia and play happy family. I'll be going to jail, eventually. If I get caught, or it leads back to me, then life will be over for a very long time in a concrete box. And Amelia will be gone. She'll eventually move on with her life, do all the things she's supposed to do, and though I want her to want those things with me, deep down, my commitment to this twisted thing has been my goal since as long as I can remember.

Only, that was before her.

"You don't hurt me, not like that."

"You have visible hickeys on your neck and my finger-prints on your ass and hips, Amelia."

"Stop it. Don't make this out to be something it's not."

I pull her close to me again, folding both arms around her. "I'll never let anythin' happen to you, got me? I only ever want what's best for you. Remember that."

She goes quiet. "Can I ask you something?"

I bring my eyes back to hers. "Of course."

"When you lost your mom...did you ever want revenge?"

It's like she can see to the heart of me, so I answer honestly. "Of course. As the years went on, the feeling grew even stronger, especially when he won't spend the rest of his life in jail."

"I'm sorry. He deserves a lethal injection."

"No, he deserves much worse than that."

She regards me for a moment, then frowns. "Gears?"

I give her a chin lift. "Yeah, babe?"

"Do you think there's a happy ending, for people like us."

I snort a laugh. "People like us? People like you, definitely."

"What's that supposed to mean?"

"Amelia, let's not dance around the obvious; you're above me, in every single way. We're complete opposites. I'm a short-order cook and a prospect in an MC with no real family, no money, and I live in a one-bedroom apartment above a pub. Is that the life you think you're gonna have with me? The life you envisioned."

Her eyes narrow. "You seem to have it all figured out, and I didn't know we were talking about sharing a life together. It's not like we've even been on a date before."

"Right, because we can't, remember?"

She jabs a finger into my chest. "One thing I really dislike about you, if you want to know, is the way you always put yourself down. You never give yourself any credit and just assume that you know what's best for me, what life I *should* have, just like everyone else in my life who wants to try to control it."

When she pulls away this time, I have to let her go.

"That isn't what I meant."

"No? Well, then, if we're so sure about each other, let's tell the club; Hutch, Brock, right now. Let's tell them we want to be together, and there's nothing they can do to stop us."

"It ain't that simple, babe."

"Riiiiight."

I can't tell her it's because I'm going to go and kill the man who ended my mom's life. The less she knows about any of that, the better. I can't embroil her in all this turmoil to come. I will not implicate her in any way.

"Amelia, the world isn't as black and white as you make it out."

"I'm not stupid. I know how this works. At the end of

the day, the club comes first. I've got it. I've been getting it loud and clear ever since I moved here. The club will always come first, above all else."

I can't let her get any farther away. Leaning forward in a rush, I grip her wrists when she tries to push off the bed. "That isn't it!" I growl. "I don't want you to ruin your life, not with me. I've got nothin' to offer you, and that ain't no sob story, *sugar,* that's the truth. There's shit I gotta do that I can't involve you in. Stuff that's dark and dangerous and a whole world away from your pretty life in the suburbs. That's the reality. And I'm a fuckin' fool, tellin' you shit like I love you when I know I can't stick around, not forever…"

She stops struggling. "Wait, you love me? For real? When you said that before, when you helped me with my car, I didn't realize you meant it…"

Fuck.

"And what do you mean, you can't stick around? Where are you going?"

"Amelia, don't make this any harder than it has to be. You know this isn't just a fling, but you also know I'm bad for you. You know it like you know the sun will set in the sky every single day. You wanted a walk on the wild side. You think you're in love with me, but it's the safety you like. I'm a safe bet, we both know it."

"You don't know shit."

I smirk. "You're smart, beautiful, honest, courageous, everything I could ever want in a woman. But I know when I'm shooting above my belt, babe. What I got is nothing more than hot sex and a foul mouth. I can't give you anythin' more than that, and we both know it."

She looks like I've slapped her. Her eyes cloud over, and I've never felt so bad in my entire life.

Stupid fuck.

I shouldn't have told her that I was in love with her. But

when I get locked away—or worse—I want her to know the truth. That I do love her, with everything good that's inside of me.

She shakes her head as I let her go, and she starts to climb out of the bed. "Clearly, you know nothing about what I want." Her tone is icy.

I run a hand through my hair. "Amelia?"

She hunts around for her clothes. "I'm going to the bathroom," she says, clearing her throat. "And when I get back, you better be gone, *prospect*."

I shake my head, letting out a breath I didn't even know I was holding.

A part of me wants to fight it, tell her she's wrong. Make her understand. But I don't do any of those things.

She stalks off to the bathroom, and I can't be sure, but I'm certain I hear some whispered words as the door quickly slams…I hope to God she doesn't hate me now.

GEARS

Two days pass by. Then three. Then five. Then a week.

I've texted her, but in true Amelia Altman style, she won't answer.

Then, the dreaded day comes.

When my phone rings and Hoax, the resident hacker and ID whiz for the Phoenix Fury, is on the other end of the line. We've met in passing a few times, before I was prospecting.

"Twelfth of December," he says, by way of greeting.

I've been waiting for this phone call since I was six years old. I never thought the bastard would only get fifteen years. What a fuckin' joke.

"Right before Christmas." I run a hand down my face.

"Happy Holidays."

"You got an address?"

"I'll text you the halfway house he's been assigned to."

Fuck.

This is getting really real.

I thought I would have more time, but it's less than two weeks away.

"Thanks, man. Owe you one."

"You got a plan? You know two heads are better than one, and all that shit."

"I gotta do this alone," I say. "This isn't the club's fight."

"No, but it could be your last."

I shake that thought off. "I'm a prospect. I ain't worth shit, and neither are my problems."

"Whatever you say, man."

"Appreciate it."

He hangs up.

Out of nowhere, Brock grabs me by the scruff of my neck as I head toward the clubhouse for the usual Friday night catch up.

"Fuck!" I yell, when I realize who it is. "You scared me half to death."

He punches me in the stomach.

Oh shit, he knows.

"This is the last opportunity I'll get," he gruffs, grabbing me by the arm as I put up my fists to defend myself. "To kick your ass."

"Don't beat him too bad," Colt says from somewhere behind. "We all wanna get a punch in. Payback for all the shit he's given us this last year."

"Get in line," Rubble says next, shoving Colt. "That little pissant owes me after that poker game where he took all my money."

I know Brock talked about me patching in a few weeks back, but I hadn't heard anything since. I assumed that it hadn't passed the table, so there was no point in bringing it up to only look like a bigger loser.

"Don't fuck with his hands," Hutch orders. "Need those fuckin' things to work. If he gets injured and can't cook, we're fucked, and then I'll have Kirsty ridin' all our asses for not takin' better care of him, like a fuckin' mama's boy."

I grin. "Hey, can't help that women of all ages have this thing for me."

Hutch points at me. "Watch it."

"Fuckin' pussy," Steel grunts. "Go for the face. That way, those fuckin' sweet butts will stay the fuck away from him. Might teach him some manners."

Gunner laughs. "More like they'll want to nurse him back to health. Right, Bones?"

"How the fuck would I know? I never got any sweet butts patchin' me up," Bones grumbles as they all form a circle around me.

"Not the face," I groan. "It's my money maker."

They all snort.

"See, he's been fuckin' breastfed by the women of the club for too long," Brock calls out. "Fuckin' pathetic, if you ask me. Man can't even go and get takeout without a mouthful of lip from the fuckin' club sisters about not puttin' pressure on the cook. Apparently, they've got 'real' customers to take care of first."

"Not my fault that the club sisters all want my meat." That earns me another blow to the guts.

Fuckin' Brock. He doesn't hit like no girl.

"Burgers," I splutter as I laugh. "I meant burgers."

"Think he's bein' a wiseass," Steel points out. "Go for the face, fucker deserves it."

"Just remember who spits in your food," I remind him, as he comes toward me. Even I can admit; Steel coming toward you with that look on his face is slightly terrifying. But I remind myself they need me alive, at least for the moment, so the Burger Joint doesn't go under.

He punches me square in the jaw. That didn't tickle.

"He's a tough little fucker," Brock remarks out of the side of his mouth. "Think you need another lesson in how to keep that smart mouth shut."

"You hit like a girl," I say, laughing. What can I say? I'm a glutton for punishment, and maybe deep down, a part of me wants him to beat the shit out of me because of my guilt. Not that I regret any of it. Not a chance. I'd do it all again in a heartbeat.

"Really?" he rubs his chin in that way that tells me he's contemplating how to hurt me in the worst way possible.

"He doesn't know when to keep his mouth shut," I hear Nitro put in, late as usual.

"And you had to put up with him at the car yard for fuck knows how long," Bones retorts. "I would've buried him out there, under the car parts."

Little do they know, Nitro and I get along fine, and he's always treated me like an equal. But, if he wants a little payback for the time when I gave him shit, then tonight is the night to do it.

I spread my arms wide, knowing I'm gonna regret this later. "Do your worst," I say right as Steel's fist comes toward me again.

～

"Gears?" Amelia runs over to me, and I'm not the only pair of eyes on her as she does so.

"What the hell did they do to you?"

"Initiation," I grunt out. "I'm patched in now."

She stops for a moment, and I can almost see the cogs in her head turning.

"Patched in?"

"Yup."

I slump back against the bar as her hand comes to cup my face. Even though I'm half brain dead and have a splitting headache, I know her actions won't go unnoticed.

"Don't fuckin' baby him," Brock says from somewhere behind the bar. A shot is placed next to me as I ignore it and look at Amelia's worried face. Her beautiful eyes cast down at me as her eyebrows knit together, then she looks up at Brock.

"Is it really necessary to beat the living daylights out of someone just to prove their worth?" she throws back. My little spitfire.

"Of course it is," he replies. "It's called *being patched in.*"

"Just because he's patched," Axton says, from the other side of me, "doesn't mean you can put your hands all over him."

"Shut the hell up," she says, ignoring them both. "I'm going to go get some ointment and ice."

"Better still, go take him to the infirmary," Steel grunts. Fuck knows where he is. "He's bleedin' all over the place like a fuckin' pussy."

More laughs ensue.

Amelia props me up as I sling an arm around her neck and I hoist myself off the stool. I swear every bone in my body hurts.

"You go get your ointment and ice," Brock says. "Just don't let him touch you, or what we just did will look like a Girl Scout Club cookie fundraiser when we're finished with him."

"Shut up, Brock," Amelia spits over her shoulder. "You did enough."

"What's up her ass?" I hear Axton murmur as we pass by.

As we go to leave, Candy and Bambi appear in front of us. "We've got it from here," Bambi says, sizing Amelia up. "Don't we, Gears?"

Before I can reply, Amelia leans toward her, and in a menacing tone I've never heard from her, she says, "Move your ass out of my way, or I'll rip your vocal cords out before you can offer more *help*."

Holy shit.

Bambi closes her mouth, then opens it again, like a goldfish. "Hey! You can't talk to us like that!"

"I can, and I did. Now move it!" she barks.

"Brock?" Candy calls. "We always get to clean the prospects up and give them a proper welcome." She glances at Amelia with a smug look on her face. "Of the oral kind."

"Ugh," Amelia replies, pushing past them without waiting for Brock's reply, nor the girls'.

They're smart not to follow us; they know their place, and Brock isn't gonna side with either of them anytime soon, so he lets it slide.

The brothers watch on with a slight look of disbelief on their faces as we disappear down the hall.

She half drags me out of the bar and down toward the storeroom where they keep all the booze and medical supplies.

"You still mad at me?" I croak as she shuts the door behind her.

"Shut up," she says, reaching for the first aid kit.

"Don't you think that was a little bit obvious?"

"I don't care."

I slump back against stool, as I hoist myself up on it, watching her rummage around. "I need to go get ice," she says. "Wait here."

I laugh. "Where else am I gonna go?"

She leaves, returning a few moments later with a bag of peas from God knows where.

"This initiation crap is so old and redundant," she says. "Beating the hell out of someone to show they're worthy enough to be in the club."

"Hey, least I'm still breathing."

She gives me a pointed look. "They're barbaric."

I pull her to me.

"Don't, Gears. This is hard enough."

"Why not?"

"Because we both know where this will lead, and where will that get us?"

"You haven't texted me."

"I'm sorry about that."

"You walked out on me."

"That's because you told me you loved me, and then said you were leaving."

"I never said that second part."

"I know what you're doing, you know."

I frown. "You do?"

"Yes. And I'm here to tell you that I'm not going away. So you can shove your pathetic excuses up your ass. You're patched in now. Problem solved."

If only it were that simple.

"Babe?"

"Don't babe me, and if you give me any more lip about me being better than you and you just being a 'short-order cook who can't give me what I need,' then I swear to God, I'll sock you in the nose."

I give her a pout. "You wouldn't hit me now, would you, *sugar*? I'm injured."

She takes me in and her eyes soften. "Sometimes I hate them," she grumbles. "For doing this."

I hold her hips, dragging her closer to me. "No, you don't. You just don't like me bein' hurt." She avoids my gaze, and I push her chin up with two fingers so her eyes meet mine. "You love me."

She shakes her head. "No, I don't."

"Yes, you do. I heard you say it."

She rolls her eyes. "They must've hit you hard in the head. Let me remind you; you told me that *you* loved *me*."

"And you said it back when you stormed off, and you called me an idiot."

"A fucking idiot."

"There you go."

"So you waited a whole week to tell me that?"

"No, I waited a week, six hours, twenty-four minutes, and three seconds to tell you that."

"Wiseass."

I take a deep breath as she holds the peas up to my face. "Hold them here while I get some water to wipe up this blood," she says. I can feel my face swelling and my split lip hurts like a bitch.

She disappears again, coming back with a bowl of water.

"You like takin' care of me, don't you?"

"I think you're all a bunch of idiots," she replies. "And, I'm here to tell you that whatever you think you have going on with this revenge pact, you need to tell the club."

I stare at her, dumbfounded.

"Amel-"

"Don't *Amelia* me. You're patched in now, and the club will help you get rid of him. I agree with you, by the way. If someone killed my mother, right in front of my eyes, no less, I'd want to kill them, too."

"That's not-"

"Don't insult me, for God's sake. I'm old enough to know what you have planned, why you can't commit, why you keep talking as if you're already gone. I put it together, Gears. You want revenge, you told me as much, and I get it, I do, but it doesn't have to be this way. You don't have to bear this burden alone. We're your family now. This club has your back. If you tell them what he did, they'll fix it."

226

Hearing her say they're my family, it warms my chest. It makes me feel like maybe I am worth something, even if they did just beat me half to death.

I shake my head. "I can't ask them to do that."

"You don't ask, you tell! You're patched in now, and they'll listen."

"You make it sound so easy." I wince as she cleans my mouth, dabbing gently.

I watch her in utter adoration.

"It *is* easy. They're your brothers, they'll back you. And so will I, Gears. I'm your woman, not just in the bedroom, but out there too." She flings her arm toward the door. "We joke around about having a date and getting to know one another, but we both know how we feel. We both fell hard and fast, I know that now. That all these feelings I have, you feel them too. I want you to claim me, Gears. I want to be yours and have everyone know I'm yours."

I'm in awe as I stare at her, pulling her closer so she's standing between my legs. "How did you get so tough?"

She snorts a laugh. "I have two menacing brothers who think I'm actually patching you up right now, instead of what I'm really doing."

"Oh yeah, and what's that?"

"This." She brings her lips to mine and kisses me softly, murmuring against my mouth. "You are so worth it, prospect, Gears, Jake… I fucking love you, and I know you love me too. We can make this work. If my brothers don't like it, they can go jump off the Canyon for all I care."

I smile, cupping her face as I drop the bag of peas on the floor. "Those are big words."

"I mean them, every single one."

"I love every one of those words, then." I kiss her again. My dick is hard, pressing up against her as she reaches between my legs. I hiss when she squeezes.

"Just checking it still works," she muses, and I smile, moving one hand down to cup her breast.

"All this fussin' makes me horny," I murmur between kisses.

"Mmm," she hums as I pinch her nipple lightly.

"You make me very fuckin' happy, do you know that?"

"Mmhmm." She cups me harder.

"Get my dick out," I tell her. "Show me how much you missed me."

She doesn't even glance at the door. It's not like anyone gives a shit about me being hurt, though they may come looking for Amelia.

She unbuckles me, and I lift my hips off the ground as I stand, unzipping my jeans. Yanking them down hurriedly, she takes my hard cock in her hand and massages me.

"Fuck," I groan. "That's it, baby, milk me with that dirty mouth."

I know we're taking a risk, but I can't help myself as she gets down on her knees. Fuck me if she doesn't take my dick into her mouth and begin to suck me like a lollipop.

"Gotta make this quick, babe." Her mouth covers my tip, working me farther down her throat.

Her garbled reply makes me snicker as I grab her hair in my hands and start to fuck her mouth. I throw my head back, unable to watch when she casts her eyes up at me.

"So fuckin' beautiful," I mutter. "Touch yourself. Let me see."

She moves her hand down into the front of her jeans and starts to rub herself eagerly as my eyes come back to hers. I watch as her cheeks start to go pink, feel her moans increasing and vibrating around me, and when I reach down and grab her hair harder, she cries out her release. My cock blocks her scream as I ram it down her throat and empty myself on a long groan.

I pull out and she starts to lick me clean, but then I'm yanking her up to her feet, needing my lips on hers. I shove my tongue in her mouth as our lips meet and she throws her arms around me.

"Never walk out on me again," I murmur.

"I need it. I need you," she replies, just as breathily.

I grab the hand that was buried in her pussy and then move it to my mouth, sucking on her two fingers as she watches, her breath catching in her throat.

"Think we need to move this to my place," I mutter. "So I can take my time eatin' you out."

She bites her lip, then says, "My place. It's less conspicuous. Until you let them all know about us, that is."

I smile, tuck my dick back in, and do up my belt, as she runs both hands through my hair, her gaze softening.

"I will," I say. "I will tell them."

"Don't you do anything reckless," she whispers. "You have to tell the club about your plans, Gears. Please, they need to know. I can't...I can't lose you..."

I cup her face and pull her closer. "You won't lose me, babe. You'll never lose me. I know you care about me, and I know it comes from the heart. You've no idea how that makes me feel."

Before she can reply, the door swings open, and I look up the same time Amelia swings her head around.

Brock is standing in the doorway.

His face goes from confusion, to disbelief, to full-on raging in all of five seconds.

"What the fuck?" he growls as Amelia and I spring apart.

Thank fuck my dick is back inside my pants.

"Now seems like as good a time as any," I mutter, as Brock's hands move to his hips; never a good sign.

He looks at Amelia, then back at me again. "You were gone five fuckin' minutes!"

"Brock…" I start, then I glance to Amelia. Her eyes are wide, and I know she's about to make an excuse. But even she can't smooth it over this time. It's time I manned up. Took control. Claim my woman and let the world know she's mine and that ain't changing any time soon.

I take her hand in mine, linking our fingers as she opens her mouth but no sound comes out. I've got nothing else to lose, this much I know. And I never ever want to see disappointment on my girl's face ever again. That cut me deep, like nothing else has in a long time.

He glances down at our joined hands, then shakes his head. Before I can get another word out, he points at me. "You got some fuckin' explainin' to do."

AMELIA

"This isn't what it looks like," I begin, but Gears squeezes my hand, and I turn to look up at him once more. I'm tempted to mouth, *"Are you fucking crazy?"* at him, but I refrain. It was my tough words that got us into this declaration of love, or whatever this is, and now we have to suffer the consequences. Even though all I want to do is shout in Brock's face and tell him to back off.

"It's *exactly* what it looks like," Gears says, and I wince, watching Brock's face.

They stand there and face off for a few solid, terrorizing seconds.

"How long has this been goin' on?" Brock asks in an eerily calm voice.

I open my mouth to lie, but Gears answers instead. "A couple of months."

I didn't think it was possible for my brother's face to get any redder than it is now, but after hearing that, it's almost purple. His wrath may be legendary, but his disappointment somehow seems worse.

"And I want you to know, before you kill me, that this isn't just a thing for me. I'm...I'm in love with your sister."

I swallow hard, biting my lip as I look up at him.

I don't know what's worse. Brock's rage, or his silence. Both are equally terrifying.

"You're in love with her?" he says *love,* like it's some kind of poisonous word. Then he glances at me. "You're not fuckin' pregnant, are you?"

My eyes go wide. "No!" I stammer. "Brock!"

He takes a couple of steps inside, and I stand in front of Gears.

Brock snorts. "You doin' that isn't gonna protect him, Amelia. Now move it."

"No!" I fire up at him. "He's been beaten enough tonight. He doesn't need any more, and if you want someone to blame, turn that finger right around and point it at yourself. You're always disapproving of everything I do; who I see, when I see them, and I'm here to tell you that I'm not putting up with this shit anymore. I'm a grown ass woman, and I don't take orders from you, or anyone in this club. So if you have a problem with me and Gears being together, then that's just too fucking bad, Brock Thomas Altman, because we're a thing and we're not going to stop doing what we're doing. Not for you, Dad, Hutch, or anyone else in this goddamn club, and if anyone has anything to say about it, then I'll tell them the same thing, which is to fuck off and let me live my life. And if that's with Gears, then that's *our business.*"

Brock frowns even more as he points in my face. "*Not* when he's the prospect. We've got rules around here, or have you forgotten that in your little love bubble?"

I stand my ground. "He's patched in now. You don't get a say."

"You were sneakin' around while he was a prospect, Amelia. That's against club rules."

"Leave her out of this," Gears replies, his voice low and authoritative. "Whatever punishment has to happen is with me and me alone. I led her astray. I'm the one who will suffer at the hands of the club. I knew the risks and I took them anyway. That's on me."

He smirks. "Like she's so innocent in all of this. You think it's okay to go around lying, to go behind our backs and just do whatever the fuck you want? It doesn't work like that."

I turn to Gears, ignoring Brock. "*You* led *me* astray?" I huff, shaking my head. "I don't think so."

"Let me handle this," Gears replies, still facing off with Brock. I know he's trying to take a stand, but provoking my brother won't win him any favors. "I knew it was wrong, and I still pursued you anyway."

"That isn't true. If anything, *I'm* the one who pursued you." He's not taking the brunt of all the blame.

Brock clears his throat. "When you're quite finished…"

"What's goin' on?" Axton says, as he and Hutch suddenly appear in the doorway.

Axton's eyes almost bug out of his head when he glances down at our joined hands.

"These two have been fuckin', and not just recently. They been at it for months," Brock declares. *Kill me now, like seriously.* "Been lyin' about it, sneakin' around like school kids because Gears isn't man enough to come and face me himself."

"I didn't know I was gonna feel like this," Gears begins. "Shit got real, for me anyway…"

The warm feeling of love I feel for this man almost bowls me over.

Brock holds a hand up to stop him. "This just gets even

better! So she was just a quick fuck because you know she's off limits."

"*You* put those limits on me, Brock," I spit at him. "Not him!"

"Butt out. You know if you're hangin' around the club, then you're club property. Like it or not, that's how it is."

Sometimes I honestly just want to slap him stupid.

Axton comes to stand beside Brock. "Amelia?" he says, as I move my attention to him. "Why would you do this?"

I shake my head, not him too. "Because I fell in love with him," I shout. "And the last time I checked, that wasn't a crime! Only in the Altman family, right? And if I'm not mistaken, you were a prospect fooling around with Stevie. How is this not the same thing?"

Everyone goes quiet.

Exactly.

"You've got double standards!" I go on, on a roll now. "It's all right for him, but not okay for Gears? The only difference is Stevie doesn't have any overbearing, annoying brothers looking over her shoulder every five seconds, telling her not to do this and not to do that. It ends here, tonight. I'm not putting up with this shit anymore."

Axton and Brock look at me with their mouths open.

Hutch clears his throat. "I think we need to discuss this when everyone is sober," he interrupts calmly.

"Fuck that. We need to take this outside," Brock tries to grab Gears's shirt, but he drops my hand and pushes him back in the chest.

"Not afraid of you," he grits out, even though it is clearly not a fair match. Nobody, except maybe Steel, could beat Brock in a fight, even when they're not beaten half to death, but like this, Gears will get knocked down and fast.

Axton grabs Brock and holds him back while Hutch gets in the middle.

"That's enough!" he says, looking from one to the other. "I said we'll discuss this later, when everyone is sober. Axton, get him the hell outta here." Axton hesitates. "Now!" Hutch barks.

I get two seconds of satisfaction seeing Brock being schooled by Hutch, but then Hutch turns his glare back on us.

Brock shrugs out of Axton's grip and stalks off. Axton turns and gives me a sympathetic smile. He knows this whole scenario is as fucked up as I do.

Pity it took me pointing it out, but I'll give him credit where it's due; at least he looks sorry for us.

When they're gone, Hutch scratches his head for a long moment. It's as if he doesn't know quite what to do with us.

"Don't think I'm gonna go easy on you because you're hurtin'," he says, eyes locked on Gears. "We have rules in this club for a reason, and frankly, I've no words for you, Gears. I thought I knew you better than this." He shifts his gaze to me. "And you should certainly know better, Amelia. You're a club sister; you know how this shit works. We can't have prospects runnin' around, doin' whatever they want, with whoever they want. You're a part of this club, whether you like it or not, and by being a part of this club, it means we're a family, and families don't lie to each other."

"We fell in love," Gears says, earning him another long look from Hutch. "We didn't mean for it to happen...we we're just...foolin' around at first. Yes, we crossed a line, but neither of us expected to feel the way we do."

My heart melts all over again. Even when Hutch looks very displeased at that declaration.

This man makes me quake in my boots a little, more

than my own father, and not because I'm scared of him, but because I respect him so much. I always have.

His rules might be stupid and outdated, but he's done a lot for my brothers, especially Axton, giving him a chance when nobody else would when he got out of prison. He's a good man, and I feel a sudden and strange sense of guilt flood over me.

I'm a grown woman who can make her own choices, yes, but I also don't want his disappointment. This club is my family. They've been there for me when, at times, my own family couldn't. Dad has just repaired his relationship with Brock last year, and recently started speaking to Axton again. But Hutch never needed any of us to prove anything. He gives second chances.

I swallow hard. Giving him lip, like I did Brock and Axton, won't wash this time.

I have to suck it up. He's reasonable… *I think.*

"I'm sorry, Hutch," I say as I feel Gears's hand in mine again. "But as sappy as it sounds, it's true. We started seeing each other in secret because we knew how it would go down. We knew you would never approve, neither would Brock, or Axton, for that matter, and for the first time in my life, I've never been so happy. I finally found a man that is decent, kind, loyal, funny, and sexy as fuck, and I'm sorry we went behind your backs while Gears was a prospect, but the way this man makes me feel, it makes me do crazy things. We tried to stay away, but we couldn't, so if you're gonna hate us, then fine, but just know we didn't do any of this on purpose, or to disobey the club."

He stares at me, and I'm unsure if I've crossed a line. It's hard to tell.

Eventually, he rubs a hand through his beard, his piercing blue eyes not missing a trick. "That's very heart-felt, Amelia, but Gears has to learn that his woman can't be fightin' his battles. That shit won't wash around here. You can't expect Brock or Axton to be happy about this when you're their little sister."

I roll my eyes. "Hutch, with all due respect, I stopped being *little* when I was twelve. I'm twenty-six years old, I can make my own decisions, and I don't need Brock or Axton acting like I'm a teenager who doesn't know what she's doing. I get they're protective, but they need to let me live my life. Maybe if they weren't so in my face, I wouldn't have to sneak around."

"Have you told them that?" He tilts his head to one side, a slight smirk on his lips.

"I thought I just did?"

"Amelia," Gears says, squeezing my hand. "I'll handle this with the club, and your brothers."

I turn to him, then back to Hutch. "What will you do to him?"

He pushes a hand through his long hair. "We'll discuss it at the table and decide from there."

My eyes go wide. "What the hell? So, you're going to kick him out anyway?"

"Didn't say that. Like I said, actions come with consequences, and when Gears came on board with the club, he agreed to an oath."

"Yes, ride or die," I blurt out. The club's motto is at the front of the clubhouse and on the emblem of their patches.

"Well, I don't think that includes ridin' you, Amelia."

Please, ground, swallow me whole.

Gears kisses me on the back of the head. "It's gonna be okay, *sugar,* I promise. You need to go now."

Hutch looks at him like he's in no position to be making promises of any kind.

I cup one side of his bruised face. "I'm not going anywhere."

His lips twitch into a smile.

I turn to Hutch, grabbing him on the arm, and say in earnest, "Please don't hurt him any more. Not tonight."

He does that thing again where he doesn't seem pleased, but he doesn't say anything.

Instead, he gives Gears a chin lift. "Be sure she gets home safe." With that, he turns and walks out of the room, leaving the two of us staring after him.

I put my head in my hands. "This is such a mess."

Gears pulls me to him as I wrap my arms around him. "Look on the bright side, it could've been worse."

"Worse?" I mumble into his shoulder.

"They could've come in a few minutes earlier, when you were blowin' me."

I glance up, and despite myself, I huff a laugh. "Jesus, do you see what you do to me? You make me into this bad girl who can't keep her hands off you, and then I mouth off to the club Prez."

"Oh, I don't mind the hands, just need more of that pussy." He presses his lips to mine, and as I press my body into his, he grimaces.

"Shit, sorry," I say, pulling back.

"It's fine, they're just flesh wounds. If your brothers ever let you leave the club again without adult supervision, maybe you can be my nurse." He cups my face, his thumbs rubbing along my cheekbones as he looks into my eyes.

"Are we crazy?" I whisper.

He smirks, shrugging. "We gotta be a little bit crazy, babe. Without that, life would be pretty boring."

I snuggle into the crook of his arm, then I hear, "Amelia Jane Altman!"

"Shit," I groan. "It's Brock again. He probably thinks we're going at it back here."

"Guess by now, the whole club's gonna know."

"I'm never gonna be sorry, you know that, right?"

He presses his forehead against mine. "That's like music to my ears."

"I guess the rocky road to redemption starts here," I sigh. "If we make it out of here alive."

He brushes my lips again. "Say that when I'm buried deep inside you, *sugar*."

His words, his actions, the way he stood up and fought for me..."The only redemption I need is you."

GEARS

I LOOK DOWN AT MY HANDS.

If someone had told me six months ago all my dreams would come true; cooking for a living instead of working at the car yard, finding the woman of my dreams, getting my own place to live, and being patched in with the Rebels, I'd have told them they were crazy.

Now, as I sit here waiting for the club to decide my fate, I know that it may not fare well for me.

I'd like to think that someone like Hutch can relate. I mean, wasn't he young once? Impulsive. Reckless. Sure, I may have a bit of a chip on my shoulder, but I don't think I'm a bad person. I want what I want, doesn't everyone?

If they can't accept what Amelia and I did while I was a prospect, then that changes things.

I also never thought I'd be in a position where I'd be having to choose between my club and my woman. I hope it doesn't come to that.

I've also considered Amelia's words in telling the club about my plans for revenge. I can't live with myself if I let that man walk. Involving the club was never my intention, but this is what being part of an MC is. We're a family, even Hutch said it, and we have to stick together. If I don't tell them what I'm up to, what does that make me?

A martyr again.

If they don't support me, then at least I've gone into this with no more lies.

Hutch would never forgive me if I went and did this without telling him the full story. He knows a little about my past, but not to the full extent. To disrespect him like that would be worse than killing a man.

It's a lot.

So I sit here, outside the meeting room doors, a million things running through my mind, awaiting my fate.

One thing I don't regret is Amelia.

Our connection is undeniable, it's palpable, and it's one I've never found with a woman before. We may have a long way to go in getting to know each other better, but I can't help how I feel. Amelia was meant for me.

I know every ounce of good I have inside me points to her.

I hate disobeying the club, but I'd be lying if I said I'd do things differently. She's not just some random fuck, she's *mine*.

I may be young, but I know what I want. Maybe I've always known. And she's the missing piece of the puzzle that's been absent.

I run a hand down my face. This wasn't in the plan, none of it was. But life has a funny way of turning things upside down when you least expect it.

When the clubhouse doors finally open, Colt sticks his head out. "They're ready for you."

I swallow hard as I stand, steeling myself for the onslaught.

When I get inside, everyone is around the table. Hutch

at the head, then to his left Brock, Gunner, Colt, Bones, Rubble, and lastly Steel, who doesn't even spare me a glance.

I stand, like an errant schoolboy waiting for punishment, as Hutch looks up at me.

Before he speaks, I open my big mouth. "I know you're disappointed in me," I start. "But I never meant for any of this to go down the way it did."

Silence falls around the room, that is, until Brock speaks up.

"But you still did it anyway, all while bein' a prospect. You still took what you wanted without any regard for the rules."

I take a deep breath and remember to keep calm. "I didn't *take* it. Amelia wanted this just as much as I did. Neither of us expected things to go this far." Somehow, by the look on his face, I don't think I'm helping my cause.

"Like I said last night," he barks. "I don't give a fuck. You went against club rules, Gears, rules that you don't think apply to you, and with a club sister, *my* sister, no less. She may be a grown woman, but she's still club property, and as club property, YOU DON'T FUCKIN' TOUCH! It's pretty fuckin' simple." His voice booms around the room. I don't think they heard him in the next county.

"I'm willing to accept the punishment..."

He laughs without humor. "Now that you got caught? How noble of you."

"I never wanted to hurt Amelia, which is why we kept it a secret. We knew we couldn't come out until I was patched in. Again, I knew it was wrong, but she's such an amazing woman...When I started havin' strong feelings for her, I didn't know how to face it..."

"Face what?" he says, as he steels his jaw.

"The fact I fell in love with her."

Brock shakes his head, having already heard this last night. And it's clear he didn't forget by the furious look on his face.

"Jesus," mutters Steel.

"Fuck," says Bones.

"What did I miss?" comes from Gunner. "I thought you were just doin' the nasty? No strings attached?"

Brock shoves him in the shoulder. "Don't fuckin' tempt me, brother, or I'll make you look like him…" He points to me and my beat-up appearance. The swelling has gone down, but I'm starting to bruise.

"Calm down and get back on track," Hutch says to Brock and Gunner, then brings his attention to me. "Gears, we all know you've done a lot for the club. Nobody at this table can say otherwise, but frankly, this is disappointing. You knew the consequences."

I stare back at him, holding my own. "I'm not gonna come in here and spout about how sorry I am, and that it'll never happen again, because honestly, that would be insulting to all of you, and you'd have every right to kick my ass. But what I can say is that I would never put Amelia in harm's way. I'd never lie or deceive her. I'd never pretend to be something I'm not, just to make any of this okay," I say, taking a breath. "She deserves better than that, and that's the man I am when I'm with her. She brings out the best in me, like I want to be better and prove my worth to her. Fuck knows I ain't got much to offer a woman like Amelia, but I'll be fucked if I'm gonna stand by and watch some other motherfucker waltz in and sweep her off her feet. Frankly, I'd rather take a bullet. If she'll have me, then I'm hers, and that's all there is to it."

I may actually die in this room.

Brock regards me with disbelief.

"The point is, you broke the rules," Steel points out

before Brock can say anything. "We don't break rules in this club. Period. You don't just get to have what you want because you want it, not when you're startin' from the ground up. It's no way to win the club's respect."

"So beat me again," I fire back at him. "You can't do any worse to me. Kicking me out of the club will fuckin' hurt like a bitch. This club is all I have. You're my family, and Amelia is gonna be my ol' lady…"

"Over my fuckin' dead body!" Brock roars.

Hutch presses an arm to his chest to prevent him from standing, and probably leaping over the table to pound my face in again.

"Least he's willin' to claim her," Gunner points out. "I mean, that's respect, if nothin' else."

"Don't be such a pussy," Steel barks across at Gunner. "We all know how your sneakin' around ended up, so let's not go there. And you weren't a prospect when you and Lil got together."

Gunner and Lily were seeing each other behind Steel's back, until they got caught and

Gunner got acquainted with Steel's knuckles.

"Exactly my point," Gunner says with a shrug. "I wasn't, but Lily was still technically off limits without your permission. We worked it out. Lily is my ol' lady now and it was worth the beatin'. We've all made mistakes. Brock and Angel broke up for years because neither one could get their shit together. Bones was fuckin' the club lawyer. You were doin' our landlord, and if my memory serves me correctly, Rubble left his old club to be with Lucy. Then there's Axton and Stevie. He was havin' fun as a prospect and she's his boss."

I never thought that, out of all the brothers, Gunner would be the one to see sense and make a case for my argument. I should've brought the popcorn.

"Like Brock said, rules are rules, Gunner," Hutch reminds him. "Everyone in this club takes an oath. What kind of club would we be if prospects just went around doin' whatever the hell they wanted with no consequences."

Clearly, they've not decided my fate if they're disagreeing right in front of me.

That gives me some kind of hope that they won't kick me out. I meant what I said; they can't keep me from Amelia.

"So punish me, I'll serve my time, if that's what it takes. I'm sorry that we didn't wait until I was patched in, but we were always gonna end up together," I tell them, looking straight at Brock. "I love this club, more than anythin' in life. And I thought that's all I had in the world, aside from my grams. You're my family. But when I spent time with Amelia, I realized there was somethin' else missing, and I never knew what it was until she came along."

Hutch looks at me for a long moment, rubbing a hand down his face.

"Have you actually ever seen Amelia this happy?" Colt says, out of nowhere. Everyone turns to him. "Seriously, I've noticed. She's got a spring in her step, like someone switched a light on inside her."

"Are you suggestin' it's because of him?" Brock throws at me.

Colt shrugs. "Seems kinda coincidental, doesn't it? And he plans on claimin' her. That means somethin' more than just a roll in the hay."

"Does Amelia want to be claimed?" Hutch asks skeptically.

"She knows club life," I reply. "She knows what it entails, and she wants to be with me, so I guess the answer to that question is yes."

"You might wanna take her on a date first," Bones pipes up. "It's one thing bein' compatible in the bedroom, but quite another when you have to keep your clothes on and find somethin' to talk about."

Brock looks thoroughly disgusted.

"He's right, son," Hutch agrees. "When it's all said and done, claimin' a woman, who's also a club sister, isn't somethin' you do lightly. Shit goes down, you're fucked."

"We know how we feel," I reply. "If it'll make you feel better, put me on probation again. If I do anythin' that you feel is unfit for Amelia or if she wants out, then feel free to kick my ass."

I know that's putting a big target on my back, but I don't plan on fucking this up.

"With all due respect to Amelia," Rubble adds. "We lose Gears, we lose our short-order cook at the Burger Joint."

"That all you're concerned about?" Brock questions, his eyes blazing.

"Nope, but Gears has proven his loyalty time and time again, and he's a hard worker. If he puts the same amount of time in makin' Amelia happy and workin' on their relationship, then I don't see why it can't work."

So I've got Gunner and Rubble on board. That's better than no one.

"You're twenty-one years old," Steel gruffs. "How much could you possibly know? And how do you know what the fuck you actually want?"

That's an easy answer. "I may only be twenty-one, but I've lived a fast life. I grew up too quick. Gettin' in and outta trouble. My mom...my Mom was killed in front of me when I was six years old, and that changed me forever. After that, I went to live with my grandma, and she saved me in so many ways."

Everyone stays silent.

Then, "I know a little about your past, but not exactly what happened," Hutch says in a low voice.

I nod. "She was beaten to death, then stabbed, by her junkie boyfriend. I hid in the wardrobe so he wouldn't find me." They all only stare at me. So I add, "I wasn't sayin' this to get sympathy, but there's somethin' you should all know before we go on…"

"Here we go," Brock mutters.

"The piece of shit who did it, he's out on parole in a few days…" I take a deep breath. "And…it's been my plan since I've been old enough to think for myself…" They all wait. "I want to put him in the ground, make sure he never lives another day breathing the same air as me, the same air he took from my mom, the life he stole when he killed her."

"Fuck," Steel mumbles.

"This is some fucked up shit," Bones agrees.

"I kept it on the downlow because I didn't know he'd be gettin' out, for one. There were rumors of it after he pleaded insanity and got a reduced sentence to fifteen years, then out on good behavior."

"So you planned on goin' to take him out?" Hutch clarifies.

I nod, no point in denying it. "I need to avenge her. It's in my blood; it's what's driven me to get this far without goin' off the rails; that one day, he'd get to see my face and I'd remind him of what he took, of what he stole from me. It's what kept me goin' when I was in a bad place. When I think about her, about how innocent she was…she just got mixed up with a bad crowd."

Brock wipes a hand over his face. "This piece of shit deserves to suffer."

"Agreed," Gunner says.

I can see they're already hatching a plan, and this isn't

what I wanted. I'm capable of putting this piece of garbage out of his misery without their help.

"I need to do this," I go on. "And that's why I tried to keep my distance from Amelia. I didn't want to get too close."

"Because you were always goin' to do it," Hutch finishes. "Weren't you?"

"I don't know," I say honestly. "In my heart, I wanted to, but takin' another man's life is no easy thing. I've never killed a man before, but all I can see is my mom's face, hear her pleas for him to stop while he said her name over and over...*Willow...*"

My eyes meet Hutch's as he frowns. "Willow?"

"Yeah, that was my mom's name. Willow Buford."

He stares back at me with an unreadable look. "Willow Buford?"

I nod.

Then, something changes in the air. I can feel my skin prickle when I add, "Did you know her?"

Somehow, his face pales. Then, oddly, his eyes assess me, as if seeing me for the first time. "You're Willow Buford's kid?"

"Yeah."

He takes a long, shaky breath. "Everyone out," he orders in a voice that booms across the room. Then pointing at me, he adds, "Except you."

I swallow hard. What the fuck is going on here? Hutch knew my mom?

"Hutch?" Brock begins.

"Out!" he barks again. "Need to talk to Gears alone. Hurry the fuck up."

Steel doesn't move either. "Think we need to discuss this as a club…"

He lands his lethal glare on Steel when he reluctantly

stands from his chair, muttering under his breath as he leaves.

The room clears out, everyone looking at Hutch like he's grown another head.

Hutch stands, goes over to the bar behind him, and pours himself a whiskey. Knocking it back, he pours another.

"How old are you again, Gears?"

I stare at his back, unsure of what's going on. "I just turned twenty-one."

With his back to me, he runs a hand through his long hair, then throws the next shot back.

Turning to me, he walks closer. "Yes, I knew your Mom."

My eyes go wide. "I didn't know she ran in the same circles..."

"It was a long time ago. She was...troubled...but a very sweet woman..." His eyes drift away as I try to gather the strength to understand what he's getting at.

"She was part of the MC?"

His eyes move back to mine. "Not for long. She stayed with the club for a few months..." He clutches the empty glass in his hand, then moves away from me, his hands planting on the meeting table as he continues. "Twenty-two years ago, Kirsty left me."

I wait. The silence deafening.

"We split up for about a year. I was drinkin' heavily, not bein' a good father to my daughter, gettin' caught up in the club and neglectin' my woman, and she'd had enough. I was angry, heartbroken, fuckin' lost, and when Willow came to the club, we talked. She was a very intelligent woman with a pretty smile. She had a kindness to her that I found endearing. She wasn't like other women; she wasn't fast or sleepin' around with all the brothers. She cooked and cleaned, and in return, I told the club she was off limits. I wanted to keep her safe, since I knew she'd run from trouble, and I didn't wanna be responsible for her bein' out on the streets. One night, we'd had a bit to drink. I was lonely, one thing led to another, and we slept together." He doesn't meet my eye, but my heart races in my chest. "I liked her, a lot. She didn't just keep my bed warm; she was a comfort when I thought my marriage was over. We didn't love each other, but we had a mutual respect. My heart was always with Kirsty. Durin' this time, Deanna got sick, and it changed everything for me. I went to the city, and I realized everything I should've already known; I had to fight for my family. I traveled back and forth until Deanna was better, and Kirsty and I ended up gettin' back together."

"Did Kirsty ever know about my mom?"

He nods. "Told her everything. I wasn't proud of it, but we were separated. When I got back from the city, Willow had left. I never knew what ended up happenin' to her, except when I saw on the news she'd been killed six years later."

I swallow hard, no words forming in my throat.

"And…it never mentioned she had a kid…they never said…"

"Grams never wanted anyone knowin', for my own protection," I say. "She changed my name, and we moved. The guy who killed my mom was shady and had criminal connections to the mafia. Grams wanted a clean slate."

He turns to look at me. "Gears."

I open my mouth, knowing what he's about to say, but not really believing it.

"Twenty-two years ago, I slept with your mom for a couple of months. I was the only man she was with. Like I said, she didn't sleep around, she wasn't like that...she left...and then you were born...nine months later..."

No.

I try to wrap my head around it, but I just can't.

It can't be.

This can't be happening.

Hutch is...

"There's a chance..." He runs another hand through his hair. "There's a possibility, Gears, that...that you could be my kid."

My mouth goes dry, the words hanging heavily in the air. So many thoughts run through my mind all at once. I can't think straight.

His eyes meet mine, and all I can say is... "Holy fuck."

Chapter 23- *Amelia*

I stare at Gears, unable to comprehend it for a moment.

He sucks in a long intake of breath. "Hutch could be my Father."

I stare at him, waiting for the punchline. Of all the things I thought he was going to say, that definitely wasn't it.

When one doesn't come, I can only say, "What?"

"Yeah."

"How is that possible?"

"It's a fuckin' long story." He puts his head in his hands, as though he's still coming to terms with it himself.

"Okay, back up, what the hell?"

"He's pretty sure he knew my mom years ago."

"So...he had an affair?" I can't imagine Hutch ever cheating on Kirsty. She's his life.

"No," he says. "They split up twenty-something years

252

ago for a short time, when Deanna was little. Kirsty left him. They ended up reconciling, but in the meantime, he slept with my mom for a short space of time. He says she didn't sleep around, that he was the only guy she'd been with, and he never knew about me. My mom never told him. It all kinda lines up with the time she spent at the club."

I sit down next to him on the couch, shellshocked.

I'd always thought Kirsty and Hutch had no chinks in their armor. They're so...*together*, so loved up.

"What about when he knew she'd been killed?"

"He didn't know she'd had a kid. My grams was lookin' after me a lot back then when Mom was drugged out. She didn't want anyone knowin' about me because she was afraid of the people my Mom associated with. Grams never knew who my Pop was, so she was very protective. She even changed my last name after my Mom was killed."

I stare at him. "I'm...I don't know what to say."

"I'm a little shocked myself."

"What did Hutch say?"

He shrugs. "Not a lot, he went really quiet. I mean, this is some fucked up shit."

"So you'll get a paternity test?"

He runs both hands through his hair. "Yep."

"It is kinda cool if you think about it."

He turns to look at me. "How is any of this fuckin' mess kinda cool?"

I cup one side of his bruised face, still mad the brothers had to "initiate" him the way they did. "Because if Hutch really is your pop, then how amazing for you to get to know him."

He shakes his head. "Why wouldn't Mom ever tell me? Why didn't she tell my grandma?"

"We'll never know that now, but I'm sure she'd want

you to know him. Maybe she was protecting you from club life. Maybe after Hutch got back with Kirsty, she didn't want to complicate things."

"That's what Hutch said."

"Well, there you go, then. Sounds like your mom was an extraordinary woman, babe."

He looks so lost in this moment, that I want to reach out to him. Hold him. Tell him everything is going to be okay. I know he's a grown man, but I also know there's trauma involved with what he saw happen to his mom when he was a child.

That's enough to make anyone go off the rails.

"You've come so far," I whisper when he looks back down at his hands. "Look at the life you've made for yourself from nowhere. Your Mom would be proud, just like your grandma is."

He smiles softly, but it doesn't reach his eyes. My heart breaks.

"I should be happy," he says after a while. "If Hutch really is my Father, then it's a good thing."

I run a hand over his stomach, resting my head on his shoulder as his arm comes around me.

"It's a lot to take in."

"He said some kind things about my Mom." His voice is barely a whisper. "She just got mixed up with the wrong crowd…"

"I know that, Gears, she was a good woman."

"It wasn't her fault…"

"None of it was."

"She…" he trails off, emotion in his voice as I squeeze my arms around him.

I give him all the time he needs. "I'm here," I whisper.

"She was just a kid herself. She was barely my age…"

"She loved you so much to hide you away. She never

wanted anything to happen to you, Gears. It isn't your fault."

"If I'd have been older…"

Sliding into his lap, I straddle him as he sits back on the couch, his eyes clouding over.

"I love you so much," I whisper, looking into his sad eyes.

He frowns, his bright, beautiful gaze seeking solace in mine. "Why the fuck do you?"

"Because you're amazing, Jake."

He gives me a small smile. "Jake?"

"Your mom gave you a beautiful name because you're a beautiful person. You're kind, generous, loyal, hardworking, but you also don't know your worth. You always put yourself down, make a joke about it, but I know you're serious. I don't care about any of it, about what you do for a living or how much money you make. I love you, everything about you, do you hear me, Jake?"

His arms come around me. "I've loved you since the moment I saw you," he says, his voice cracking. "And that's why I never wanted you involved in my shit in the first place, I didn't want to implicate you…"

I put a finger over his lips to quieten him. "I don't want to hear that. I know we're getting to know each other, but I'm with you, Gears. I'm with you all the way, with whatever you decide to do."

"Even kill a man?" His eyes meet mine again. "Really, Amelia? Could you be with a killer?"

I press my lips to his, kissing him softly. His lip is still busted, and black bruises are appearing on his skin. "You're no killer. That bastard deserves all he gets. I understand why you want to do this, anybody decent person would. What you went through…no child should ever have to go through that."

"Things have changed," he mutters, his hands moving to my ass.

"What did the club say?"

I know the boys have their oath about *club business,* but all the women in this MC know how pillow talk works. Each and every one who has an ol' man would be subject to some of the club information.

He gives me a look.

"What?" I say, feigning innocence.

"You really think I'm gonna involve you? The least you know, the better."

To say I'm shocked is an understatement. "What happens now? You take that paternity test…"

He blows air out from his cheeks. "But I'm pretty sure we're not gonna need one. I could tell by the look on Hutch's face that he was comin' to terms with it. He's my pop, baby, I can feel it."

"Jesus, Gears. So, did he seem happy about it? After the initial shock?"

"Hard to say." He shrugs. "He went very quiet."

His eyes drift away for a second.

Finding out who your father is, is supposed to be a happy occasion, especially when it turns out to be man like Hutch.

"It's early days," I tell him. "It would be a shock to the both of you." I watch him for a moment, then add, "Are you happy it's him?"

He looks up at me again. "Yes, but then a part of me thinks I've failed."

I frown. "How so?"

"Maybe I'm not the son he imagined he'd have."

My heart aches for him. I know how much this club means to him.

"Don't ever say something like that," I whisper, cupping

his face. "You're a good man, Gears. You don't have to keep proving it, not to me, not to anyone. You're patched in now, and you wouldn't be part of this club if they didn't value your worth. You know that, you just won't allow yourself to believe it's true."

"I'm not lookin' for no pity party." His eyes look so earnest, I want to cry. I know how losing his mom hurt him so much; it scarred him for life. But to have found Hutch, if he really is his father, well, that's a blessing.

"And I'm not giving you one, but you're allowed to feel emotional about it. It's a pretty big thing to learn, as well as your fate with the club."

He snorts. "They're undecided. The meeting got adjourned because I blurted out my mom's name and that's when Hutch kicked everyone out to ask me questions."

"So, if you're Hutch's kid, that means Deanna is your half-sister."

He nods. "I always wanted a sister. I never imagined in my wildest dreams that it'd be Deanna. Holy fuck."

I can feel the uncertainty coming off him, and I want to take it all away. I want to give him back what he's given me: confidence. The ability to feel loved, to feel like I matter. To believe in myself. Nobody can take that from us. I won't let them.

"Holy fuck is right, but we're gonna get through this. I promise."

His lips twitch.

"What's so funny?" I bump my hips into his as his hands settle on my ass.

"You."

"Me, what?"

He leans up and presses his lips close to mine. "I like a woman with a little spirit, and I like the way you say 'we', *sugar.*"

257

"I know what you're doing," I say, loving how he feels beneath me. I reach between us and palm his cock. "And *this* isn't going to distract me from our conversation."

He pumps his hips, once, twice, my eyes going wide. "Gears!"

He smirks. "You were sayin'?"

"You can't distract me with sex, all jokes aside."

"I can try, though, right?"

"No," I chastise. "But I really do believe everything happens for a reason. If Hutch is your dad, then you were obviously meant to find him, in this time and space, and just imagine…you'll have so much to catch up on. It'll be amazing."

He squeezes my ass cheeks. "This is why I fell for you, you know."

I can't help but push my body into his, two can play that game.

"What is?" I reply as he groans, his cock grinding against my pussy.

"This. You talkin' me up."

I laugh out loud. "Is that what I do?"

"Yep, does wonders for my confidence."

I stare at him as he looks back at me, his expression so full of hope. "I just want you to believe that you're worth it," I whisper. "It's all I ask."

His demeanor changes, his eyes growing serious. "I'm workin' on it. In the meantime, we wait for the paternity test."

"I still can't believe it, then there's Kirsty."

"Yeah, that's gonna be interesting."

"Very."

"I can't imagine callin' her like…Mom."

I chuckle. "You don't have to. You had a mom, Gears,

and she protected you, that's how much she loved you. That's what matters."

"You're right."

"I'm always right."

I begin to unbutton my blouse as his eyes follow my movements.

He smirks. "So now you're gonna distract me with sex?"

"No." I shake my head. "But you deserve to let off some steam after learning all of that in one day."

"I could get used to that," he says as I push him back against the couch.

He kisses me, slowly at first, as I continue to work on my blouse. Pulling back, he glances down at my bra, his hands moving to yank the cups down as he leans in and sucks a nipple into his mouth. I gasp at the contact, then he repeats the touch on the other side.

All the while, I press into his hardness, wanting him so bad.

He reaches between my legs, cupping my sex through my jeans as I run my hands through his hair, gripping him tighter as he licks and sucks my nipple.

"Yes," I cry out. "Oh God, yes…"

He chuckles, reaching down I hear his belt buckle come undone, then his zipper…then he lifts his hips and I yelp as I fall forward. Laughing, I slide back off his knee, allowing him to pull his jeans down to his knees as I help him, then pull my own off, along with my panties. Still wearing my open blouse and my bra, I climb back on him, fisting his cock.

He groans as I sheath him. "I love this cock," I whisper against his mouth.

"This cock loves you," he whispers back.

I yank his shirt at the hem as he lifts his arms, and I pull it over his head. I need him fully naked. Glancing down at his body, I run my hands over his chest as his hand reaches between my legs again. This time, he glides his fingers through my folds as I groan.

"So wet, baby."

"I'm always wet for you."

"You certainly are." He chuckles.

He plays with me as his cock nudges my inner thigh, the tip all sticky from his precum. I want to lick him, suck him off until he shoots his load all over me, but I know we both need a quick fuck to relieve the tension.

"Make me come," I groan. "Hurry, I need you inside me."

He rubs my clit, swirling his fingers around as I tilt my head back and pump my hips against him, the sensation rolling through me as my orgasm builds. As I start to moan, my cheeks flushing when my climax hits, he grabs the base of his cock, positioning it at my entrance, and shoves inside me. I cry out.

My climax isn't even done as I start to ride him, it only gets stronger. His hands grip into my hips as he grunts, slapping my ass as he moves me up and down.

His huge cock fills me so tight, his piercings massaging my walls as my sensitive clit rubs against him each time I sink down.

"Oh…" I cry. "Oh, Gears…oh yes…right there…"

He bounces me faster, pushing up inside me as he curls one hand around my neck and keeps the other at my hip, our skin slapping together as we take from each other what we need.

My orgasm explodes as I dig my nails into his shoulders, pressing harder when he calls my name on a stifled grunt, shooting his hot cum inside me.

We still, our bodies tangled, our hands everywhere, our breathing ragged.

"Okay, you distracted me," I pant.

He laughs against my neck as I collapse against his chest. "You ride me so good, Amelia."

"Let's go to bed," I reply, my body aching because I need so much more. "I want to do all of that again, but in slow motion."

"Now there's an idea I can get behind." He squeezes my ass as I laugh, his warmth filling me.

There's no more talk about club business. Or Hutch. Or paternity tests. Or any of that shit. Tonight, it's just us. Exploring. Taking. Giving. And it's exactly what we both need.

2 2

GEARS

Two weeks later - The Shady Inn, Phoenix

I walk into the pub, taking a seat at one of many vacant stools at the seedy bar.

The stench of stale beer and cigarette smoke permeates the air.

I order a drink, after having to produce my ID, then a few moments later, the seat next to me moves. I stare straight ahead, watching the bartender mix my drink.

I don't know how a person is supposed to feel in this kind of situation, but I swear, every single muscle, nerve, and cell in my body is on fire.

I've waited so long. More than half my life has passed and now I finally get to put things right.

"You Jake?" the gruff voice asks next to me.

I don't glance at him. "That depends, you got the cash?"

"I got it."

"Then I'm Jake."

In my periphery, I see him glancing around. "You picked a fuckin' dive," he mutters, like he's used to dining out at Caesar's Palace every night.

"Fit for the dregs of society. I chose it for a reason; these walls don't talk."

The bar is owned by the Sons of Phoenix Fury. Friends of the Rebels. The club Prez and Rubble are tight, as well as with Hutch.

So, what happens within these four walls stays here. A lot like Vegas, in a way.

I grapple with the idea of tearing his vocal cords out, but instead, I crack my neck. *Follow the plan. Do not do anything reckless yet.*

That's a big *yet.* I plan on doing plenty.

The bartender slides my drink across from me as he looks to the stranger beside me with a chin lift.

He orders a beer with no pleasantries exchanged.

"You look a little young," he goes on. I can tell by the look on his face in the mirrors across from us that he's on edge.

He looks like a man who's been in prison a long time, a man time forgot about, yet for me, it wasn't enough time. An eternity wouldn't be long enough.

This fucker is mine.

"A little young for what? Dealin' drugs in a bar?" I still don't look at him. I don't want any more memories of his face than what's completely necessary. But this needs to be done, and it'll be done my way.

It didn't take much convincing to get the club on board. Not after everything.

My mind drifts…

It took a week, but the paternity tests came back indicating that Richie Hutchison was, in fact, my father.

Shit a fuckin' brick.

I don't know how long a person can be in shock for, but we both just sat there in silence for a while. Nostalgia, or something, crossing Hutch's features. When he'd finally spoke, he said, "You have her look, your mother. She was beautiful."

When I swallowed hard, I didn't know what to say, so I made a joke. "Are you sayin' I'm beautiful too?"

He chuckled. "I can see you got my smartass side."

The pain in my chest, the one I'd had since my mom left me, it didn't seem so painful anymore. As awkward as it was, we're family.

It was like a burden had been lifted, one that I never knew I'd been carrying.

"All jokes aside, Hutch, I couldn't be fuckin' happier... that you're my dad, I mean." I'd meant it. Maybe it made me sound like a fuckin' sap, but he'd just looked at me from across the table, the paternity results on the wooden table before us. The gavel to one side. And for the first time in the entire time I'd known him, he was lost for words.

"My son," he'd said, then, "Jake." As though he was trying out the words for the first time, and I suppose in some ways, he was. It had a whole different meaning now.

"Does this mean I get to call you Pops?"

He chuckled again, his eyes clouding over ever-so slightly. I'd never seen him this vulnerable, either.

I mean, Steel and Brock were two of the toughest men I'd ever met, but Hutch was on another level. To see him like this...I didn't know how to describe it. I think we were both just as shell-shocked as one another.

"Not if you expect me to answer," he'd replied.

I chuckled too.

"How did Kirsty take the news?" I asked, not able to keep the question to myself that had been burning in the back of my throat for a week now.

"She was shocked, to say the least, but we will get through it. She's always liked you, go figure. She's a woman who likes to take *care of everyone. She saw somethin' in you and convinced me to give you a chance. I thought it was just the pretty face, but turns out, she's got good taste after all since we share the same genes."*

"Does she want to get to know me, too?" I hope this won't change things with them, or if it does, only for the better. Kirsty and I have always gotten along and been able to share a joke. She was the one behind the scenes, telling Hutch to give me a chance at the Burger Joint. I'll always be grateful for that.

The corner of his eyes had wrinkled as he smiled. *"Of course she does. She's chomping at the bit to insert herself into your life. You know women, especially women of this club. Always tryin' to fix shit and poke their nose in."*

"You mean, insert herself further into my life?"

His eyebrows raise. *"I forgot, she lured you into takin' the reins at the Burger Joint, and she was instrumental in you movin' to the Crow. Maybe the woman had a sixth sense all along."*

"So, she's cool that there was another woman..."

"She knows it was while we were split up, and out of respect for your mother, I won't go into the details, but I was fucked up when Kirsty left me. Got into booze pretty heavy, got into a lot of shit that wasn't good. I was hurtin', my family was gone. Deanna was only four, and I thought I'd lost it all. Your mom was a distraction from all of that, yes, but I liked her. She was a good woman; we were kind of there for each other. Then she left, and for some reason, she never told me about you."

I felt that knot in my chest again when we spoke about her.

"Truth is, Gears, I'm proud of you. You've come a long way since you snitched on Jack and came to prospect with the club."

"Is that how I'll be remembered? The snitch," I replied, running a hand through my hair.

His eyes met mine. *"No, but we both know that honesty and integrity run through our veins. You acted out of instinct and chose loyalty; that's why I wanted you as part of my club,* because those traits are so rare to find these days, especially in the young. What Jack did was wrong, and it took a lot of guts to come to us, instead of takin' cash on the side and lookin' the other way. It's easy to tuck tail and run when shit goes down. It's harder to step up to the plate than it is to hide."

"That and the fact I didn't wanna be on the other end of your fists, or Brock's, or Steel's."

"There is that." He chuckled again.

"It was only a matter of time before Jack got found out. Besides, my grandma always taught me to be truthful, no matter what."

He'd given me a look of approval. "She did a good job. I'd like to meet her, and thank her. It couldn't have been easy."

"She never knew about you," I said. "My mom never told her who my real father was. Like you, I don't know why, but I'm sure she had her reasons."

I'll never truly understand it, but I don't want to hold bitterness toward a woman who I lost so long ago. None of that will bring her back.

"For what it's worth, I'm sorry, son. Truly. For what happened to her, for what you saw, for what you went though. I'd be lyin' if I said it didn't disappoint me that she never chose to tell me. It does. But know this; that if I'd known about your existence, I would've come for you, Gears, I would've been there in a heartbeat. You would have had me, like it or not."

I nod, knowing it's true. "I know you would have. You're the most genuine man I've ever met, which is why I'm glad you're my old man."

He snickered. "Watch it with the old shit. I'm still young enough to kick your ass."

Of that, I was completely certain.

Sure, we had a lot of catching up to do, but when he'd stood, and walked me to the door, his arms had embraced me in a hug I'd never had the pleasure of knowing before.

267

It was solid. Warm. Heartfelt. And slightly terrifying.

Aside from my grams, I didn't respect many people, but knowing this man I'd looked up to for such a long time was actually my father, it made me want to do better.

I wanted to make him even more proud of me, and not just for helping out at the Burger Joint or doing whatever the club needed as a prospect, but in life.

He's that kind of man.

You don't ever want to fail him.

All the talk of Amelia and me being kicked out of the club was long gone, too. The patched members would be aware of who I was, as Hutch was calling a meeting at church.

And then there was the problem sitting right in front of me...

My mind back on the job, I take a slow sip of my drink. Enjoying the sweet sting in the back of my throat. In truth, I'd already had a few before arriving. For what I was about to commit, I had to be on form. And that wasn't being sober. Some things are best served with a little intoxication.

I can safely say, I can't wait for today to be over. I want this behind me. I want *him* gone, from my life, from my nightmares, from every waking moment my mind drifts back to of my mom and what could've been.

She didn't deserve to have this fucker's hands on her and his be the last face she saw. She didn't deserve to never see me grow up. He took that from me, he took it from the both of us. Nothing can bring her back.

"...you hear me?" he says, repeating himself because I didn't care enough to even pretend to listen. "What are you, some kind of freak?"

Oh, he's about to find out just how much of a freak I really am.

Before I get to answer, Steel parks himself on the other side, so their elbows are almost touching. Subtle.

Of course, any excuse for the big man to knock a skull against a bar and watch a man bleed, he's right there. I've only seen the man smile a couple of times, and one of them was when he was inflicting pain on Jack, when he broke all of his fingers with a hammer. And that was Steel on a good day.

"Crowded around here," fuckface mutters. "We gonna do this, man, or what?"

I turn to him. "Oh, we're gonna do it. Just like you did to my mom, except worse, because that's all a piece of shit like you deserves."

His brow furrows. "What the fuck are you talkin' about?"

"Willow Buford," I say, the words sounding steadier than I feel. Our eyes finally meet. "I'm her kid, the one who witnessed you murdering her that night, fifteen years ago."

He has the audacity to curl his top lip into a sneer like some rabid dog. Before he can blink, Steel stabs a knife violently through his hand, nailing it to the bar. He screams out, trying to frantically remove the blade, cursing, spitting, and screaming.

"Jesus, *fuck!* Who the fuck are you? What do you want?" he spits.

"He doesn't listen very well, does he?" Brock adds, coming up behind him.

"I'd say that's a no," Hutch agrees, flanking him as he stands behind Steel. "What do you think, *Jake,* should we gag him now or after we cut every one of his fingers off so he never gets to hurt another woman again."

"Help me!" he snarls around the room. Nobody is there.

The bartender is gone. No patrons remain in the vicinity, and all the doors are locked.

Having friends in low places, or in this case, one percent clubs, sure has its advantages.

"Nobody's gonna help you," I say, throwing the rest of my drink back, then I stand.

He tries to stand too, but Steel shoves him back down onto the stool. Blood runs down the bar from his hand. That's gotta hurt like a motherfucker.

"Move again, and I'll cut your fuckin' nuts off," Steel snarls.

I move closer.

"What do you want from me?" he cries.

I face him, the blood pumping through my veins rushing in my ears. I've been waiting a long fuckin' time for this. "Justice, for my mom."

"I didn't...wait, you've got the wrong guy."

"I don't think so," I reply. "I may have only been six years old, but I'll never forget your face."

"I was high!" he screams, agitation setting in as sweat pours down his face. He's in pain, and panicking, not a good combination. If this fucker passes out, I'll miss out on all the things I'm going to do to him to make him suffer.

At one point in my life, I wondered if that made me as bad as him. Inflicting pain and suffering on another human isn't something I usually enjoy, but I came to the resolution that some people just need to be put down. If he's six feet under, then he won't be able to hurt anyone else.

"Is that any excuse?" I say. "And what's worse; you tried to cover your tracks."

"I told you, I was high. I didn't know what I was doing! The bitch owed me money. She wanted to get high and then not pay. I wasn't running a goddamn charity."

I punch him square in the face. Blood starts to gush from his nose as he wails.

"Frankly, I'm disappointed. I thought for sure you'd put up some kind of a fight."

"Bit hard when his hand's now attached to the bar," Steel grunts. "Here, let me help with that." He yanks the knife out just as abruptly as he stabbed him with it, and more wailing ensues, blood gushing everywhere. He stumbles to his feet.

"You fuckers!"

Brock cracks his knuckles. "Oh, I'm gonna enjoy this." He smirks.

"Any last requests?" I ask, shoving him in the chest as he staggers backward, trying to swing at me, but missing. Seriously, he had all that time in prison to work out. While he's never gonna get out of this alive, I didn't expect him to be so fuckin' weak.

He opens his mouth, ready to spit another mouthful of abuse at me, but this time, I don't let him. I sock him in the face again, and again and again until he falls backward, and I follow him to the ground. "Scratch that," I growl, landing a blow to his rib cage. "There's no redemption for fuckers like you. Just remember that, because I'm about to send you to hell."

Revenge is definitely a dish served red hot, not fuckin' cold.

Fifteen years.

Finally, the day has come. I won't waste it.

AMELIA

48 HOURS LATER

I STARE AT THE TELEVISION, HUNTING FOR THE REMOTE control so I can turn the volume up.

My eyes go wide, and I slap a hand over my mouth as I see David Logan's face on the screen.

"...a drug bust gone wrong. David Logan was found dead in an abandoned house notorious for drug deals in the downtown Phoenix area. It is alleged Mr. Logan was shot and killed by Dexter Shepherd, a recently released prisoner who was granted bail only two days ago.

Mr. Shepherd was incarcerated after the brutal murder of Willow Buford fifteen years ago..."

A dozen emotions run through my mind. Shock. Horror. Complete bewilderment.

David's dead? *What the fuck?*

I mean, it's not like I've seen him since that night all those years ago. I had heard he'd flunked out of school. Even back then, drugs played a part...then I get to thinking...could Dexter Shepherd be the man who killed Gears's mom?

That's a little too coincidental...

Shakily, I turn the volume down and hunt around for my phone.

I never told Gears anything about David, just his first name, and that he'd done this before…surely, he had nothing to do with it. But the more that I think I about it, the more things start to add up.

This happened recently. Gears has been out of town for two days, and so has everyone at the club…

Why did my gut tell me that Willow Buford was Gears's mom?

When I find my phone, I dial Gears. My hand shakes as I wait for him to pick up.

"*Sugar,*" he says, and I can hear the tiredness in his voice.

"Gears," I whisper. "I just switched on the news."

"Yeah?"

"Did you have anything to do with…with David?"

There's a long pause. "I'll come over. Don't want to talk over the phone."

So many memories wash over me, least of all the night David raped me and left me lying on the bed like I was a piece of garbage he could just dispose of. A cold shiver runs through me. What he stole from me, namely my innocence, can never be replaced. It's not like he was even sorry, blaming me, shaming me. He took everything from me, and I let him get away with it.

"Was it you?"

"Amelia." His tone is firm.

"So, you're back from Phoenix?"

He stifles a yawn. "Just got back literally a half hour ago. I'll come over."

I've missed him. It's felt like a lifetime since I saw his face, and I shouldn't be so needy, but I can't help it.

With Gears, everything is uncharted.

"I'll come to you."

He hesitates, then says, "All right."

Within fifteen minutes, he opens the door of his apartment, his hazel eyes assessing me as I stare at him.

"Hi," I whisper.

"Hi," he says.

I glance down at his hands. They're swollen and bruised.

"Shit, Gears."

He smiles softly. "What, this? This is nothin', babe."

I stare at him.

"You gonna give me some sugar?" he goes on when I don't make a move toward him.

"Gears."

"Don't Gears me, I've been missin' you for two whole fuckin' days, Amelia. I need to touch you."

I swallow hard, moving into his arms as I cup his face, kissing him gently. "I missed you too."

He pulls me to him, so our bodies are pressed together. He's everything I remember; warm, protective, and safe.

"I want you to tell me the truth."

"Fine. That wasn't a real kiss, Amelia. Startin' to think I lost my touch while I was away."

He kicks the door closed with his boot.

"I meant about the news."

This time, he cups my face, spinning me and walking me backward until my back hits the door.

"What do you want to know."

"Did you kill David?"

He shakes his head, "No, but I did kick the shit out of him."

I place a hand on his chest, holding him back as he frowns. "You knew I wouldn't let that piece of shit get away with what he did."

"Gears, you didn't really…" I pale. "Do my brothers know about him, about what he did?"

He cages me in against the door. "No, I would never do that to you. It isn't my secret to tell, but knowin' he was still out there…I told them a friend of mine was sexually assaulted by this dick, and he's done it multiple times."

"You killed a man."

"No, Dexter did."

"Do I even want to know who Dexter is?"

"The man who killed my mom."

I take a deep breath. "Willow Buford?"

His eyes are fierce when he answers, "Yes."

I take a deep breath. "Jesus."

"Did you know David Logan was also arrested for using the date rape drug? More than once."

I bite my lip.

"And he gets his kicks watchin' underage girls," Gears goes on. "He likes kiddie porn, Amelia, how fuckin' sick is that?"

My bottom lip begins to tremble. "How do you know all this?"

"I have a friend in the Sons of Phoenix Fury MC. He did some diggin'."

I take another deep breath. "So you killed David?"

"No, I told you, Dexter did."

"Gears, I'm not following."

He tilts my chin, forcing my head up so our eyes meet.

"You're my ol' lady now, Amelia, or you will be soon when I claim you. And like the rest of the Rebels, I'll protect my woman at all costs. It may mean we need to get a little creative at times, but there is nothin' in the world that's gonna hurt you anymore, *sugar.* I want you to always feel safe. I hate that he took that away from you. I hate that he was the one who put fear in your head that you carried that around for such a long time, but that ended two days ago. He's a piece of shit. Trust me when I say I did the world a favor."

My eyes brim with tears. "This is big, Gears." I still hold my palm against his chest, and he doesn't move any closer, but he also doesn't step back. "You set this up, so it looked like Dexter killed David, and not you?"

He shrugs. "Drug bust gone wrong. They each had a gun, and they got into an altercation when Dexter didn't pay up, as most ex-cons don't when they have no money. Terribly sad."

I run a hand through my hair. "What if...what if it comes back to you?" Fear runs through me that he'll get caught and be put in jail himself.

"It won't," he says firmly. "I'm not gonna tell you any more. The less you know, the better. But I do believe in karma, baby, and they both had it comin', trust me on that. The club had my back, and that's all I'm gonna say on the matter. Two birds, one stone. Two problems erased." He moves one palm from the door to cup one side of my face. "I will always keep you safe, Amelia. I will always look out for you, no matter what."

I pull the hem of his t-shirt, balling my fist up in it. "You did too much."

He snorts. "Surely, you're not gonna be mad at me for dealin' with this. Nobody knows the real reason. I told you before, the club thinks he raped a friend of mine, not you. If you don't wish to tell your brothers the real truth, then I respect that."

I shake with rage, remembering that night and how he treated me. Little did I know he never got any better as he got older.

I look down at the floor and let go of his shirt. All the fire within me dissipates.

"You don't know what he took from me," I whisper. "How bad things were and how I was too ashamed to tell anybody. Looking back, I wish I could turn back time because I'd definitely do things differently."

He strokes my cheek with his thumb, his eyes soft as I melt against the door. "It's all over now," he says. "Nobody will ever hurt you again. I want you to know that."

I gaze up at him, so taken aback by his words that I can't even speak. I just nod.

Then, he takes my hand, leading me to the bed as he sits me down. "How about I get us a drink?"

I swallow hard. "That'd be great, thanks."

It's not every day your lover goes and kills two people. One all for you.

A few moments later, he comes back with a bottle of vodka and two shot glasses. He pours us each a shot, then sets the bottle down on the side table, handing me my glass.

"I think it's time we had a new beginning, Amelia," he says. "We both deserve it."

I smile softly.

"We do," I say, holding my shot to his as we clink glasses. "I don't know how I feel about what you did, but I'm glad that neither of them can hurt anyone else ever again.

I don't want you to think, though, that I need rescuing. I'm a tough cookie, Gears. I've had to grow up in a military family, and after what David did to me, I was in a dark place for a long time. But I did all of that on my own. I got through it, and it was hard, but I got there."

He watches me closely for a second, still holding his shot glass out. "I know you don't need rescuing," he says, his eyes never leaving mine. "You are a strong, beautiful, capable woman. I know how far you've come, *sugar.* I see that strength you have inside you, it's one of the things I love about you. But, make no mistake, I will be *that* guy if anyone tries to hurt you ever again. It's who I am, and bein' part of the MC, it's part of the deal. You won't ever have to ask or wonder because I will be there for you. As a man, your man, that's my job now, and you gotta let me do it."

I let out a long breath, then I take my shot, wincing as the back of my throat burns. I watch as Gears follows suit.

Still standing over me, he smirks when I gag just a little.

"Bit of a lightweight, aren't you, baby?"

I laugh, holding my glass out. "Maybe we should find out."

He takes the glass out of my hand. "No, I think one shot is enough for the moment."

"Why?" I pout.

He sets the glasses down, then crashes down on the bed next to me. "Because I can think of a million ways I can get a smile on your face right now, and you passin' out from too much alcohol ain't one of them."

I turn on my side to face him, and he does the same, propping ourselves on our elbows.

"You're an incredibly decent man when you're not murdering people."

He rubs his chin, his lips curling into that mischievous smirk I love so much. "You know, some say bein' decent could be a downfall." His fingers brush the exposed skin above my hip between my jeans and my top.

"Why would being decent be a downfall?"

He looks up at me with those eyes I could get lost in. "Because they don't expect you to do this." Rolling on top of me, I yelp, and he pins my hands to the bed by my wrists. He kisses me hard, pressing his cock into my stomach as I groan under his touch.

"I was thinking we should have a date first," I say when we pull apart, my lips tingling from his touch. "Like, get to know one another." Of course, I'm only half kidding. I do want to know him, all about him, but not having his touch for two days has already taken its toll.

He moves his mouth to my neck. "Sounds fine to me."

"That means no sex," I clarify.

He continues his sensual assault. "Mmhmm."

"Which is what you're doing now."

He lightly bites my neck, sending desire straight between my legs.

He works his way lower, skimming over my breasts as keeps going south.

When our eyes meet, he gives me that sexy look that I know only too well; he's gonna do whatever the fuck he wants.

"No sex?"

I nod. "Yup."

"These your new rules?"

"It's what people do when they date; they get to know one another before they get physical."

He snorts. "Why would anyone want to do that?"

"To see if you're compatible."

He gives me an eye roll. "You been readin' too many of those romance books again, *sugar?*"

I bite my lip. "No, but you said you've never had a girlfriend before, so these are things you should know."

"Yeah?"

I stifle a giggle. "Yep."

He hooks his thumbs into my jean belt loops, tugging at them as he raises his eyebrows in question. "So no sex?"

I nod again. "Afraid so."

"Huh."

Then, he starts to unbutton my jeans.

"Hey! You're breaking the rules." I laugh, trying and failing to grab his hands.

He kisses the apex of my thighs through my jeans, nuzzling his face into my pussy. "Guess I'm just gonna have to give you oral until you beg me for my cock then, baby."

Should I feel guilty, remorseful, *something* because of what happened to David?

He was murdered brutally, by my boyfriend...*in an act of revenge,* my mind kindly reminds me.

I do believe Gears; that he'll always be there for me. I feel it in everything he says and does, how he treats me, how we can talk for hours, how he can make me laugh, no matter what. The sex is just a bonus, as is the fact he's so good at it.

I only hope I can give him all the things he needs in return. Time will tell.

This journey is ours together.

"I guess you better start practicing," I say, gripping my hands in his hair. "You can buy me dinner after."

He laughs too, then unzips my jeans and reminds me of all the reasons I appreciate a younger man, especially one who can eat me out like no other man ever could.

The rest can wait.

~

Epilogue - *Amelia*
Six months later...

I stare into space while I wait for my takeout, remembering dreamily how I spent the last few nights; in Gears's bed, wrapped around him.

Smiling to myself, I remember his body, how energetic he is in the bedroom and how adventurous he likes to be. It makes my body tingle, my pussy throb, and my nipples pucker.

Even now, six months later, things have only gotten better. We're like a couple of teenagers who can't keep their hands off one another.

Not only have I gotten to know Gears, but even the deepest, darkest parts of him that he thought nobody would care about. Those are the things I love the most. Those are the times when he's the most vulnerable and opens up to me. It's never easy, but I knew from the beginning, Gears was no ordinary man. And, like me, he has many layers, and some of them are complicated and scary. But he's opened up, and so have I. I've learned to trust again, and because of that, we've grown so much closer.

Considering I'm his first real girlfriend, he's doing a pretty damn good job.

He also hates it when we're apart, like now; when I'm away for a couple of days for business.

I'm doing a course, courtesy of Kennedy, but it means I'm out of town.

And he can't stand it.

My phone buzzes, and as I read the text, I can't help but smile.

Gears: Hurry the fuck up, I need to see you naked.

Yep, some things never change.

Since we got caught that night by Brock at the clubhouse, we've barely spent a night apart.

No matter what, they couldn't keep us away from one another, and I wouldn't want it any other way.

He took me on a date, and we made out on the couch after like naughty teenagers, going down on each other but not actually having sex. In fact, dating Gears was the highlight of my year. Until, after the third or fourth date, when he hauled me over his shoulder and spanked my ass, declaring he'd had enough and couldn't wait any longer. The man can certainly go all night.

I text back.

Me: Keep your hair on, I'm getting dinner.

The grey bubbles appear to tell me he's typing back.

Gears: I'm already naked and touching myself.

I swallow hard.

The server calls out my order, and I thank them, hastily making it out of there and back to the hotel.

I send a quick text as I'm walking.

Me: What are you doing?

Gears: Wishing my palm was that dirty mouth of yours

I quicken my pace, dashing through the lobby of the hotel, stabbing at the buttons for my floor.

Me: I'm hurrying

Gears: Feels so fuckin' good, *sugar*

My mouth waters at the thought of him pleasuring himself in my absence. It makes me feel powerful, like I'm the only woman who can make him feel this way.

When I finally get into my room, I toss my key down, along with my takeout bag, and hit dial.

He answers on the first ring.

Another thing I'll never tire of: his gorgeous face.

"Took your time," he drawls. He's shirtless, and I can see the top of his arm moving back and forth.

"Lower the camera," I say. "I need to see you."

He smirks, tilting the phone. Sure enough, he's fisting his cock, squeezing it as he sheaths himself up and down.

I know I've seen his cock a zillion times these last six months, but I still get a thrill at seeing him like this. I love it when he's out of control.

"God, you're so perfect," I blurt before I can stop myself.

He grins. "Babe?"

"Huh?"

"How about you get undressed too?"

I slide the straps of my dress off my shoulders.

"You better have underwear on," he growls. "Show me."

I pull my dress all the way down, revealing I have no bra on.

"Amelia," he warns. "What did I tell you about that?"

I bite my lip.

It has a built-in bra, but I don't tell him that.

"Oops."

"Oops?"

"Did you forget your panties too?"

"I remembered those," I say. Turning, I lift the back of my dress up and flash him my ass.

"You're wearing a G-string?"

"They make me feel sexy."

"I don't want you feelin' sexy when I'm not there."

I giggle. "Are you gonna punish me when I get home?"

Thinking about me over his knee while he spanks my ass red almost makes me convulse right then and there.

"You know what it does to me."

I set the phone down and rip my dress off, his eyes trailing down my body. I stare at him, then dip one hand down the front of my panties.

"I'm so wet, Gears."

"Sit back on the bed and rip those panties off so I can see you." His urgent tone is telling me that he's close.

I do as he says, and his eyes lower to my pussy. I circle my clit, groaning as I do.

"I need it, Gears."

"Tell me, baby."

"I need your cock."

"Fuck."

I insert two fingers, moaning as I begin to fuck myself, his eyes never leaving my pussy.

"Don't come," he says. "Go get your toy."

"Gears! No! I need to come!"

He stops what he's doing. "Go get it. I need to see it inside you."

I groan, and with reluctance, I shift off the bed to go to my open suitcase, pulling out my purple dildo from inside.

I come back to the camera.

"Turn it on. Hurry," he says as he begins to pull his cock again.

I stare at it, wishing I was there to take him into my mouth.

I do as he asks, swirling the tip through my folds, circling my clit as I groan. The sensations ripple through me.

"*Gears...*"

"Not yet."

I ignore him, taking my pleasure as I cry his name. Pushing my tits out, I stretch my body, one hand planted on the bed as I ride the wave.

"Naughty girl," he says, though he's now fully jerking himself violently. "You'll get an extra spanking when you come home. Put it inside."

I comply, inserting slowly, making sure he sees every inch as it disappears inside me.

"You feel so good," I tell him. "Oh, Gears."

"Baby," he mutters, his voice low and hoarse.

"I can't hold off," I cry.

"Ride it," he says. "Turn around and mount it. Show me your ass."

I don't know how long I can hold on, but I turn, spread my legs, and sit on the dildo, gripping the headboard as I throw my head back and ride the damn thing. I've never done it in this position before. Gears always likes to use it on me while he plays with my ass.

"Oh, oh, oh," I cry. "I'm coming…I'm coming…" I let go as my orgasm hits me hard and sweeps me into oblivion.

He grunts, and I turn to look over my shoulder as he shoots his load all over his stomach.

We're both panting and sated as I roll onto my back and reach for my phone. "You're a dirty man, Gears, did anyone ever tell you that before?"

He smiles. "Long as it's you sayin' it, that's all that matters."

"Such a romantic."

"Gonna go clean up. I'll call you back."

"I'd rather like to watch you shower," I admit, knowing I could definitely go another round.

"That'll only lead to me fucking my palm again, and I want the real thing. When are you back again?"

"Tomorrow night," I say. "Less than twenty-four hours."

He grumbles again. "Back in five."

I blow him a kiss as he hangs up.

I lie back on the bed, hugging myself. Knowing I have a man like him waiting for me when I get home is all I've ever wanted. Out of all the things I've accomplished in my life so far, he's the best.

My man.

My heart.

I'll love him forever.

❧

Another three months after that

Gears

Brock passes me the new baby as I flinch. I don't know what the fuck to do with babies. At least this one's quiet, not like Ethan Wolf, who's almost two and has a set of lungs on him like his papa.

"Don't drop her," Brock warns, careful not to swear in front of the other kids.

Amelia coos and strokes little Amber Jane's cheek adoringly. "She's so perfect. You guys did so good," she says, looking up at Angel and Brock.

"Yeah, she looks like Angel, so that's gotta be good," I agree, earning me a smack on the arm from Amelia.

"Thank fudge for that," Brock mutters.

"Ooh, is there fudge, Dad?" Rawlings pipes up, bouncing across the room with a bag of Cheetos, holding Kirsty's hand. Kirsty also holds Ethan Wolf at her hip, and he starts to grizzle and wriggle around.

"Not at this time of the mornin," Brock replies.

Seriously, I don't know how they do it. Kirsty passes Ethan to Brock, and he immediately stops his tantrum.

"You got this baby shit down pat." I smirk.

"Mom, Dad, Gears said *shit*," Rawlings repeats.

"Raw," Brock warns. "And, Gears, you should know better with kids present."

My shoulders shake as I laugh. "Sorry, I forgot."

While it's far too early for Amelia and me to be talking about kids together, she's said a few times she's not really sure about having children. I know the kids Brock and Angel have are thoroughly spoiled rotten, so at the very least, she makes an awesome aunt.

I've never really been sure about kids myself. To be fair, I've never really considered it. Life's pretty sweet as it is at the moment.

I moved in with Amelia just a few weeks ago, giving up

my place at the Crow. I much prefer the quiet of Amelia's place, and her big bed.

Making a life with her is the most natural and easy thing in the world. We argue a shit ton, she still can't cook, and I leave my shit lying around just to annoy her, but the makeup sex is worth all of it. I just want to keep making her happy. Be there for her when she's had a shit day, or something didn't go right. I've been learning that women are interesting creatures who cannot be tamed. And really, would I even want my naughty, rebellious sugar to be tamed? I don't think so. It's much more fun teaching her and finding new ways to make her happy…and to have her ass stinging with spankings.

I pass the baby to Amelia when she starts to stir.

"Not afraid of a little baby, are you?" Angel mocks.

I snort. "Nah, I just don't want her throwin' up on me or some shi…uh…other gross thing."

Amelia giggles. "Like pooping?"

"Exactly."

"Ethan did that a lot," Rawlings tells us. "It was so disgusting."

"So did you," Angel reminds her. "When you were a baby."

Rawlings pulls a face as she makes a gagging noise, and we all laugh.

When Amelia hands Amber over to Kirsty for a hold, I pull her closer to me, her back against my front.

"Excited I'm in your bed tonight?" I whisper in her ear.

Her breath hitches. "Of course," she whispers back. "Though you are a duvet thief."

I snort a laugh. "A duvet thief?"

"Yup. I wake up cold in the middle of the night."

I bump her from behind. "We know how to fix that."

We watch on as Amber gets passed around, and I feel the warmth in my chest.

My family.

Finally.

And it feels fucking fantastic.

Grams has even been over to the clubhouse a couple of times and has met Hutch and Kirsty, and she wants to come and see the new baby next. My dad and Kirsty have welcomed me with open arms. I know it couldn't have been easy for her, but she's a strong woman.

Deanna was just as shocked to learn she had a brother, as were the rest of the club with the news. We've hung out a couple of times and she's pretty cool, though she likes to think she's the boss of me because she's older.

I kiss the top of Amelia's head. "Happy?"

She squeezes my hands with hers. "Very."

I kiss her neck, ignoring Brock's frown. "Good."

A couple of weeks later, when Angel's feeling up to it, we have a barbecue at the club so everyone can meet the new baby properly.

I sit at the bar, a beer in one hand, as I watch my woman from across the room.

She's a vision in her short dress, a little too short, if you ask me, but at least that'll be easy access for later when she's ridin' my cock.

I take a long pull, and turning, she meets my eye and gives me a wave. I give her a wink, assessing her with my eyes, telling her how much I like what she's wearing.

She's come so far after all the trauma she's suffered. Some may say I crossed a line, taking care of David like I did, but I don't give a shit. I'd do it all again if I had to. One less asshole on the streets is a good enough reason as any.

The love I feel for her isn't just physical, and I really don't think it ever was. We've been each other's rocks, getting through this maze called life together. We've both had a lot of firsts with one another, and I wouldn't want it any other way.

She's the love of my life. My queen. I want to give her everything, and I'll make sure she wants for nothing.

I've been working on my issues about not being good enough, and even though I know Amelia could get any man she wanted, I have to be secure in the knowledge that she picked me. It's only ever going to be her.

"Another beer?" Summer asks as I down the last mouthful.

"Thanks, sweetheart."

"No problem." She snaps the cap off and slides the bottle toward me.

Rubble plonks down noisily next to me.

I turn to him. "You all right, bro?"

He looks like he's run a marathon. A few moments later, Lucy comes out of the ladies' room, adjusting her skirt, looking just as hot and bothered as he does.

I snicker. "I guess I just answered my own question."

He turns and orders a beer from Summer. "We're tryin' again for baby number two," he explains. "When a woman's at the right time of the month, you got a small window to get shit happenin'."

I flinch. "Ew."

Summer hands him the bottle and he takes a pull. "Fuck, that's nice and cold."

"Looks like you earned it."

"More like she did," he says, a smirk on his lips.

I move off the stool to go take a leak, then go out back to check on Buzz. He's manning the gate tonight. Security has been at an all-time high this last year.

With everything that's gone down with this club, directly or not, you gotta take precautions.

Which is why I'm surprised when I see Buzz scratching his head, talking to some tall dude who's telling him something I can't quite make out.

I move toward the gate.

"Hey, numb nuts," I say as Buzz turns to face me, relief flooding his face. "You all right?"

"Uh, this dude here wants to come in," he says as I check out the guy. Bigger than me. Broad, with cropped hair, a short beard, and bright blue eyes.

"Who is he?"

"I've tried to call Steel," Buzz goes on, in a flurry. "Didn't know what to do."

I roll my eyes. "Who the fuck are you?" I give the dude a chin lift. "We've got a family barbecue going on at the moment, and I don't believe you have an invite."

He stares me down, brave fucker. I might be smaller than him, but Lord knows I won't say no to a fight if he continues to look at me like that.

"Don't need one. I need to talk to Jayson. It's urgent."

I put my hands on my hips and give him a chin lift. "What's so fuckin' urgent that it can't wait?"

He runs a hand over his short hair. "I didn't wanna do this here…"

"Fuck's sake, spit it out. I ain't got all night, got a party to get back to."

He doesn't seem agitated or like he may be violent, but you can never be too sure.

"I'm family," he says, like that's an explanation.

"Fine. I'll give him a call. What's your name?" I reply, not sure who this fucker thinks he is barging in here. If he's 'family,' then he'd have Steel's number.

"Knox," he says, taking a deep breath. "Knox Steelman."

Huh? "Okay…and you are his…"

"Brother."

I frown. "Brother? Steel doesn't have a brother, just a sister."

"I have a sister, too?"

I pull my phone out of my pocket. "I don't know what the fuck's going on, but you're not comin' in here until I speak to Steel," I say, hitting dial and hoping he'll pick up.

After the fourth ring, Sienna's voice sounds down the line. "Hey, Gears," she says.

"Hey, Sienna, I need to talk to Steel. It's important."

"Uh, he just went to the men's room, where are you?"

"I'm out front. Can you send him out here as soon as he's done."

"Is everything okay?"

"Everything's fine," I reply, keeping one eye on Knox. "Just tell him to come to the gate."

"Gears…"

"Does Steel have a brother?" I blurt out.

"Uh, no," she replies. "Why would you ask that?"

"I've got some guy out here called Knox, and he seems to think he's Steel's brother."

"My father and his father are the same person," Knox adds helpfully.

"Shit," Sienna mutters, the phone muffling. It sounds like she's walking. "I'll go find him."

I hang up the phone, turning my attention back to Knox.

"You're either very sure of yourself or completely fuckin' stupid," I tell him. "Steel is the strongest motherfucker I know; it'd be in your best interest to walk away now if this is some kind of hoax. You don't wanna make an enemy out of him. The wisest course of action is to run."

"It's no hoax," he says. "And I'm done runnin'. I'm not goin' anywhere until he comes out here."

I shove my hands into my pockets, giving Buzz a look

as he palms the back of his neck. Confrontation isn't exactly his strong suit, though we're working on it.

"Fine, it's your funeral," I say. "You know they don't call him Steel because he's a soft cock, right?"

Knox takes a long breath. "I know that, but it can't be helped. He's the only one who can help me."

I don't know what this fucker's problem is, but he's starting to grate on my nerves.

"Like I said, it's your funeral."

I turn and see Steel coming toward us; a wall of muscle, his jaw set and his eyes blazing. Oh, holy fuck. I wouldn't wanna be Knox right now.

"What the fuck?" he grunts, storming our way as I instinctively move out of the firing line.

As he gets closer, I say, "This is Knox. He's claimin' to be your brother."

"The fuck?" Steel barks.

To his detriment, he stands his ground, and that's never easy with Steel in your face.

"I wanted to talk," Knox says, backing up just a little. "This is where they said you'd be."

Steel sizes him up and doesn't look impressed. "Yeah, well, you've got about ten seconds before I put my fist down your throat."

His eyebrows twitch ever-so slightly. "I'm your brother, Jayson...Our father led a double life. He had another family, one neither your mom nor mine knew about."

Out of all the things I thought he was going to say, that wasn't it.

I watch the change on Steel's face. He's always hard to read, but this time, I think he just looks plain mad. Grabbing Knox by the lapels of his shirt, he hauls him closer, getting right in his face.

"Knox?" he snorts. "You've got some explainin' to do."

BONUS EPILOGUE

ONE YEAR LATER - THANKSGIVING

I look down the table that everyone is gathered around, busy catching up.

My pop and Gran talking. Amelia. Brock and Angel. Deanna. Rawlings. The other kids are having a nap.

Deanna and I have been getting along great.

Right after Hutch and Kirsty sat down with me and her to tell her what happened all those years ago, I wasn't sure which way it was going to go. My mind wanders...

"So I seriously have a brother?" She looked from her dad to her mom then to me.

Hutch palmed the back of his head, looking a little uncomfortable. "Like I said. I loved your Mother, even when we were separated, I was lost when we broke up. I didn't realize until it was too late exactly the turn my life had taken, and I blamed everyone else except myself. Does that excuse that I slept with Gears' mom? No, because I should have fought harder and not let either of you go...when you got sick Deanna..." He'd trailed off.

Deanna, a lot like her mom in more ways than one, listened intently as if trying to understand.

I mean, even though they were technically separated, nobody wants to think about their parents with each other, much less other people.

"The short answer is yes, you do," I said, just as Kirsty flicked her eyes to me with a smile.

She accepted me straight away, with open arms. I couldn't wish for more, but it's awkward with Deanna. I don't really know if she's gonna be a bitch about this or be cool with it.

I'm here. I can't change the past or control what our father did.

She turned and looked at me. "Well I'll be damned."

"Is that good or bad?" I frowned.

She shrugged. "That depends on if you're gonna be an ass to me."

I put a hand over my heart. "Hey, I'm not an ass to anybody, only the boys when I was a prospect but they deserved it." She punched me on the arm, it really fuckin' hurt. "What was that for?"

"Welcome to the family, bro. I always wanted a sibling to boss around and make my slave."

Hutch and Kirsty chuckled. "Deanna, be nice to Gears, we want him to come to dinner again," Kirsty said, giving me a warm smile.

The lump in my chest got tighter and tighter. To be sitting here, with my family, the family I never knew about.

I shoved a forkful of steak and potato in my mouth and said, "You won't be gettin' rid of me that easily, don't worry."

Deanna winced. "Eww gross. Can't you eat with your mouth closed?"

Kirsty linked her fingers together and pressed her chin against her hands, watching us with amusement. "I always wanted a big family, didn't I Richie?" she said, turning to him.

He looked at her fondly. "Not through a lack of trying..."

"Oh for god's sake!" Deanna complained. "Mom and Dad,

seriously, we're eating here, nobody wants to think about you two doing.... that, pass me a bucket."

They lean toward each other and kiss quickly. "One day you'll find a man just like your Father," Kirsty said, looking at Deanna. "We've had our ups and downs over the years, but this is a chance for us all to be a real family, to reunite and realize how blessed we are."

This woman is a fuckin' saint.

"Kirsty's right," Hutch said, as he'd looked at me. "This is a chance to start fresh. To reconnect and build something together. I want to cut down a little at the club, I'm not gettin' any younger, and I'd like to get to know my son."

Hearing him say I was his son made my throat dry and my heart race. The fact I have a father hasn't really sunk in yet, much less I have a sister and Mama bear Kirsty.

"I want to get to know you too," I managed, when I'd finally found my voice. "It's all been a pretty big fuckin' whirlwind."

"That it has," he replied. "So, I take it we're all okay welcoming Gears into the family?"

"I'd love nothing more," Kirsty went on, tears in her eyes, clapping her hands together.

"Hell yeah!" Deanna shoved me again and I could tell she's going to be annoying.

"That settles it. Jake 'Gears' Hutchinson, welcome to the family." He held his beer out to me and I clinked my bottle with his, then Kirsty's and Deanna's wine glasses.

I'm too caught up with emotion to eat, but I think they understand. It's all been pretty sudden and pretty full on this last week.

"Okay Gears, hurry up and eat will you?" Deanna said, turning to me.

I frowned. "Why's that?"

"I always wanted a little sister," she laughed. "And I'm dying to braid that hair of yours."

I shove her this time. "Very funny."

"What?" She pulled my hair like a little kid and I smacked her hand away.

"Oh my God, you two." Kirsty shook her head, but she beamed in the process. I know she's happy with the union, and that Hutch got to meet the son he never knew he had.

I only hope I can be the kind of son he'd always hoped for....

Hollering jolts me out of my reverie.

"Gears!" Kirsty bellows from the kitchen. "Can you get in here? This bird isn't getting itself out of the oven."

"Coming!" I yell back. I give Amelia a chin lift and make my way to the kitchen. "Your ass on fire, Mama bear?"

She turns to look at me, giving me that 'Mom' look she does so well. "I need the turkey out, the damn things heavy."

"Got it."

I reach down to the oven and take the bird out, placing it on the center of the island bench.

"You know what I've been thinking this whole time when I see you in the kitchen?" she goes on, coming to stand next to me.

"What's that?"

"Why you're so good at cooking and your Father's so shit."

We both laugh.

"I guess I got some genes from my Mother."

She smiles.

"Actually, Kirsty..." She looks at me with a frown but I plough on. This woman has been instrumental in making sure I fit in, that Hutch and I get to spend as much time as possible. She's the glue of this club and this family, it's obvious to everyone she comes into contact with. "I was kinda hoping for something from you."

"Oh yeah, what's that, honey?"

"It's just…it feels kinda weird calling you Kirsty."

"Uh huh," she starts fussing with the bird.

"And while I do like the nickname Mama bear." I see her smile but she starts making the potato salad while she listens. My heart thrums loudly in my chest and the blood pounds in my ears. "But I was wondering if it would be okay if…if I called you Mom?"

She stops what she's doing and her hands still. For a second, I don't know if she's going to clout me around the back of the head or hug me. When her eyes meet mine, they're glazed over.

"Oh Jake!" she cries, ushering me to her for a hug. "I've been waiting for eighteen months for you to ask me that! I didn't like to pry or assume anything… I know I'm not your real Mom, and I could never replace her."

"I know that. I will always have my birth Mom; nobody can replace her. I know she'd be so proud of me, like Gran is. But you've been the kind of second Mom I could only dream about. It'd be easy for you to reject me, after how I came into the world…"

She lets me go, reaching for a paper towel to dab her eyes as I continue.

"But getting to know the Hutchinson's has been pretty great."

She sniffs into the paper towel, dabbing her nose. "Hutch and I tried for more kids for years, but we just weren't lucky enough to be blessed with anymore," she stammers. "We joke all the time to embarrass Deanne about just how hard we tried, but the truth is, it was heartbreaking. I wanted more kids. I wanted to adopt but with Hutch's record from spending time in jail, no adoption agency would look at us. Having you come into our life, Jake, I can safely say that you're the son I always wanted. You've brought such joy to all of our lives, just by being you. I knew there was something special about you when you came to Hutch about what was happening at the car yard with Jack."

I've never had a woman get so emotional over me. A protective urge comes over me that I reserved only for Amelia. "I'm the lucky one, to have inherited this awesome family," I say.

Tears leak from her eyes. "I should have known, though. Hutch is the most handsome man I've ever laid eyes on, he still is. He stunned me when we first met, I was besotted with him. When I first saw you, I thought; my God, he looks just like Richie did when he was your age, exactly the same. I don't mind admitting that I thought you were a handsome boy, I still do.

But you're also a little softer around the edges than Hutch, I think you must get that from your Mom."

I nod as I don't really know what to say. I've only seen a few photos of her. "As long as I don't go grey like him when I'm his age," I laugh, looking down at my hands.

"Jake, I'm so glad you came into this family. I hold no animosity toward your Mom or Hutch for that matter. I left. And out of something so tragic, she gave us you. I'll always be grateful. Hutch says she was a beautiful soul, just like you. She'd be so proud of the man you've become."

I feel a lump in my throat at her words and when she calls me by my real name. "Thank you," I choke out. "You don't have to be so cool about this, yet you rise above it all, with grace and elegance."

She smiles and I reach over to wipe her mascara from under her eye that's run slightly. "Well, what kind of a Mom would I be if I turned my back on Hutch's kid? On *our* kid."

It feels so good to hear her say that. Out of everyone, I

was sure Kirsty would be the one who would push against this. She surprises me at every turn.

"You deserve a medal feeding this family, especially with Brock's appetite," I say, trying to lighten the mood.

"Well, we did cook for an army, and Steel and Sienna are coming over a little later, so there'll be plenty to go around."

I hold her by the shoulders. "You did good, *Mom*."

"To hear you say that…"

"No more crying," I tell her firmly. "Dad will think I've upset you and then he'll cut my nuts off."

She shakes her head and points to the bird. "Carry that to the table and set it down, Hutch can do the honors."

"Yes Ma'am." I do as she says, Hutch giving me a big grin as I set the tray down and get back to the kitchen.

"Do you need a hand with anything?" Angel asks.

"No thanks, we've got this," I reply.

"They're regular master chef's together," I hear Deanna say. "They're always coming up with new recipes and shit, the other day Gears made a souffle…"

I smile at the memory. I enjoy cooking with Kirsty, she's excellent in the kitchen and Gran comes to help me bake the pies for the Burger Joint.

When I come back and place the potato salad and green salad down, I kiss Grams on the top of the head. She pats my arm.

"You're a good boy, Jake," she says, smiling over at Amelia. "You did good."

Grams and Amelia spend a lot of time together too. We take her to the movies and Amelia likes to take her shopping with Kirsty and Deanna, and she's even been to a couple of barbecues at the club.

I look at her and I feel an enormous amount of gratitude. Without her, I wouldn't be here now, around this table with the people I love the most.

"So happy you could come," I tell her as Amelia smiles at us warmly.

"Yes, this is the best thanksgiving yet," she beams. "And we haven't even tried the food yet."

"So glad I didn't eat anything for lunch," Rawlings says, running the breadbasket in from the kitchen. She likes to help sometimes too. "Gears, did you make jello?"

I look over to her. "Of course I made it, it's your favorite."

"What color?"

"Red."

She beams and we high-five.

I glance at Hutch. "You givin' your Mama a hard time?"

I hold up both hands, palms facing out. "Wouldn't dream of it."

He smirks as I go and fetch the rest of the hot food, and Kirsty brings the salad.

I hold the door open for her with my foot, "Such a gentleman," she says, as I follow behind.

When I finally take my seat, Amelia finds my hand under the table and gives it a squeeze. "You did an amazing job," she whispers.

I plant a kiss on her cheek as she giggles. "Kirsty outdid me," I tell her. "But that's nothing new."

The Burger Joint is bigger than ever. We've added a takeaway window to the front of the restaurant and we've hired three more cooks. I've been taking some night cookery classes to brush up on my skills, but most things I've learned to be honest have been from my Grams and Kirsty.

I love what I do. If you'd have told me a year ago we'd be expanding and I now oversee the production in the kitchen, rather than cooking every night, I'd tell you you're crazy. I still love cooking and I jump in on the busy nights. But I also like having time to make sure every meal, even if it is just a burger, is the very best it can be. And I also love tinkering with new recipes.

"Got a new fudge Sunday I'd like to try out later," I whisper to Amelia as she turns to look at me, that devilish look in her eyes. She knows what that means. After the one hot night where we got it on after I fed her my desserts, it's kind of a regular thing now. I love eating ice cream off her body, somehow it tastes that much sweeter.

"You're a very bad man," she whispers back.

I lean over and kiss her.

"Eww," Rawlings says, covering her eyes. "Gross."

We pull away and I can't help but smile over at her.

"You think it's gross now, but just wait till you're a teenager," I say, knowing Brock will be on my case in all of two seconds.

Like clockwork he says, "Like hell she will be. She doesn't need to date until she's at least thirty."

Angel gives him a slap on the chest playfully.

Rawlings shakes her head. "Dad, seriously?"

"Fine, forty-five, is that better?"

Rawlings giggles.

Amelia and I may not have marriage or kids in our immediate futures, we're both still young with so much to achieve in our careers, but I know that I want to build a life with her. One day she will be my wife, if that's what she wants. Moving in together has been the best thing to happen to me, to us both, and we don't have to rush anything.

We'll figure it out as we go along, with her by my side, I know that I'm the very best version of myself, and I've never been happier. We somehow keep the magic alive and she hasn't found anything about me that she doesn't like, so that's a bonus.

I've also been saving up and we're going on our first holiday together in the new year. It's a surprise for Amelia's birthday. I can't wait to get her in a bikini and fuck her in our own private pool in the Caribbean.

Yeah, life's pretty sweet.

As I glance at my girl, talking across the table to Grams and Kirsty, I smile to myself.

I'm a lucky bastard.

My eyes meet my dads across the table and he gives me a chin lift, a proud look on his face.

This is where I'm supposed to be.

With these people.

My family.

At last.

ACKNOWLEDGMENTS

Thank you to my fabulous Alpha reader Michelle and Beta reader Alana for all that you do

Thank you, Kiki, for proofreading and keeping me sane

Thank you to Savannah @ PeachyKeen author services

To my sister D, thank you for all the late-night pep talks

Hugs to my editor Mackenzie @nicegirlnaughtycdits for your patience, especially when I'm behind schedule (again)

Much appreciated to my ARC lovelies who signed up and my existing ARC team who keep wanting more, I'm so grateful

Thanks once again for all my blogger friends, fellow authors, and all the amazing people on my journey. I'm so grateful for your support

Thanks LJ from Mayhem Cover Creations for the cover design for another fantastic cover

Appreciation has to be given to my cover model Chris Lynch from Wander Aguiar Photography- the second I saw Chris I knew he was Gears!

A huge, big hug to all my readers. I love you so much, thank you for letting me be an author and for all your support.

If you can spare the time to leave a review on GR and/or Amazon if you loved Gears or any of my books that would be greatly appreciated and helps me so much as an indie author. Links are on the following pages.

I can't wait for you to meet Knox; his book is scheduled for 30 March 2023 (pre order details below with the sneak peek)

Be sure to check out my private Facebook group (links below) as I update this page regularly before anything gets released on other social media channels.

Love from Australia, MF xx

ABOUT THE AUTHOR

Mackenzy Fox is an author of contemporary, enemies to lovers, motorcycle and dark themed romance novels. When she's not writing she loves vegan cooking, walking her beloved pooch's, reading books and is an expert on online shopping.

She's slightly obsessed with drinking tea, testing bubbly Moscato, watching home decorating shows and has a black belt in origami. She strives to live a quiet and introverted life in Western Australia's North-West with her hubby, twin sister and her dogs.

FIND ME HERE:

Tiktok: https://www.tiktok.com/@mackenzyfoxauthor
Tiktok backup account: https://www.tiktok.com/@mackenzyfoxbooks
Face book: https://www.facebook.com/mackenzy.foxauthor.5
Instagram: https://www.instagram.com/mackenzyfoxbooks/
Goodreads: http://bit.ly/3ql07a7

Don't forget to join my private Facebook Group: The Den – A Mackenzy Fox Readers Group here: https://bit.ly/3dgQfKk

Sign up for my newsletter:

https://landing.mailerlite.com/webforms/landing/g2l8y8

Find all my books, ARC sign ups, book links and giveaways here in one easy spot: https://linktr.ee/mackenzyfox

Checkout my website:
https://mackenzyfox.com

WANT MORE?

KNOX SNEAK PEAK (UNEDITED) SUBJECT TO CHANGE

BLURB

Knox:

A new town.

A motorcycle club.

A brother and a sister I never knew about.

I thought I had a handle on my life, it turns out, I don't.

I came here to learn the truth. To start anew.

I didn't expect the black haired woman at the bar with the beautiful blue eyes.

Rebekah.

It was supposed to be one night.

A night of lust and passion with a stranger.

Then she turns up in Bracken Ridge.

And everything I thought I knew, turns upside down.

She moves me any which way she chooses.

I'm under her spell.

Powerless to stop it.

She's mine.

And I ain't running.

Rebekah:

I ran from my past.

From a religion I never chose.

From everything I thought I knew.

But my past caught up with me and I ran out of hiding places.

I didn't think I'd ever feel safe with anyone, much less a stranger.

We spent a drunken night together and now he's here.

My new boss.

And I can't stop looking at him.

He's tall. Broad. Masculine.

Everything a man should be.

But I have dark secrets.

If they came out, I risk losing the one thing that's good in my life.

The one man who listens, who cares about what I say, about *me*.

I've never had that.

And now I've had a taste, I want more.

Of him.

I want it all.

KNOX

I stare at the man they call Steel.

My brother.

We share the same father, or did, until the dead-beat died. And I've only just learned this information myself, finding out by chance when sorting through my father's things.

In truth, I wondered why he owned a small business in Bracken Ridge, left to my mom when he died. I came here wanting answers and came up with a whole bunch of questions.

Jayson Steelman's a big, intimidating guy. He's tall as me, but wider. His face strong, his jaw tense with deep, blue eyes. Eyes that give nothing away. Except he may want to kill me. That part I got loud and clear.

"Who the fuck are you?"

He may be hard of hearing though since I've already told him exactly who I am. I get this is weird.

"I'm your brother, Knox."

He frowns a whole lot, his stance rigid like he's getting

ready for a fight. I didn't think it would come to this, but after finding out Jayson Steelman was the muscle for the local motorcycle club, I may just have to make a run for it. Somehow, my feet stay planted on the ground. I came here for answers, and I'm going to get them.

Before he can respond, a girls voice calls out behind him. She comes running out of the clubhouse toward us.

"Steel?" she calls. "Sienna just told me…"

He gives me a distasteful look before turning to her. "Get the fuck back inside, Lil, I'm dealing with this!"

"Is it true?" she says, halting when she reaches him, peering over his shoulder on her tiptoes.

"He's our brother?"

This is my sister?

"No, he isn't, now listen for once in your life and do as I say."

She frowns, trying to push past him to get a better view but he holds her shoulders so she can't move.

He's protective, nothing wrong with that. I admire it, even.

"Steel! Let me go!"

A tanned blonde haired dude comes sauntering out and gives Steel a chin lift. "What's going on?"

"Will you take your woman back inside, Gunner, I've had enough of her lip and not listenin'."

"I want to talk to him!" she explains. "It's not fair I get kept out of these things!"

"Fuck sakes," Steel mutters.

"Lily, let's go." Gunner eyes me cautiously but steers her back toward the clubhouse, unwillingly.

Steel finally turns back to me.

"Fuckin' women," he grumbles. "Now, get to your point and do it fuckin' quickly 'cause the only dead-beat man I know as a 'Father' was a no good son of a bitch who's been dead for years."

I swallow hard. "Hank Steelman is my Father. We live in Phoenix, he came and went a lot for work, never heard of Bracken Ridge, or knew about you, it was just me and my Mom."

I reach into my inside jacket pocket and pull out a picture of me when I was about ten and hand it to him. "That's me, and my Pop."

Steel takes the photo and stares at it. It could just be me, but he seems to pale just a little bit. "Alright, you've got my attention." He turns to the guy called Gears and the prospect on the gate and says, "fuck off."

Gears shakes his head, and maybe I should've head heeded his warning and left while I had the chance. Then again, I didn't come all the way out here to run away without any answers.

Yeah - this guy has a few traits that remind me of Hank; they've got the same build, he was a grumpy ass with a sharp tongue. Nothing pleased him. I don't know how my brothers temperament is, but hot tempers run in the family.

Steel loos back up at me. "Hank had a secret family?" I'm sure he's doing the math in his head. "How old are you?"

"Thirty." I'm guessing Steel's older than me, maybe thirty five or six. "What about your sister?" *Our* sister.

"She's twenty-four." Steel palms the back of his head. "Fuck sakes."

"I'm sorry man, for what it's worth."

"So your Mom only liked married men?"

My eyes go wide and my blood starts to boil. "My Mom had no idea Hank lived a double life." I stare at him and don't back down.

I can hold my own. Not that I'd want to start a fight with Steel, hat would be crazy. But if it comes down to it, I won't go down without giving it my best shot.

I didn't come here to fight. I came here to get answers...

Pre order here – releasing 30 March 2023

ALSO BY MACKENZY FOX

Made in the USA
Middletown, DE
25 September 2023